JACK & BET

Also by Sarah Butler

Before the Fire
Ten Things I've Learnt About Love

Sarah Butler

JACK & BET

PICADOR

First published 2020 by Picador
an imprint of Pan Macmillan
The Smithson, 6 Briset Street, London EC1M 5NR
Associated companies throughout the world
www.panmacmillan.com

ISBN 978-1-5098-9815-2

1 3 5 7 9 8 6 4 2

A CIP catalogue record for this book is available from the British Library.

Typeset by Jouve (UK), Milton Keynes
Printed and bound by CPI Group (UK) Ltd, Croydon, CR0 4YY

Visit **www.picador.com** to read more about all our books
and to buy them. You will also find features, author interviews and
news of any author events, and you can sign up for e-newsletters
so that you're always first to hear about our new releases.

In memory of Jeanne and George Butler

JACK

Jack Chalmers was a man of few words, married to a woman of many. Hardly unusual, though it would be fair to say they had been married for longer than most. Seventy years tomorrow. They were having a party, because Bet had insisted. There were so few people left to invite, but his wife had been adamant – had talked about olives and music and dancing with such excitement he hadn't liked to say no.

But tomorrow was tomorrow, and today Jack was doing what he did every morning: walking from the new flat – they had lived there almost five years, but both still called it new – to Elephant and Castle shopping centre. It wouldn't exist for much longer; that's what people said. They had been promising to knock it down for years, but there it still was, with its blue paint cracked and stained; a line of gold-tinted windows around its upper edge; the long curved ramp leading to red-framed doors; and inside, floor tiles flecked white and orange, grey and black; the air still and bright. Wires looped from wooden carts up to plug sockets on the orange pillars. Stall-holders heaped their wares – handbags, African headscarves, plastic-wrapped duvets – onto flimsy tables. The fake plants hanging from the pillars in their silver cornet-shaped pots looked like they needed a water.

It seemed to him that every day he got a little bit slower, a little bit less stable. He would stop, often, leaning his weight onto his stick, breathing carefully. There were people who brushed past, their shoulders or bags knocking against him, tutting or swearing under their breath. London was such a rush-about city – everyone would be happier if he stayed at home. But he had his health to think about. Men died before women – he had read the statistics – and he wasn't about to leave Bet on her own.

Every day he walked the same route: along Amelia Street, under the railway bridge to the Walworth Road. Left to the crossing where he waited for the green man who hardly gave him enough time to get from one side to the other. The red-brick building opposite had a blue sign: Sexual Health Clinic. Bet would laugh if he told her, but it took him a little by surprise each time he saw it. The library and the museum next door had their arched windows boarded up. He remembered the scream of fire engines and the harsh, sour smell, which had reached all the way to their flat. They said it would reopen the same as before, but too many promises had been broken around there already for anyone to be convinced.

It was the walk from the library to the shopping centre that was the most difficult, passing along the edge of their old estate. It had almost gone; just sky and a distant view where there used to be blocks of flats. Now the Shard stabbed up from the horizon. Sometimes it caught the sun, turning silver or copper or gold; sometimes it was half hidden by clouds. He didn't like it, but it was easier to look at than piles of rubble behind metal fences. Like a bombsite – all those walls and windows and roofs broken into pieces, and the bulldozers still going, scraping away at what was left with their sharp teeth. Jack's hearing was not what it used to be, but even for him the sound was too much. Easier to look at the Shard than the stretches of hoardings with their pictures of trees and promises of a brighter future. He was too old to be getting angry about such things – that's what his son, Tommy, said – and there was nothing people like them could do in the face of all that money. Things changed. Moved on. He should know that by now.

There were other routes he could take: down Penton Place and along Newington Butts, past the French restaurant where the party would be the following night, past St Mary's church-yard and the old leisure centre. And yet this was the way he walked. He wouldn't stop visiting a friend because he was ill, he told himself. Someone had to pay attention.

They knew him at the shopping centre. The African man in the mobile-phone booth raised a hand as he passed. The Indian man at the stand where he bought the paper asked after his family. And they knew him at the Sundial. He went in every day for a coffee: white, two sugars.

The cafe was busy. A queue at the till; someone shouting in the kitchen; the woman serving looking tired and harassed. Jack ordered his coffee. When he turned from the counter he saw that the table he usually took, in the far corner, was occupied by two builders in boots and fluorescent jackets. In fact, now he looked, he saw that there were no tables free, just a couple of tall stools at the thin shelf that ran the length of the back window. He was too old to be sitting on a stool. He stood, his cup shaking a little in one hand.

'Here.' A woman waved at him, then pointed to the seat opposite her. She was young, with cropped dark hair and pale lips, a silver ring at the edge of one eyebrow. Did he know her?

'You can sit here,' she shouted. A couple of people glanced up, then went back to their phones and their breakfasts.

Don't talk to strangers. Tommy had gone through a phase of telling them the details of every scam he read about – people pretending to be plumbers, engineers, council workers, wheedling their way into old people's lives and then robbing them blind. Jack looked at the girl, who was still smiling, still gesturing. There was something about her – maybe her eyes, or the shape of her cheekbones that reminded him a little of Bet. And there was nowhere else to sit.

'Thank you,' he said as he lowered himself onto the chair and laid his stick lengthways at his feet.

'I am Marinela.' She had one of those Eastern European accents, Polish or Lithuanian or he wasn't sure what. She stretched out a hand and Jack took it.

Don't talk to strangers. They used to say the same thing to Tommy when he was little. If someone offers you sweets, say no. If someone wants you to get into their car, or go to their house, say no. Now it was the other way around – Tommy always worried about them. Wanted them in some home with wipe-down chairs, a fenced-in garden, locked doors. For your safety, he said, for your peace of mind. But Jack couldn't think of anything worse – sitting around in overheated rooms, waiting for mealtimes, nowhere to go, nothing to do.

'Jack,' he said.

'Jack,' she smiled. 'You have a good face.'

Jack touched his cheek and the girl laughed.

'It is a very good face.'

Maybe she wasn't quite right in the head. Jack took a too big, too hasty mouthful of coffee and felt it scald his tongue and the top of his mouth. He cast his gaze around the room. The two builders were staring at their phones; three old ladies sat with cups of tea and eggs on toast, their shopping trolleys parked at the side of their table; a man with white wires trailing out of his ears nodded in time with his music. In the far corner, a thin, dark-skinned boy assembled yellow cardboard boxes for the day's fried chicken, stacking them up like bricks, as though he was barricading himself in. Jack wondered if he called out

4

whether someone would come to his aid. But what would he say? A pretty young woman is talking to me? Whoever came would laugh, tell him it must be his lucky day.

'Maybe I say it wrong?' She looked worried and Jack felt immediately guilty.

'I don't think anyone's ever told me that,' he said, trying to make light of it.

'Well, it is true. I look at faces. You see this woman where we pay, she has a very interesting face. You would not say she is pretty, no, but look at her eyes, and then the way her mouth moves when she is thinking. And then the boy with the boxes – yes, I would like to photograph him.'

Jack had always hated having his picture taken. Most of their photos were of Bet – Bet holding Tommy; Bet by the window in the old place on Larcom Street; on the balcony of their flat on the estate; Bet wearing that green dress, the one that had been sent in a box filled with tissue paper.

'I study photography,' the girl said. 'One day I want to be famous photographer.'

It seemed as though all the young people these days wanted to be famous. When he was that age he'd just wanted to get back from the war and find a decent job. He'd driven buses in the end. It wasn't what Bet had planned – she'd wanted him to do a degree for heaven's sake, become a teacher or a lawyer even – but it was reliable. It paid the bills. And he'd liked it: the mess of London reduced to a handful of routes; getting to know the regulars; watching the seasons change; it had suited him.

'You live here?' the girl asked.

Don't talk to strangers. Don't tell them your bank details, your phone number, your address. You have to be careful, Dad.

'Just down the way.' He moved one arm in the vague direction of the Walworth Road.

'Me too.' She smiled. 'I live here nearly two months. When I hear of Elephant and Castle I think it sounds beautiful. Like nightclub.'

Jack smiled.

'Maybe it is like nightclub – very busy, very noisy. But it is a little bit grey I think. And this shopping place, it reminds me of home – in Romania. Here, have some of my cake.' She took a knife from the container in the centre of the table and cut the doughnut on her plate in half, pushed it towards him. Jack looked at the semi-circle of white icing dotted with coloured sprinkles. He couldn't remember the last time he'd eaten a doughnut.

'No, no.'

'Please.'

He didn't want it, but he took a bite because she was watching him. It was dense and chewy, with just the icing giving a sharp kick of sweetness. He laid it back on the edge of the plate, as far away from her half as he could. A lot of fuss about not very much, but then Americans always were that way inclined, in his opinion.

'It's a doughnut,' he said.

The girl frowned.

'Not a cake. We call these doughnuts. Cakes are more—' He stopped, wishing he had never started. 'They're more spongy.'

'Spongy,' the girl said, the word sounding even odder from her mouth.

'My wife used to make the best Victoria sponge you've ever eaten.' Bet hadn't baked since they'd left the estate. The move had taken it out of the pair of them and they'd never seemed able to settle properly in the new place. Or maybe it was because of her eyes. Or maybe she'd just decided she had made enough cakes in her life. 'That's a sponge cake,' he said. 'Two sponges with jam in the middle. Icing sugar on the top.'

'At home we have good cakes.' The girl took a bite of her

doughnut and grimaced. 'Better than this. My favourite is *pra-jitura cu visine*, you would say cherry cake.'

Jack glanced up. There *was* something of Bet about the girl – nothing specific, just an air, a boldness maybe, a desire to be right.

'I take photographs of Elephant and Castle.' She spread her hands on the tabletop. Short, neat nails, each painted a different colour: red, green, yellow, blue, pink. 'There is the place being knocked down?'

'That's right,' Jack said.

'It is ugly and beautiful at the same time, I think. All the dust, and the broken things. Everything behind fences. I watch it go a little bit at a time.'

Jack and Bet had been so happy when they moved there. It was a new start. Another one. They'd not said as much, but they'd both felt it, he could tell. A new home, bright and light, up on the eighth floor with views all the way across London. Hot running water. The gardens in between the blocks filled with new trees. They felt like they were living in the future.

'We lived there,' he said.

'In the place?'

'They only built it forty years ago,' Jack said. 'If you ask me it's criminal, knocking it down.'

'It was not bad place?'

Jack shook his head. 'No. No, it was not a bad place.'

The girl reached across the table and placed her hand over his. A shock of warm soft skin. 'That is very difficult,' she said, 'for it to be taken down. I am sorry for it.'

He slipped his hand from under hers and put it back in his lap.

'What was it like?' she asked.

Jack shrugged. 'It was where we lived.'

'But you liked it?'

He liked the light. He liked the view. He liked how Bet was – as though she had shaken free of something that had been weighing her down for years. He liked the neighbours, at least to start with.

'It wasn't perfect,' he said. 'Nowhere's perfect. But it wasn't anywhere near as bad as everyone made out. Why are you taking the photos?'

'I take them to try and know where I am,' she said. 'I don't know if I say it right. But it is to look properly. I look when I take the photos, and then I use the darkroom to make the pictures and I look again. And then somehow I know more.'

'You don't have one of those digital ones?'

'I have one, yes, but I like the film most. I am old-fashioned, no?'

Jack remembered the little capsules of film he'd take to the chemist's and the glossy envelopes of photographs he'd get in return. Sometimes, looking through, there were ones neither he nor Bet could remember taking.

'Are you good?' he asked.

The girl laughed. 'I do not know. Maybe one day I show you pictures and you can decide. Jack, I am buying more tea. Can I buy for you?'

Jack looked at his empty cup. 'My wife is at home,' he said. 'I always make her lunch.'

'Just one drink? You have made my day happier, I would like to.'

He hesitated. If he had another coffee he'd have to use the toilet. Twenty pence a go they charged these days, and the place wasn't clean. Still, he liked the girl and she was looking at him, waiting for an answer. 'A coffee,' he said. 'White, two sugars. Thank you.'

The girl grinned and went up to the counter. She wore black jeans – the kind that clung to your legs, closer than drainpipe jeans ever did – and a black long-sleeved top. No jumper, even though they were at the tail end of a chilly September and there was no fat on her to keep her warm. Maybe she wanted something from him. Money, or a visa, or a place to stay – he didn't know what it was these people needed. He could get up and leave, he thought, but he was so slow she would catch up with him and ask why, and anyway, he liked her.

She came back with a cup of black tea and Jack's coffee. They sat opposite each other, sipping their drinks, suddenly awkward. Jack looked out of the cafe window into the shopping centre, at the sandwich kiosk with its silver chairs and tables; a big glass box filled with soft toys, a metal claw hanging above them; the stall where the Chinese woman used to sell dragon oil and tea, which was now filled with cheap jewellery.

'Tomorrow is my wedding anniversary,' he said, for something to say. 'Seventy years.'

The girl smiled.

Jack ploughed on. 'We're having a party,' he said. 'Bet wanted a party.'

'What is she like?'

'Bet?' He thought of her sitting in the living room of the flat, the pot of tea he'd made before he left cold now on the little glass and wicker table. 'She's beautiful,' he said.

'It is a long time with one person.'

And they hadn't got all of it right, not by a long shot. But they'd lasted. That counted for something.

'Sometimes it feels like no time at all,' he said.

'You must be very happy together.'

The girl made it all sound so simple, so straightforward.

'Maybe you could take her photograph,' he said without thinking. 'At the party? You could come to the party and take her photograph.' It would be a surprise. A present from him. 'I will pay you, of course.'

She smiled. 'Yes, I come. But I don't want money.'

'I have to pay you.'

The girl shook her head. 'Maybe sometime you buy me a cup of tea and tell me about the place that is knocked down. Maybe this is the payment.'

It would make just the right present. He could get it framed, put it on the mantelpiece next to their wedding photo. He could do a copy for Tommy. Bet would say she was too old, too worn-out to have her photo taken, but she would love it. He could see her already, smoothing down her hair, adjusting her collar, turning towards the camera, smiling.

BET

Jack kept saying they weren't the type to throw a party. He'd wanted a quiet pub lunch, or if there had to be a bigger gathering then a daytime thing at Draper's Hall or Crossways, but Bet had insisted on something classier. Community halls always looked and smelled like community halls, however hard anyone tried; she didn't want stewed tea and plastic chairs and strangers' attempts at art pinned to the walls. They would book the upstairs bit of the French place for an evening, she'd told Jack. A man on the piano. Some bits to eat. And now here they were. Bundles of silver helium balloons tied to the banisters. Bowls of pretzels and olives on each table. She'd had to fight with Jack for the olives. What's wrong with crisps, he'd wanted to know, but then he'd have had sausage rolls and cheese and onion quiche if she'd let him. This is special, she'd said, and he'd given in, the way he always did.

The restaurant sat in the wedge of space where Newington Butts split into Kennington Park Road and Kennington Lane, the road like a zip opened up either side of the building. Bet sat at the window of the second-floor bar and looked out towards the busy roundabouts; the majestic Tabernacle church; the 1960s shopping centre; the new black and white glass tower; and beyond them, Borough, Waterloo, the Thames. She had to fill in some of the details from memory. There was something wrong with her eyes – a small dark smudge at the centre of her vision: it had appeared a year or so ago and had been getting ever so slightly bigger these last few months. Not that she'd told Jack or Tommy it was getting worse. They were such fusspots at the best of times, and it wasn't anything she couldn't manage.

Jack sat on the opposite side of the table, hands cupped around his beer. 'This is nice,' he said. 'Good to see people. There's Deepa just arrived – she's looking thin – and Stuart – you remember Stuart from the committee?'

Jack had got involved with all that business on the estate. So many committee meetings. So many arguments with the council. It made her tired just to think about it.

'And this place is nice. It looks nice, Bet.'

She could smell onions frying down in the restaurant, a faint whiff of cleaning fluid. Bars used to smell of smoke. They were better that way. She picked up an olive and placed it in her mouth. She wished she liked them, but she didn't – bitter, slimy things. These were black, not like the green globes speared with a cocktail stick and plunged into a Martini. Bet lowered her head and prised the stone from her mouth. It was uncouth, she thought, holding it between her finger and thumb and wondering what she should do with it. In the end she simply placed it onto the tabletop, then lifted her drink to swill away the taste. It was a gin and tonic, weaker than she liked, but still she closed her eyes with pleasure at the twist of gin and lime, the tonic's fizz against her tongue.

'Seventy years,' Jack said. 'It doesn't seem possible.'

Everything had gone so much faster than she'd expected. When she was a girl she thought she'd be a film star, or maybe a ballerina; she never thought she'd be nigh on ninety years old, sitting in a room above a restaurant in Elephant and Castle, celebrating seven decades of marriage.

'Feels like yesterday,' Jack said. 'Everyone says that, but it's true.'

Bet looked away from him, at the dark wood tables and matching dark wood floors, the little stage where an upright piano stood, its lid closed.

'It rained,' she said.

Jack laughed. 'Couldn't ruin it though, could it?'

Bet remembered the sky banked with black clouds, rain slapping at the windows. Early that morning, she had lain with her eyes open, doing all kinds of deals with God, or whoever else might be listening, if they would just stop the rain. Everyone made light of it, but she was cold in her dress, and the hem sucked up the muddy water and then brushed wet and heavy around her ankles.

'You looked so beautiful. You still do, love.'

She had worn her mother's wedding dress, washed and starched, nipped and tucked so it fitted, though she was in a rage about not having the coupons for something new. This was the beginning, she had promised herself, the start of the rest of her life. Something that momentous required a new dress, not a hand-me-down from a woman who had never seemed particularly happy about her own marriage.

'We're lucky, aren't we?' Jack said. 'Both of us still here.'

Her eyes going and her legs not much better. The two of them old as the bloody hills. Bet swallowed. 'We are.'

It was not a crowded party. Some old workmates of Jack's from the buses, and a handful of neighbours from the estate – those who hadn't ended up so far away it felt impossible to keep coming back. She could make out Mike's voice – brash as ever – but couldn't hear his wife, Sue. They had lived three doors down from her and Jack. Mike had made a drunken pass at her once. But that was all long ago.

Everyone else they would have wanted to invite was dead.

When Bet said things like that, Jack told her she was being miserable, but she was simply stating fact. She was not someone who dwelt on the idea of her own death. She had tried once: she'd read an article which said that people who thought about dying every day led happier, more fulfilled lives. She did it for a week: sat down for five minutes after lunch and imagined breathing her last breath. But it made her feel worse; gave her the sensation of being trapped in a small space. Nothing to do with coffins, or burial, it was more a creeping feeling that she had got things wrong.

'Mr and Mrs Chalmers!' It was Stuart, balder and ruddier than the last time she'd seen him, his words already slurred with drink. 'Congratulations!'

Jack was on his feet, shaking Stuart's hand, Stuart patting his back. 'You old devil. You need to tell me what your secret is.'

'Love,' Jack said, and Bet found herself having to blink away the tears that rose without warning.

If she hadn't married Jack, she wouldn't be here. She might still be living in Yorkshire; or sitting in an upstairs bar on the other side of London; or in another city; or even another country. She would look different: she wouldn't be wearing this dress – dark grey, sensible; or this particular shade of lipstick – pearl blush. Tommy wouldn't exist, though she supposed there might be others, a daughter maybe, or one of each; she might have got things right with them.

'You seen what they're doing to the old place, Bet?' Stuart said. 'It's bloody criminal. They should be locked up, them on the council, and the developers besides. You heard about old Mr Tooley?'

Old Mr Tooley was younger than her and Jack. His wife had died of cancer, Bet remembered; she was fine one week, dead the next, just like that.

'He died,' Stuart said. 'Broken heart. I'm serious. They

moved him to some tiny flat out in Morden, didn't know a soul. I used to visit when I could, but you know what it's like. He just gave up. You could see it, clear as day.'

If she hadn't married Jack, she might be dead. It was possible – every choice you made closed off all the other things that might have happened instead. The magazine article had said that by thinking about dying every day you'd stop wasting time regretting things. Bet had liked the sound of that, but it hadn't worked.

A burst of laughter erupted on the far side of the room, one woman laughing louder and longer than all the rest. Someone behind the bar dropped a glass and then swore – she heard the shards scatter across the hard floor.

She had married Jack. Seventy years ago today. And so here she was. Here they all were. And she was wearing the sensible grey dress because Jack's fumbling compliments about the one she'd put on earlier that evening – layers of thin peach gauze, pleated at the neck line, beaded around the hem – had made her feel even older than she was. He was not the kind of man who was able to say things straight: Bet, you look ridiculous. She'd had to learn to decipher his meaning.

She hadn't noticed the pianist arrive, but there was a sudden flurry of notes, which resolved themselves into 'My Funny Valentine'. Bet had always found it a sad tune, but the pianist was keeping it light. Someone over by the stairs started to sing, petering out after a couple of lines. Bet let herself sway a little from left to right. She was thinking about Bertie's in Soho, all those years ago – Dougie on the trumpet, leaning back so far you'd think he'd fall over, cheeks puffed, eyes scrunched. Max at the bar, shaking ice in time with the drums. And the girls, beautiful in their long dresses and fitted gloves, their jewellery sparkling just as bright as any diamonds, their lips painted into red smiles. Sometimes her memories of that time were entirely within reach, sharp as Technicolor; other times it might all have happened to someone else.

'Now, I've got a surprise for you,' Jack said. 'I met a girl.'

Bet started and Jack laughed, put his hand on her forearm.

'She's a student,' he said, as though that explained it. 'Photography.'

'What are you talking about?'

'I asked her to come tonight and take your photo. She's here. She's just arrived. I'll bring her over.' And he was up and gone before Bet could say anything.

She watched his slow walk between the tables to the top of the stairs where a young woman stood holding a black camera bag. The light would be hopeless for taking photos. Bet would look like a ghoul. But they were walking back towards her now, and Jack's face was alight with excitement.

'Bet, this is Marinela.'

'Hello, Bet.'

She was foreign. 'Jack didn't say he'd met you.'

'At the cafe,' the girl said.

'It was full. She let me sit at her table.' Bet could hear the plea in Jack's voice.

'I don't think the light is right,' Bet said.

'No, no, it is good. I have flash, and a reflector.' She had one of those rings in her eyebrows – Bet wondered if it had hurt to have it done.

'You like having your photo taken,' Jack said. 'She does,' he told the girl. 'She could have been a model. Whereas I'm like a bit of cardboard if you point a camera at me.'

'I think here by the window?' the girl said. 'With the city behind?'

Which is what Bet would have chosen, but she said nothing. The girl was young, twenty maybe, or a touch older, her skin smooth as new butter, her back straight. She looked so easy in her body Bet couldn't decide if she was delighted by her or horribly jealous.

'A drink,' Jack said. 'I should have asked. What do you want to drink?'

'Water is fine.'

'For God's sake, it's a party,' Bet snapped. 'Get the girl a gin and tonic.'

She thought Marinela was going to object, but instead the girl touched Bet's sleeve and laughed. 'A gin and tonic,' she repeated and laughed again and Bet found herself smiling too.

Marinela unfolded a large silver circle and propped it behind Bet. She fussed about with a tripod, fixing her camera to it, moving it a little, then she stepped towards Bet and held a small black device with a white button up to her face.

'You can stay in this seat, yes, but maybe turn it a little this way. That is good. And look just here.'

The girl held up a hand and Bet looked past it, at a group of Jack's old workmates standing by the bar clutching pints; at Deepa talking into her mobile phone.

'Nice,' Marinela said. 'You are a natural.'

Bet smiled again. Jack was right, she loved having her photo taken.

'Look here again. Lift your chin a little. Yes.'

There was Tommy, just arriving, searching the room to find her and Jack. There, Jack was going to him, shaking his hand, patting his back, turning to point towards Bet and Marinela. Bet shifted her attention to the girl's hand. White, slender fingers.

'Where are you from?' she asked.

'Romania.'

Bet couldn't think where Romania was. 'You like it here?'

'I think so.'

Bet had been desperate to move to London. She could still

remember the feeling, as though London was a magnet and she was a tiny bit of metal stranded in Yorkshire, being pulled towards it. When she'd arrived – Jack's new bride – there had been five years of war and the place looked exhausted: piles of rubble and broken glass; the remaining buildings dark with coal dust. The people walking with their heads down, wearing drab old clothes. Even the river had looked like used bathwater. But none of that had got in the way of her excitement, her sense of being at the start of something new.

'I say to Jack that I take photos of the place they are knocking down. But you lived there?'

Jack had told her about the bulldozers, the fences, the dust, but she hadn't seen it. She stayed in mostly. Her legs hurt if she was on them too long and she was damned if she was going to use one of those chairs.

'It got to him more than me,' she said. 'The council made promises, they broke promises. That kind of thing happens all the time, doesn't it? You'd expect women to take it worse, but I think it was the men. The ones we knew anyway.'

'It is hard to lose your place. Look to the left again, please.'

Bet turned and saw Tommy striding towards them. He had dyed his hair. Too dark. It made his face look pale and a little drawn.

'Mum!' He leant down and hugged her – his aftershave strong enough to make her cough.

'I'm having my photo taken.'

Tommy took an exaggerated step backwards, holding up his hands.

'This is your son?' Marinela asked.

'Tom. Tommy to these two.' He held out his hand.

'Your mother is good model.'

'Is that right?'

Bet looked towards the window and followed the lights of

the cars streaming towards the roundabouts. She wanted Tommy to go away. She wanted the girl to carry on.

'This is nice, Mum. All this.' Tommy waved his hand towards the room. 'Not bad for Elephant and Castle.'

'He's such a snob,' Bet told Marinela, who lifted her eyebrows but said nothing.

'You're having fun?' Tommy asked.

'I'd like another drink. Will you get one for Marinela too?'

'No, no, it is fine. I am nearly finished. I think now maybe I take one of all of you?'

'Jack hates having his photo taken,' Bet said.

'That would be great,' Tommy said. 'Wouldn't it, Mum? I'll go and get Dad.'

Bet watched him walk away. Her boy, except he was sixty already, his hair grey beneath the dye, his body thinner and less straight than it used to be. He had been such a slight child, she had always thought she might break him if she wasn't careful.

The pianist was playing a tune she didn't recognize. There was a soft burble of conversation; the noise of glasses knocking against tables, and chairs scraped across the floor. She wondered if people were having a nice time, or wishing they were at home watching TV. She wondered if they liked the olives and what they were doing with the thin pointed stones at their centres.

'You know I'm useless at this,' Jack said, as he approached, holding onto Tommy's arm, but he was smiling.

Marinela arranged the two men behind Bet's chair, like an old Victorian portrait.

'This is good. Very nice,' Marinela said from behind the camera.

Bet felt Jack's hand brush against her head and shifted away from his touch.

'You are very handsome family.'

Tommy had had three wives but no children – Jack had always been sad about that. And maybe it would have been good to have a brood around them, grandchildren and great-grandchildren filling in the silences, distracting them from each other.

'All finished.' Marinela stepped away from the camera and grinned.

I used to be like you, Bet wanted to tell her. She couldn't say how, exactly, but it was something about the girl's eyes – an openness, a kind of excitement.

'You can stay,' she said. 'Have a drink, Jack will buy you a drink, won't you Jack?'

The two of them walked towards the bar and she watched them go – you'd think they were grandfather and granddaughter if you didn't know.

Bet turned to Tommy. 'She seems like a nice girl.'

Tommy walked around the table and sat down. 'Are you having a good time?'

Bet sipped her drink. The ice had melted and she could barely taste the gin. She wanted one of Max's cocktails. A Martini or a proper gin sling, ice cold, strong enough to make you splutter. A cocktail and a cigarette. She hadn't smoked in years. She considered asking Tommy to get her one, but you couldn't even smoke indoors these days, now it was officially bad for you. Back then, Bet and the other girls only thought about how gorgeous it made them look, the smoke swirling up around their faces as though they were film stars.

'I should have brought diamonds, shouldn't I? Or is seventy platinum? In fact I've messed up and not brought a thing. I'm so tied up with all this flat-hunting. I looked at a place in Kensal Rise on Monday. One bed. Three hundred and thirty grand. In Kensal Rise!'

'You're coming back to London, then?'

'If I can find something other than a damp shoebox to live in.' Tommy drummed his fingers on the tabletop. 'The commute is killing me.'

His latest wife had been called Diane. Ten years younger than Tommy. A yoga teacher. Into juiced spinach and God knows what else. Bet had never liked her. They'd lived in a big house in some Surrey village with a green and a pond and a forest nearby. She half-listened to Tommy complaining about house prices and lawyers' fees, and wondered whether he'd have been different if he'd been a dad. It changed some people – softened them. But maybe he'd have been like her: hopeless at it. She'd never got it right with Tommy. She'd try to say something helpful and it would come out sounding like a criticism. She'd plan a surprise and it would turn out to be exactly the thing Tommy hated the most. Jack on the other hand was a natural – she used to watch the two of them together and wonder at how easy it seemed, how straightforward.

'You used to have such tantrums,' Bet said.

'What?'

'You used to scream until I was sure you'd burst. Sometimes I'd lie down on the floor next to you and scream as well.'

'He was a kid,' Jack said. She hadn't noticed him approach. 'Kids scream. Now, Bet Chalmers, shall we dance?'

She was wearing heels. They were not high, but she could hardly walk in them. Damn it, it was her party – she would dance in her stockings if she wanted to. She slipped off her shoes and got slowly to her feet. She looked for the Romanian girl but couldn't see her. Of course she'd left – a girl like her wouldn't want to hang around with a bunch of old people.

As Jack and Bet approached the dance floor, people started to cheer. Bet felt it move through the room and rise in volume. Everyone was looking at them. It was like stepping into a greenhouse, the warmth seeping straight into her blood. Her stockings caught on the rough floor. Her legs felt heavy and old. But now Jack's hand was on her waist, and for a moment it didn't matter that he thought the peach-coloured dress was too young for her; it didn't matter that when she looked up a dark smudge sat in the centre of his face. Because she was nineteen years old again, dancing at the village fair with a handsome stranger, and the world was crystal clear.

'Did you like your surprise?' Jack's mouth was down by her ear and she could feel his words come out in hot puffs onto her skin.

'I'm too old to be having my photo taken.' Bet leant her head on his shoulder, the material of his jacket coarse against her cheek. He ran his hand down her arm and she thought, suddenly, of their first time, weeks before the wedding, in the back of a borrowed car. He'd wanted to wait, but she'd said why, why wait for anything, there was a war on, they might die before she had a ring on her finger. Laughing as he slid his fingers up her legs, as he stumbled over the fastenings of her stockings. She couldn't believe her bravery. She couldn't wait for her life to start.

There were a handful of couples on the dance floor. Mike and a woman who was not Sue; Deepa and her son – half her size, wearing a waistcoat and tie; a man Bet recognized from Jack's work.

'Where's Romania?' she asked.

'Near Hungary.'

Bet closed her eyes, breathed in Jack's familiar scent and listened to the notes of the piano trickling across the room.

'Where's Hungary?' she asked.

'Near Austria.'

They were barely moving, nothing much more than a sway to one side and then the other.

'Tommy thinks I should make a speech,' Jack said.

'There's no need.'

Jack had given a speech at their wedding. Bet had imagined he would be funny, sophisticated, bold, but he was shy and tongue-tied and she'd had to try hard to stop herself feeling disappointed.

'It might be nice? I could thank everyone for coming.'

It would be embarrassing, Bet thought – he would stumble and mutter and blush and she would be desperate for it to end. But she couldn't bring herself to say as much, and so she rested her cheek against his and said, 'If you want to. Only if you want to.'

MARINELA

There were clubs like this one in every city in England. Black-painted bricks. Blacked-out windows. Two suited men on the door with earpieces and thick, folded arms. This particular club was down a side street in Euston, next to a newsagent with posters advertising cheap international call cards. A string of pink bulbs had been slung across the entrance, and the club's name was written, pink on black, book-ended by the silhouettes of two women.

Inside, on stage, Marinela hung upside down from a pole. She wore black hot pants and a black corset; black high-heeled boots with fake-leather straps twisting up the length of her calves. The music was loud enough for the beat to be felt as well as heard, as though the very building had a pulse.

She was halfway through her dance. Afterwards, she would go out onto the floor – the other girls called it 'the pit' – and hustle for table dances and VIPs if she could get them. The stage dance was a calling card, an advertisement – the trick was to convert it into cash.

She could feel the blood making its way towards her head, the heavy swoon of it, as though she had drunk too much. The room looked different upside down: the ceiling scarred with lumps and holes, bits of tape and a trailing electricity cable; the empty tables like black islands, edged by red-leather shores. Two of the occupied tables already had girls writhing around them. At another, five men were deep in conversation. They'd have cash, but she would need to wait – there was nothing guaranteed to lose you a dance more than interrupting business chat. You waited, and you watched and you judged when was the right time to move in.

Some of the men didn't even look towards the stage. They talked to their friends, or picked at their nails, or checked their phones, the screens glowing in the dark. Some of them stared without seeing. Others looked – hungrily, angrily, sadly; it was all the same to her.

She started to make her way down the pole, still upside down. Slow, slow, keeping her face still, hiding the effort of it: thighs, back, arms, the thump of her heart. None of what she was doing was real. That was the biggest, the most important, trick of all: to know that everything was a facade.

Just before her head reached the floor, she flipped herself upright and dropped to her hands and knees. She tuned herself back into the beat – the hiss snap of the snare drum like someone sucking their teeth. The stage was wooden – rough and slightly sticky. She crawled forwards, squeezing in her elbows to make the most of her cleavage, watching out for splinters. If she thought it would make a difference she'd tell her boss he should cover the floor with a harder varnish, but the management liked making money, not spending it.

The music had started to feel too loud, the beat too heavy, though it was the same as it ever was, the singer's voice like thick syrup. She fixed her eyes on a man with a bald head and a blue tie, and smiled. He raised his hand, a house note held between finger and thumb. The girls traded them for real money, and lost a cut to management along the way. If they were found taking real cash it was confiscated. They were the rules. She moved towards the man, slow, slow.

The first night she'd worked there, only a month or so ago, she'd considered leaving before her stage slot, and once she had stepped out into the lights she'd nearly walked straight off again. There were other ways to make money. But they were more time consuming, and what did it matter, really? It was just skin.

She was almost at the edge of the stage, the bald man reaching his hand towards her, when it started.

For a moment, she was simply lost. A sudden gap opened up between her body and her mind so that one could not reach the other. It was like watching herself in a bad film. The man was pushing the note into her almost undone corset. She was sitting back on her heels and batting her eyelids.

The man held out another note and made a circular motion with his finger. She lowered herself to her hands and knees, turned so she faced away from the punters, and rocked herself backwards, forwards, backwards. When the man tucked the note into her hot pants, his fingers made a swift furtive move forwards, but she could not feel his touch. She could not feel the wooden boards underneath her knees and palms. She was not present. There was simply her body, carrying on doing what it was doing, and her mind, locked up somehow, crashing against the inside of her head.

It had happened once before, at her grandmother's funeral. A day hot enough to turn the milk sour; hot enough to make the sweat creep out of every pore. She told herself that was why it had happened: she was hot and upset and she had not eaten. It was nothing important. And it had not happened again, until tonight. Had she eaten today? She couldn't remember.

The music rushed at her and then backed away. Rushed

forwards again, as though it had turned into something with shape and speed.

She unfastened her corset, but could not feel the black lace in her hand, and when she unclamped it from around her body, she could not feel the release, or the air on her breasts. The house note dropped onto the floor. Marinela picked it up and tucked it into her waistband. She could not feel anything.

At her grandmother's funeral she had stood at the front of the church and just as the priests started their chanting, she had lost herself. She'd felt as though part of her was dead; and the bit that wasn't – the bit that was standing there with a tissue crumpled up in her hot hand – had become unreachable. It lasted for hours. All through the service, the burial, the walk back to Bunica's house for wine and *koliva*. She moved the way a real person would move, but she felt none of it.

She was back at the pole now. Climbing. She could not feel the metal between her thighs; could only hear the music rushing and waning, rushing and waning; and now she tipped herself upside-down again, one leg straight up, the other bent into a triangle. The lights had started to spin.

The bald man clapped. She saw him. She heard the pat pat pat of his hands hitting each other. But it was as though he was far away, as though she was looking at him through the wrong end of a telescope. She tried to imagine photographing him: her holding the camera, focusing on his eyes, asking him to lift his chin, still his hands. She tried to bring the thought closer, but it slithered out of her grasp and was gone.

She was back on her feet. Moving towards the exit. The next dancer pushed past her onto the stage – she had taken too long, but if she went any faster she might fall, she might never get up again.

'Are you OK?' It was Jess, one of the other girls. She

sounded as though she was talking into a voice-distorter, the words swelled and then sagged, their edges uncertain.

'You look like you've seen a ghost, love.'

Marinela wanted to take hold of Jess's arm and hold on. She wanted to ask her to help.

'I. Am. Fine.' She concentrated on making each word and then pushed them out of her mouth as though they were stones. 'Just. Tired.'

'Well, sit down, then. Have a minute before you go out there. Do you want a glass of water?'

She nodded. Jess brought her a glass, and she drank, but she couldn't feel the water in her mouth, or dropping down her throat.

Try to breathe. Try not to fall. She asked Jess to retie her corset, speaking in the same careful way.

'Don't you think you should go home, love? I can cover for you. I'll make up something to tell Paul.'

Marinela stood, nearly stumbling, because the ground was no longer flat, no longer stable. She shook her head, forced a smile and left the room, stepping carefully over the shifting floor towards the door into the main space.

And so it went. It was remarkable what you could do when you were dead. A ghost. She was smiling at the bald man. She was climbing up onto a tabletop, picking her way through champagne glasses and breaking nothing. She was touching her breasts. She was touching her thighs. She was undoing her corset, a little more, a little more. She was telling a man who asked if she was Russian that yes, she was Russian, because why not? She was anything they wanted her to be.

When she got home, there was another party. There had been one the night before, and two nights before that. When she'd signed the tenancy she hadn't thought to ask about such things. Strangers in the hallway, on the stairs, in the kitchen. The music was almost as loud as it had been in the club. A couple leant against her bedroom door, kissing. She stood in front of them and waited until they pulled apart, glaring and indignant. In her room, she locked the door, drew the curtains and swapped her clothes for an oversized T-shirt and a pair of Stefan's boxers. She took a packet of crisps from the plastic box of food she kept under her desk and sat cross-legged on the bed eating them without registering their taste. Sleep now. She would shower in the morning. She would be back to normal in the morning.

And she was. She woke up herself again. Alive, present. On a Friday morning, early October, in a shared house halfway between Kennington and Elephant and Castle.

Upstairs, her housemate Danny was doing his exercises; the ceiling shook with each jump and the windows shuddered in their frames. A police car whistled past outside and a pigeon cooed somewhere close by. The sounds were as they should be; each in its place. Marinela touched her forehead with both hands and then ran them down the length of her body, lifting her knees to her chest so she could reach all the way to her toes.

She rolled over and twisted around so her feet met the floor, an old green carpet turned grey at its edges. Hers was the front room on the ground floor. Large, with elaborate plaster cornicing, a vast ceiling rose, cracked green and yellow tiles in the fireplace. Grand once, but shabby now – a weedy light fitting dangling from the middle of the room; a damp patch spreading across the chimney breast; the paint peeling away from the ceiling.

Her face was tight and raw, her eyelids tacky with mascara. She opened her bedroom door and stood for a moment, looking out at the narrow hallway with its scuffed walls and piles of unclaimed post, breathing in the smell of last night's cigarettes and alcohol. The bathroom was littered with beer cans and plastic glasses. Sticky footprints marked the lino. Marinela stood under the shower and let the water rush hot over her skin. She stayed there longer than she usually would. It was a sensation she remembered from the last time: a brief and absolute wonder at being back inside her body.

She made coffee – strong and black – and took it to her room, sat propped up against her pillows, staring at the empty, magnolia-painted walls. She had dreamt of Romania again. It was always the same dream: she wore only one shoe, and a coat way too big for her, walking through the fields at the back of her grandmother's house. Sometimes there was snow; other times the corn was thick rustling green and thistles shot their purple flowers towards the sky. Last night, it had been raining, puddles forming on the track as she walked, the raindrops denting their surfaces. And Stefan had been there. Wearing a suit but no tie; his feet bare, mud between his toes; his greying hair darkening against his scalp.

Marinela sipped at her coffee and listened to the pulse of a heavy bassline from a passing car. Stefan had given her a dictionary. It sat on the mantelpiece, next to a couple of library books. He had written a message on the first page. *For my darling Sparrow, a hundred thousand English words for you. All my love, always, Stefan.* She'd ripped it out when she arrived in London, but the ink might as well have seeped through to the page underneath because she still saw it every time she opened the book.

She had promised herself not to message him, but every day there was something new she wanted to share – the water-worn bricks she'd found on the muddy beach at the edge of the Thames when the water was low; the shopping centre at

Elephant and Castle that reminded her so much of home; the piles of rubble where there used to be flats. Jack and Bet.

Maybe she should have waited. Believed him. Had more patience. He would leave his wife and they would get married. But then she'd seen him with that other girl on the lake and she'd gone home and started looking for courses. Any course. In any city that wasn't Bucharest.

Marinela finished her coffee and took her camera from the desk. It was only a ten-minute walk from the house to where Jack and Bet's estate used to stand. Morning commuters hurried, heads down, headphones in, towards Tube stations and bus stops. Shopkeepers pulled up shutters; laid out plastic bowls of fruit on wooden trestle tables; ran cloths over fridges, tables, counters. The air was wintry, but the sky was clear of rain clouds and there was something promising about the day.

She crossed the road at the lights, stopped by the tall hoardings with their pictures of trees; new tower blocks with gardens on their roofs; people sitting and smiling, running and smiling, walking and smiling. The bulldozers were already at work.

She'd looked up images of the old estate online. Tall, brown-grey blocks. Concrete walkways. Rows of lower buildings with gardens. Graffiti. Trees. It didn't look so different from some of the housing projects back home, though most of those were painted white, to lessen the summer heat.

There was nothing to see now above the tops of the hoardings – just the sharp tip of the Shard, a few light clouds gathering around it. She turned down a side street, where mesh fences revealed piles of rubble, the lower sections of some buildings still standing. Machines dotted the site – articulated limbs and heavy claws. She stood and watched one pawing at a wall, surprised as she always was at the weight and volume of the noise when a section broke and fell to the ground. Over by the railway line, new buildings were already growing, white concrete skeletons swathed in scaffolding and tarpaulin.

She started to take photos. Concentrating first on the machines and the way they moved amongst the wreckage like animals; then on the remaining buildings – the details of inside walls: red paint; yellow; green; the scars of old shelving units and kitchen cabinets.

She was trying to widen a small hole in the fence so she could fit her lens through it when a woman strode up to her. Short. Dumpy. Her hair a frizz of dyed red.

'It's not a fucking freak show,' she shouted. 'People lived here.'

Marinela stared at her, frozen. She wanted to say, I know, I know someone who lived here. I know that.

'Go on. Piss off.' The woman waved her hands at Marinela as though she was a stray dog, persistent and unwanted. 'I've had enough of you lot.'

Marinela turned and walked away without saying anything. When she looked back, the woman was still standing there, arms folded, staring at her.

JACK

Jack and Bet had moved from the estate into a one-bedroom ground-floor flat, just off the Walworth Road. They'd been offered a handful of places and this had been the best of them. It was Victorian, with high ceilings and draughty, single-glazed windows. Jack wasn't complaining, but there was damp in the kitchen, and the hallway was so narrow it was hard for two people to get past each other. Whenever Tommy came round there was an awkward shuffle, Jack having to open the door and then back away so that Tommy could get inside.

'So we're agreed?' Bet said. They were sitting in the living room, on two of four green velveteen armchairs. It was a dark, cramped room, edged with still-unpacked boxes, the window giving straight onto the street. Jack couldn't remember what was in the boxes. Tommy was always nagging them to sort the place out, but they never seemed able to get around to it.

'We're not going,' Bet continued.

'No.'

'And you're not going to switch sides halfway through?'

'No.'

'Promise?'

Jack looked at his wife. She wore a blue wool skirt and thin beige stockings which stopped just short of the skirt's hem. 'He's only trying to help, love.'

'Promise.' Bet glared at him and Jack had to stop himself from standing up, walking over to her and kissing her full on the lips.

'I promise,' he said.

Bet smoothed her hair. She'd put on a dash of make-up – light beige on her eyelids, a dusky pink lipstick.

'You look lovely,' Jack said.

She lifted her head, her eyes distant. 'I wonder if that girl will bring the photos.'

'I'm sure she will.' He hoped they were good. He hoped Bet would like them.

'I don't know why you didn't take her number.'

'She'll drop them round, she said.'

Bet frowned. 'Where was she from? Russia?'

'Romania.'

Bet nodded and turned towards the television. There was one of those build-your-own-home programmes on. A couple wearing hard hats talked about foundations while a cement mixer churned behind them.

Jack remembered them building the estate. He'd stood with half the rest of the neighbourhood watching them bulldoze the terraces; and then came row upon row of prefabricated concrete boxes, stacked up on top of each other like children's building blocks.

'Jack.' Bet's voice was raised.

'Hmmm?'

'The door.'

Tommy had a key, but he always knocked, always waited until Jack almost had his hand on the door before he let himself in.

Jack got to his feet.

'Remember what you said,' Bet shouted as he reached the hallway.

'Dad!' Tommy stood in the open doorway, a breath of cool air coming into the flat ahead of him.

Jack smiled and extended his hand for Tommy to shake. Other families hugged and kissed, he knew that, but it wasn't their way – didn't mean he loved his boy any less, mind.

'I have lunch.' Tommy brandished two plastic bags and headed straight for the kitchen. 'You want to eat in here?' he called.

'Fine.' Jack followed him into the kitchen, sat at the table and watched him unpack quiche and crisps, bread rolls and cheese onto the kitchen counter like it was some kind of picnic, or party. Tommy usually wore a shirt and beige trousers, but today he was in jeans and a blue zipped sweatshirt – the kind of clothes meant for younger people.

'You look different,' Jack said.

Tommy touched his hair, smiled.

'Is she nice?' Jack asked.

Tommy blushed, laughed. 'Dad!'

He was sixty years old. Jack couldn't think where he got the energy.

'You like her?' Jack said.

'I've met her twice.'

'Who?' Bet was at the kitchen door.

'No one. How are you, Mum?'

'Who were you talking about?'

'Sit down, love.' Jack made to get up and help her to a chair but she waved him away. 'You're always in cahoots, you two.' She shuffled across the room to the table.

Tommy sighed. 'I had a date.'

'Oh?' Bet lowered herself onto the chair opposite Jack.

'Two dates. She's called Liz. We met on the Internet. She's

nice. There's not much else to say. Early days. Here, have a look at this while I'm sorting lunch.' Tommy took a brochure out of one of the bags and handed it to Jack. Springfields Retirement Complex. The paper was thick and glossy.

'I've looked at a few, and this one's the best so far. A bit out of London. Nice gardens. I need to give the council a call about the fees and what have you. We might need to top up what they offer.'

Jack put the brochure on the table in front of him. He didn't look at Bet.

'The Internet?' Bet said.

'I can try and help out with the money.'

'You're buying a flat,' Jack said.

Tommy laughed. 'Not any time soon I'm not.'

Jack opened the brochure. Columns of small black writing and a picture of a sprightly looking grey-haired couple walking across a manicured lawn towards an out-of-focus building. He turned the page. A large room with a blue carpet and French windows, smiling old people sitting around a table playing cards. It gave him the willies – looked like some kind of cult.

Bet coughed. Jack looked up and she glared at him then looked towards Tommy. 'Your dad's got something to say.' She folded her arms. 'Since you don't seem to take any notice when I say it.'

Tommy came to the table with the bread board. 'We agreed we'd talk about it.'

'Your mother and I have been—'

'A grown-up conversation discussing the pros and cons.'

'We do fine, Tommy,' Jack said. Here he was again, stuck between the two of them as always. He didn't want to move any more than Bet did though.

Tommy turned away, came back with a plate of cheese, a bowl of crisps. 'You agreed.'

'That's the mixing bowl,' Bet said, looking at the crisps.

'It's a nice place.' Tommy lifted the brochure from the table and opened a page. '"We treat each of our clients as individuals, creating tailored care plans to meet specific needs,"' he read.

Bet snorted.

'It's good of you to do that research,' Jack said. 'We appreciate it.'

Bet coughed.

'But like I said, we've talked about it, and it's not for us.'

Tommy sat down, sliced open three bread rolls and handed them one each. He cut pieces of cheese and filled his roll with slow deliberation.

'So, the pros,' he said.

'Your father said no.'

'The pros are: a clean safe place to live.'

'Are you saying the flat's dirty?' Bet snapped.

'Emergency alarms in every room. Someone on duty twenty-four seven.'

'We're fine.' Bet's voice rose and now Jack was trying to catch her eye but she wouldn't look at him.

'Other people to socialize with.'

'Your father hates that kind of thing.'

'Meals cooked for you.'

'Old Mrs Broughton got put in one of those places,' Bet said. 'A week later she was wetting the bed and God knows what else.'

'Maybe she didn't go to a good place.'

'And that couple from the estate, what were their names, Jack? Dennis and Lydia? Louise? Anyway, their son shipped them off to some place and they weren't even allowed to stay in the same room.'

'We can iron all of that out,' Tommy said. 'We can find somewhere that suits you.'

'Here suits us just fine.'

Tommy closed his eyes. Jack tried to see the little boy he used to take down to the Thames, who sat on his shoulders and pointed at the boats, and the seagulls dipping and diving in their wakes. They'd spend hours searching for 'treasure', bring back bags of water-worn pebbles and lumps of rusted metal for Bet to pretend to admire.

'Somebody watching everything we do,' Bet said. 'Trying to get us to make Christmas decorations out of toilet rolls. No privacy.'

Tommy took a crisp and the three of them sat in silence listening to the crunch of it between his teeth.

'You're ninety years old,' he said when he'd finished.

'Not yet,' Bet snapped.

'As near as damn it. You should be taking it easy, getting looked after. I'm trying to help.'

Jack held up a hand. 'It's very kind of you, Tommy. We appreciate it. But you've got to understand, your mother and—'

'What about her eyes?'

'There is nothing wrong with my eyes.'

'That isn't true, Mum. I've read about it, and it's going to get worse.'

'We manage.'

'You don't need to just manage. You deserve more than to just manage.'

Bet folded her arms. 'No.'

'Jesus.' Tommy shook his head. 'I'm not giving up on this, Mum.'

'It's our choice.'

'I'm going to take you to the GP next week,' Tommy said. 'Get them to do some tests.'

Jack looked at his bread roll. He had eaten half but couldn't imagine being able to eat the rest of it.

'I won't go,' Bet said.

'Then I'll get them to come here.'

It had been a year, maybe more, since Bet had started complaining her glasses were dirty even when she wasn't wearing them. She'd stopped talking about it, but Jack had noticed her turning her head this way and the other more and more, trying to see whatever she wanted to see out of the corners of her eyes. She'd started cooking simpler meals – claiming she couldn't be bothered with anything fancy in a voice that meant she was, if not lying, then definitely avoiding something.

'I'll have some of that cake.' Bet gestured to the fruitcake still in its cardboard box. Tommy didn't move to open it.

'Maybe—' Jack started.

Bet threw him a look. He reached for the cake and busied himself cutting three thick slices.

'Maybe having your eyes checked out again wouldn't be a bad idea.' He didn't look at her.

'You promised,' she said, quietly.

'Not the home, just the doctor.'

'It's all part and bloody parcel of the same thing.'

'He's trying to help, love.'

'Well I wish he'd stop.'

'Bet.' Jack reached for his wife's arm but she drew away, took a slice of cake and bit into it, crumbs tumbling onto the tabletop.

'You don't even like this flat, Mum. You never have. You've never even unpacked properly,' Tommy said.

Piles of boxes stacked up in the living room, and more next to the wardrobe in the bedroom. They'd been too old to move. And it felt as though the whole process – the bidding for flats and waiting for phone calls and having to decide what to take with them and what to get rid of – had put another handful of years onto each of them.

'This is our home.' Bet folded her arms. 'We got chucked off the estate. We're not getting chucked out of here.'

Tommy slumped back in his chair. 'All right.' He held up both hands. 'I give up. I give up for three months. Then we're having this conversation again, and then three months after that, and then three months after that. You'll thank me for it in the end.'

They sat for a while, eating their cake in silence. It was Jack's job to change the subject, to coax the two of them back onto speaking terms. He took a bite of cake, looked at his son and wife. She would start on at him as soon as Tommy left. You promised, she'd say. You promised me. He glanced at the brochure. He could imagine Bet thriving in such a place – full of people and gossip and activity. He would lose her if they went, he could see that. They were better off where they were.

BET

It was the third such letter she'd received. Official. The council's logo at the top of the page. The mail came when Jack was out on his walk and Bet always made sure to sift through it before he got back, just in case. Reading was getting harder, but with a bit of concentration she could make out most things.

She sat in the kitchen with the letter on her lap. Jack would be at the shopping centre by now. She pictured him walking, his body tilted forwards, his shoes scuffing the tiles, stopping to sit on one of the red metal benches. The shopkeepers must know him. Maybe they looked out for him every morning. There's Jack, they'd say to their colleagues, or just to themselves. Or if they didn't know his name – there's the old bloke. A black coat in winter, navy blue jacket in summer. Maybe it comforted them to see him.

A scheme to tackle empty properties – that was what the letter was about. *It has been noticed . . . There is support available . . . Islington council are committed to . . .* She chewed at her bottom lip. They couldn't make her do anything. Maybe she should write and tell them to stop sending the letters, but someone might telephone in response, or, worse, come round. It was easier to just do what she always did.

Bet eased herself out of the chair and walked to the sink,

took the long-handled gas lighter they'd used to light the hob since the internal mechanism broke, and clicked it once, twice, until a flame emerged from its end. She held the top corner of the letter and let the flame lick across the bottom. It took a moment, the paper blackening and smoking before the flame got hold and crept quickly up towards her fingers. She held on for as long as she dared, then dropped the letter into the sink, where it burnt out. When she turned on the tap, the ashes clogged the plughole and she had to rub her fingertip around and around until they broke apart and disappeared. She took the last remaining bit of paper – a blank white strip – ripped it in half and half again and threw it into the bin. There. She fought the window open to let out the smell, washed and dried her hands and sat back down, exhausted. In a moment she would go into the living room. Jack had left a pot of tea on the coffee table, the same way he always did, the white spout and handle sticking out from the red cover. She would pour herself a cup, put the TV on and maybe let herself close her eyes for a moment.

Something woke her. She sat upright, flustered, feeling a tightness in her neck and back. She had fallen asleep there in the kitchen, her head lolling onto her chest.

'Jack?' she called, but there was no response.

It must have been a sound from one of the other flats. Noises moved across the building in the oddest ways – someone's footsteps sounding as though they were in your hallway when they were in a different flat entirely. Voices and music; the shove of furniture or boxes; something thrown. There was a pattern to the sounds, she'd found; she'd come to recognize the way people walked – light or heavy, quick or slow – and the music they liked to play – mournful violins; heavy drums; something quick and bright and Spanish-sounding.

But then she heard a door knocker lifted and dropped and

realized that it was her door not someone else's. She felt herself freeze, the way she'd seen rabbits do in the fields back in Yorkshire, a split-second hesitation before they turned and fled.

It would be no one. Someone selling tea towels, or double-glazing; or asking her to give money for cancer or heart disease or disabled children; or to sign some petition, or answer a questionnaire. She was not quick on her feet. By the time she got to the door whoever it was would have gone and she'd be tired and put out. She closed her eyes. Her heart was beating too fast. Such a fool, but she wished Jack was there.

She heard the letterbox being pushed open, and then a voice, 'Bet? Jack?'

It was the Romanian girl. Bet opened her eyes. Mary, she thought. No, another name. She remembered the click of the camera shutter, the whirr as the girl wound on the film.

The letterbox snapped closed and was pushed open again. 'It's Marinela. I have the photos.' Bet pictured her bent down on the other side of the door and wondered if she felt the ache of it in her back.

She lifted her stick from the floor and leant her weight into it, one hand over the other on its rubber handle. She did not call out.

When she opened the door, the girl was still there, shifting from one foot to the other. She thrust a bunch of roses at Bet.

Bet curled her hand around the stems and heard the crackle of the plastic wrapping. She lifted the flowers to her nose, close enough to feel their soft petals on her skin. They smelt of plastic, traffic fumes, outside – not of roses at all.

The sound of a far-off crash made both women tense. It would be a wall, Bet thought, a wall and its windows tumbling to the ground. When the wind blew from that direction it brought the noise with it and the image of the machines ripping the flats apart, exposing wallpaper and bathroom furniture, kitchen fittings and carpets. She imagined their old kitchen sink falling from the eighth floor onto a pile of rubble below, breaking into sharp pieces.

'We were happy there,' Bet said. 'The view was something else.' She blinked and looked at the girl. 'Come in then.'

They did the awkward hallway shuffle and Bet ushered Marinela into the kitchen.

'You can put these in some water.' Bet handed her the flowers and sat down. 'Cut the stems first, it makes them last longer. And a teaspoon of sugar. Did you know that? There are scissors in the top drawer, by the sink. Vases in the cupboard underneath.'

Bet sat and watched the girl carefully clip the bottom of each stem and place them into the water one by one. When she was done she lowered her face to them.

'Maybe if they have no thorns they have no smell,' she said.

Bet shrugged, and said, 'They're lovely,' because the girl sounded disappointed. 'Tea? There's a pot next door, but it might be cold by now.'

'I will make.'

There was a time when Bet would have protested, but she was tired and her head hurt, and so she smiled and said thank you and told Marinela where to find the cups, the tea bags, the milk. The room still smelt of burnt paper, she was sure of it.

'Do you smoke?' Bet asked, when they were settled in the living room with their tea, the roses in a cut-glass vase she hadn't used in years placed on the low coffee table. 'I used to love smoking. Haven't had one in years. I don't suppose you do, do you? People don't seem to these days.'

'I do not have any.'

Shame. She would have liked to pull in a lungful of smoke, hard enough to make the cigarette crackle red at its tip.

'You want to see the photos?'

Bet nodded, though she wasn't sure if she did. It was one thing to sit in front of the camera, imagining yourself to be some kind of model, and quite another to see a picture of yourself fixed onto paper, wrinkles and all.

Marinela handed her a brown-paper envelope and Bet tipped the photos onto her lap. Black and white. She hadn't expected that.

'My eyes aren't what they were,' she said, picking the top photo from the pile and holding it to one side.

Christ, she looked old. She blew out air from between rounded lips.

'I should be in a museum,' she said.

'No, no.' The girl leaned towards her. 'This is so beautiful. You are beautiful, Bet.'

'I am eighty-nine.'

'It is very impressive. No? And look at these. Jack as well has a very good face.'

There were two photos of just Bet, and two of her, Jack and Tommy. In one, Jack looked down at her and Tommy looked straight at the camera. Who knew what either one was thinking. However close you were to other people – wife, mother, mistress – however many years you'd known them, you never truly knew what went on inside their heads. In the other photo Jack and Tommy looked at each other. In cahoots. She'd been so angry with Jack the other day, saying Tommy should send for the doctor, and call social services no doubt. He'd apologized as soon as Tommy had left, said he'd just been trying to keep the peace, but she still didn't speak to him for the rest of the afternoon.

'You like?' The girl sounded uncertain.

'Yes. Yes. Of course. They're very good.' She had been young once, she wanted to tell this girl. She had been just like her – smooth-skinned and agile. She used to step out onto the street with perfect hair, perfect stockings, perfect face. She loved the thrill of it – walking across the city, sitting on the top deck of a bus, her hat in her lap, lifting her hand for a taxi in the early hours of the morning. There was nothing but a shimmer of excitement reaching from her stomach to her throat. And it wasn't as though she felt much different now – not inside. Inside, she was still twenty years old.

'I will give you my phone number,' Marinela said. 'In case you want any more of the photos.'

'There's a notepad by the phone.' Bet pointed towards the small table by the living-room door.

The girl wrote her number and handed the sheet of paper to Bet.

'Where is Jack?' she asked.

'At the shopping centre. He walks there every day. Keeps him going, he says. You'd think he'd pick somewhere more inspiring.'

'You don't go with him?'

Bet tapped her fingertips against her right thigh. 'Legs,' she said. 'You think everything will just carry on working. I know I did when I was your age. But things pack up on you.' She lifted her tea and took a sip.

'You are angry?' Marinela asked.

Bet blinked. She was angry. About the letter. About Tommy. About most things, now she came to think of it. 'No,' she said. 'I'm still here, aren't I? You get to be more grateful when you're my age.' Which was a lie, but the girl would never know. 'You're going to get a job then, are you, taking photographs?'

Marinela laughed. 'This is not easy.'

'But you're still studying it?'

'I want to be better. Maybe if I am better I can get job. And nicer place to live.'

'When I was your age, most of us just wanted to get

46

married and have babies. Not me. I wanted more than that, but,' she faltered. 'How old are you?'

'Twenty-five.'

'Well, there you are.'

'How old were you when you had Tommy?'

Bet blinked. These young people thought nothing of asking personal questions. 'Well. We were a little late to all that in the end. My mother had given up asking,' she said. In truth she'd never been sure she wanted children, but after all that mess with Kit, it had seemed the only option – the only thing that could fix what she had broken.

Marinela smiled. 'You have other children?'

'Just him.'

Jack had wanted more. Bet had not. Now there were pills and the like that a woman could take to make sure of it. She'd been lucky – she'd always thought of it in that way – but sometimes she wondered if Jack had been right after all. Maybe it would have been easier with two, or three, or even four. She'd never found Tommy easy, never felt that immediate connection her friends talked about. Maybe if she and Jack had had more it would have helped somehow.

'And he doesn't have children,' she went on. 'They talked about adoption once, him and his second wife, but they got divorced instead.' She had always thought she might make a better grandmother than mother; she would have appreciated a second chance.

'In Romania they wanted women to have many, many children,' Marinela said. 'But my mother only had me.' She paused. 'And now I am in London and she is sad.'

'Why did you come?'

Marinela laughed and then shrugged.

Bet waited.

'A man,' Marinela said at last. 'I came because of a man.'

47

'Here?'

'There. My parents don't know about him. He's older than me. A lecturer at the university.'

Kit had wanted her to run away. From London to New York. He'd promised a place to live, money, adventure. He had not promised to leave his wife. And Bet had almost gone. She had got herself a passport, packed a bag, and then sat on the old brown velveteen sofa in the attic room in Larcom Street and watched the clock on the mantelpiece turn its thin brass hands around and around; holding her breath as the flight time neared and then passed, that other potential life dropping back into the past, turning into a thing that never happened.

'You left him?' Bet asked.

'He is no good.' Marinela shook her head. 'I had to go.'

'But you miss him?'

Marinela blushed and looked miserable.

Kit had telephoned that same evening – long distance, Bet could almost see the money evaporating as they spoke – Kit careering between incomprehension and anger, Bet trying to speak as softly as she could so Jack wouldn't hear. It's the right thing, it's for the best, she'd said, and yet only half of her believed it, and for a long time – years – afterwards she kept wondering if she'd made the biggest mistake of her life.

'I should go,' Marinela said. 'It has been good to see you. You will say hello to Jack from me?'

And there she was, gathering herself, the way people did, patting at her clothes, tucking her feet closer to the chair, ready to stand, moving her tongue around her lips with the faintest of sounds. Bet had a sudden, intense desire for her to stay.

'You don't like where you live?' she asked.

Marinela blinked. 'It is fine. A house.' She waved vaguely towards the Walworth Road. 'Very noisy. They like to have parties, the people I live with. And the kitchen—' She shrugged. 'But it is fine. Really. Thank you for the tea, Bet.'

The idea of the dress came from nowhere, just landed in Bet's mind. 'How tall are you?' she asked. 'Five three? Five four?'

Marinela frowned. 'I only know centimetres. Wait.' She pulled her phone from her pocket and swiped and dabbed at the screen. 'Here. Yes. Five feet, three inches.'

Bet smiled. 'Perfect. I have something for you.'

She could sense the girl trying to work out how to say no.

'It's a dress,' Bet said.

'Dress?'

'From a long time ago.' Bet laughed. 'Sixty years. No, even more than that. It's the only one I kept.'

Marinela walked towards her and put her hand, light, on Bet's shoulder. Bet caught her scent – not perfume, more like soap or shampoo, a faint herby smell – mint, and maybe sage.

'You cannot give me a dress,' she said.

'But otherwise it just sits and rots.' Bet could hear the desperation in her voice and hated herself for it. 'I can't wear it,' she said.

'But you can give it to someone you know.'

Bet moved to one side so Marinela's hand fell from her shoulder. 'At least look,' she said. 'If you don't like it, don't take it.'

Marinela followed her to the bedroom. She was humouring her, Bet knew, but she was fixed now on the idea of the dress, of Marinela wearing the dress.

The bedroom had a brown carpet and heavy pink linen curtains. The bed, with its high mahogany headboard, was neatly made – Jack's doing – a white sheet turned back over a dun-coloured blanket. There were low wooden cabinets on either side, each with a squat white lamp and an empty water glass.

Marinela liked the dress. Bet could tell from the way she pulled in her breath once she'd followed Bet's instructions and brought it out from the back of the wardrobe. Bet walked over to her and touched the thin plastic that covered the silk. It was as though the colour shot straight from her fingertips to her brain: like dark green glass with a light shining through it.

'It's beautiful,' Marinela said.

Bet nodded, but she was thinking about Bertie's, the clink of cocktail glasses and the burble of conversation. The doors closed and the curtains shut – nothing to think about but the here and now, the tickle of a man's moustache as he lowered his mouth towards your ear to speak; the first sharp shock of a Martini on your tongue; the way that green dress seemed to hold her in a constant embrace. It brings out the colour of your eyes, Kit told her, that first time.

'Very beautiful,' Marinela said.

You are very beautiful. Kit had said that too.

'It's yours,' Bet said. She was tired now. She wanted the girl to leave so she could lie on the bed and close her eyes, collect herself before Jack got home.

It seemed, for a while, that Marinela would insist she could not take the dress, but Bet kept saying she wanted her to; she'd had such fun wearing it; it was pointless to have it sitting in the wardrobe doing nothing.

In the end she said, 'If you don't want to wear it, sell it. People like all the old things these days, don't they?' The clothes, at least, if not the people who used to wear them.

And Marinela stepped towards Bet, the dress between them rustling in its plastic covering, and kissed her on the cheek.

'Thank you,' she said, and Bet felt a smile pull at her mouth.

They walked to the front door and Marinela stepped outside, the dress folded now and held against her chest. Bet hoped for a moment that the girl would lean forward and kiss her cheek again, but instead she said, 'Goodbye, Bet. Thank you. Maybe I will see you again soon.' And then she was gone, and Bet was left alone in the doorway of the flat, thinking about Bertie's, and the green dress, and the way Kit had looked at her that first time they'd met – listening to the grumble of machines pulling the old estate down block by block, flat by flat, concrete wall by concrete wall.

MARINELA

Marinela had heard nothing from Bet for over a week, had almost forgotten about her and Jack, caught up as she was with her latest university assignment – a project about nature in the city, which had her searching out hidden rivers, and flowers that found their homes in between paving slabs and bricks. And then, Bet had called, her voice thin and unsure of itself, sounding somewhere between excited and desperate, asking Marinela to meet her at an address in a place called Angel. Marinela had no lectures that day, so she'd said yes. She had promised herself, when she came to England, to say yes as much as she could. Plus she liked Bet – her sharpness, the way she took care over what she looked like. There was something about her that made Marinela feel the same comfort she'd felt with her grandmother – though the two women were nothing alike.

The steep escalator lifted her from the Tube station to the street, where a flower stall and news-stand crowded the pavement. She followed the route on her phone: along the main road with its smart shops and smart pubs, then right along quieter residential streets. Well-heeled. That was what the English would say. The streets wide and clean and quiet; the houses prim and polished with their arched windows and fresh paintwork and ordered gardens. She eventually reached the right road, which sloped steeply upwards, lined on both sides with tall white buildings.

Bet was standing outside number twenty-four, in front of a glossy black door with an oversized brass doorknob. Straight-backed, alert, her head lifted towards the road. She wore her blue wool skirt and cream blouse, and a thin blue cardigan. She had on sensible-looking shoes, but no coat.

'Bet? You are alone?' Marinela hurried up the steps and took Bet's hand. Cold. Her skin was soft and cushiony, and yet Marinela could feel the bones too. She imagined them: thin and yellowy-white, delicately jointed.

'We're all alone,' Bet said, 'when it comes down to it,' and then she laughed. 'Did you see the sphinxes?' She pointed across the road and Marinela turned and saw that each house opposite had a sphinx and a short obelisk either side of its door.

'Some builder's whim,' Bet said. 'I always found them a bit solemn.'

Marinela bent to kiss her cheek. 'You are cold! Where is your coat?'

'They say it'll snow, but it won't. Too early. Thank you for coming, dear.'

'It sounded important. Is there a problem?'

Bet frowned, and then said, 'Well,' as though the word meant something different. She reached into her cardigan pocket and pulled out a small bunch of keys attached to an orange plastic tag. They shook a little in her hand, metal clattering against metal.

'Bet, you are cold. I can unlock.' Marinela reached for the keys but Bet pulled away, closing her hand into a fist and holding it to her chest. After a moment she laughed again and said, 'Silly me. Silly old me.'

'Are we going to see somebody?'

'Just a minute.' Bet held up her hand. 'Just give me a minute.'

And so Marinela waited, standing with Bet, facing the wide black door and the buzzers with thin labels in the slots next to each button – some typed, some handwritten, some blank.

Eventually, Bet roused herself and said, 'Flat seven. Third floor. There's no lift, or at least there wasn't.' She approached the door and spent an age finding the right key. Marinela did not offer to help.

Inside was a wide entrance hall with a couple of bikes propped against one wall and a buggy parked in front of them. The stairs reached up and around, carpeted with brown and cream stripes that made Marinela dizzy. Bet was out of breath halfway up the first flight.

'I used to run up here,' she said. 'Light as a bird.' She laughed and then started coughing, and Marinela thought that perhaps she might die. Then there would be trouble. They would think she had hurt her. She could imagine the son shaking his fist, red in the face, bits of spit coming out with his words, saying it was all her fault, everything was her fault.

The place smelt of damp. The carpet was specked with dirt, dried leaves, little offerings from the outside. Dark scuffs marked the walls, from knee to hip height – grubby hands, furniture, bags of shopping.

There were two flats per floor. Number seven had a white door, aged a little yellow, a number seven made out of black metal, no mat.

Bet stood outside with the keys in her hand. 'I haven't been here for sixty years,' she said. 'More than that.'

Marinela waited.

Bet turned and Marinela wanted to step forwards and hug her, tell her that whatever was bothering her was of no real importance. Instead she put her hand on Bet's forearm and gave a gentle squeeze.

'There was a man,' Bet started, and then looked at the door of number eight as though someone might be standing behind it, listening. She lowered her voice. 'Kit. It was a long time ago. I was just a girl, really. I never meant it to happen.' She let out a breath. 'I suppose that's what everyone says. Did you say the man in Romania was married?'

'Will we go in and sit down?' Marinela said.

Bet opened her mouth as though to say something, but no words came out.

'Bet?'

She shook her head. 'I'm not sure I can.'

Marinela put her hand gently over Bet's, lifted her fingers away from her palm and took the keys. Bet did nothing to stop her, and so she slotted the key into the lock and opened the door.

The flat smelt damper than the stairway, and the air inside was icy and stale. Marinela took Bet's elbow and they stepped into a narrow plum-carpeted hallway, an empty white shelving unit against one wall and a tired-looking paper light shade above. The hallway opened onto a large room. First a kitchen, then a table by a tall window, and then a bigger living space around the corner, with a tired-looking sofa, and an empty cut-glass vase balanced on top of an ugly tiled fireplace.

'Come. Sit.' Marinela guided Bet to the sofa and sat down with her, still holding her arm. 'Shall I get you water?'

Bet said nothing and so Marinela stood and went to the kitchen. It looked old-fashioned: yellow cabinet doors with metal hinges and thin wooden handles; a freestanding oven with a grill suspended at the top; a white laminate surface, stained and chipped, wallpaper dotted with pink and blue butterflies. She opened cupboard door after cupboard door and found only a pot of salt; a blue plate; a pile of elastic bands; a pair of wooden chopsticks, and then, eventually, a small, clouded glass. She turned the tap. The pipes made a dry coughing sound but no water came out.

'There's no water,' she said, re-joining Bet on the sofa.

'It's different,' Bet said. 'The furniture's different.'

Marinela looked around the room. Apart from the sofa, and the table by the window, it was empty. The carpet was grubby; the wallpaper, striped cream and candy pink, was faded and marked. A thick layer of dust covered everything – Marinela could feel it at the back of her throat. She thought about Jack and Bet's flat in Elephant. The yellowed net curtains. The whole place still only half-unpacked, though Bet had told her they'd lived there for five years. And so hot it smelt – of old skin and old carpet and old dinners.

'You lived here?' Marinela asked.

Bet pressed her lips together, moved them against each other as though she wanted to push her teeth all the way through. 'I never meant for it to happen. I only went for the job because Nell insisted. It was all a bit of a joke at the start. Getting measured for dresses. Doing my hair. It was just a bit of fun after all that war. And the flat Jack and I lived in was so dark and dirty. I cleaned, I cleaned the whole time, but it never seemed to make any difference. And then I went to Bertie's,' She took a breath as if stepping out into a spring morning. 'And everything glittered.'

'The dress you gave me?'

Bet nodded. 'We were hostesses. Not dancers. No.' Bet raised her eyebrows. 'The dancers were a different kettle of fish altogether, you can imagine. We were serene, sophisticated, charming.' She laughed. 'It's all so long ago I don't know why I'm telling you.'

'You met the man?'

'At Bertie's, yes.' Bet looked towards the window, her eyes distant. 'Kit. Kit the American,' she said after a long pause. 'I don't know what I was thinking. But it went on two, three years. He wanted me to go to New York. New York.' She smiled. 'Imagine that.'

'I have never been,' Marinela said.

'I didn't go. I meant to but I didn't. I stayed. We had Tommy. It was for the best. Really.'

Marinela watched Bet's thin fingers playing with the hem of her cardigan, saw a faint flush on her cheeks. 'And the flat?'

'I hadn't heard from him for years, and then one day a letter arrives. I don't know how he found me. I suppose there are ways, if you have money. And he always had money. He knew he was dying. That's what he said, in the letter. It would be weeks, maybe a few months. He'd been thinking about me.' She pressed her hand to her mouth. 'He said he'd never sold the flat, that he'd kept it because it was like keeping a bit of me.' Bet let out a laugh. 'I mean? But anyway, he'd rented it out for years, but now he was going to be dead, he wanted me to have it.' Bet released her breath, then took another. 'This was only five, six years ago. I was an old woman. I didn't know what to do.' She turned her face towards Marinela. 'I'm not a bad wife. I've tried not to be a bad wife.' She seemed to crumple a little, sink further into the sofa.

She was young once, Marinela told herself. She was beautiful. Sexy. Unfaithful. She thought about Jack – the way his eyes smiled when he looked at Bet. She thought about Stefan. Sometimes he'd told her things about his wife – unflattering things: snoring, moodiness, frigidity – and she had hung on his every word, wanting more.

'This is where we came, Kit and I. After the first few months. This was our place. It was his idea. I was furious at first. I liked the hotels – they felt less, I don't know, less real.' She put the fingertips of one hand against her forehead. 'It's worth an awful lot of money. You wouldn't believe how much money. It's quite terrible. And the council write to me about it being empty and I just burn the letters.'

'Jack doesn't know?'

Bet closed her eyes and then opened them, clasped her hands on her lap as though she was in church, or waiting for a bus. 'I've been thinking about this all week. I've been thinking and thinking and I thought that maybe you might like to live here.'

Marinela stared at Bet. 'Me?'

'You said the place you live is noisy,' Bet said. 'And . . .' She hesitated. 'Well, you seem like a nice girl. You almost remind me of myself when I was your age.' She laughed again, an odd, forced sound.

'I don't understand.' Marinela shook her head.

'There's only one bedroom.' Bet moved her head in the direction of the closed door on the other side of the flat. 'With a funny little dressing room off it. I suppose you might need to buy some things. I don't know what's here.'

Marinela felt a sudden surge of homesickness. A physical sensation: an ache right there in her heart. She wanted to be on the balcony of her parents' flat, looking out towards the factory with its long line of impossible shapes. She wanted the smell of her mother's cooking – vinegary tripe soup, or *mititei* cooked until the meat charred. She wanted the sound of cars racing down Bulevardul Dunărea and the stink of their exhausts.

'I have a plan, you see.' Bet smiled and patted Marinela's knee. 'Tommy wants us to move into a home.'

'You have a home.'

'No, a *home* home. An old people's home. Overcooked vegetables and incontinence. Bingo and quizzes. That kind of a home.'

Marinela scanned the room. For a moment she let herself imagine sitting at the table with a glass of beer, reading. It was a quiet place – she strained to listen: a car outside, a distant plane; that was all.

'If you could come and do some cleaning,' Bet said, 'maybe cook dinner sometimes, for me and Jack. Then in return you can live here. You'll have to pay the bills, and talk to the water people, get the electrics back on.' She moved her head as if trying to free it from something. 'But I'm sure you can work all of that out, can't you?'

Marinela leant towards her. 'I do cleaning and cooking and you let me stay here?'

'Exactly. I tell Tommy I've got some help. He stops trying to shunt us off to the funny farm.'

'Farm?'

'What do you think? Why don't you have a look around?' Bet said, and when Marinela didn't get up, she puffed out impatiently. 'Go on.'

So Marinela stood and walked through the kitchen to the hallway. Behind the first door was a small bathroom with a short bath, old metal taps, a thin sink and white toilet. The floor was covered with still-bright yellow lino. Behind the second door she found the bedroom. An iron-frame bed, with a bare mattress and two uncovered pillows. The door to the dressing room was open, the room empty. Marinela stepped inside and ran her hand along the length of one wall. It was big enough for a darkroom.

The bedroom window looked across two rows of gardens towards the backs of a line of smaller houses, the sky cushioned grey above them. She sat on the edge of the bed, her hands in her lap, her eyes closed. She could live here. Alone. Just her and the walls. Peace and quiet.

After her grandmother had died, Marinela had taken the

framed photograph of her on her wedding day, which had sat by her bed. Her grandmother's hand was tucked under her husband's elbow, both of them smiling stiffly towards the camera. Marinela had never met her grandfather. He was gone before she was born. That was the word they always used about him, gone. She'd assumed, for a long time, that he must be dead, but that day, clearing out Bunica's house, she wondered if he had simply left. When she asked her mother, she told her not to be so wicked, which did not answer the question.

When she went back into the main room, Bet was still sitting quite still on the sofa.

'You can't say a word to Jack about it,' Bet said without looking in her direction.

Marinela sat down next to her. She thought about Jack. He didn't seem like the kind of man who would cry, but she could picture the hurt registering in his eyes, around his mouth. 'I am not sure,' she said.

'When I got that letter from Kit, and the one from the solicitor, I told Jack everything. I'd hidden it all those years, and then I had to tell him.' Bet stopped, stared towards the fireplace without seeming to see it. 'But we were both so old. It was all so long ago it didn't make any sense. He told me to give it back and I tried. I wrote and I wrote. But they never wrote back.'

'So it's just here? Empty?' Marinela thought about her grandmother's house in Tuluçesti – they hadn't been able to sell it and so it just sat there, rotting.

Bet nodded. 'I took the bus here once, but I couldn't make myself come in.' She shivered. Marinela shrugged off her coat and put it around Bet's shoulders, then took Bet's hands in hers and rubbed them together to make a bit of warmth.

'There was money too,' Bet continued. 'He left me money, so the council tax and everything comes from there.' She slipped her hands from between Marinela's and tugged at the coat so it sat more closely around her. 'I told Jack I gave it back.'

They sat in silence for a long time. The ache was still there, flat across Marinela's chest.

'You're young. You don't want to be looking after old people,' Bet said. 'I understand. You probably have a job anyway, I just thought—'

'No. No.' Marinela looked at the empty vase on the mantelpiece and imagined filling it with sunflowers, tulips, daffodils.

'I shouldn't have left it empty so long. There are people with nowhere to live in this city, aren't there? But it just felt so complicated.'

'What will you say to Jack?'

Bet turned towards her.

'If I lived here and I helped you in the flat, what would you say to him?'

Bet took Marinela's hand and squeezed it. 'Thank you.'

It was messy. Awkward. But it was too late. Marinela had imagined packing her bag and leaving her ugly room in the noisy house. She had imagined unpacking the bag here and then standing by the window with her eyes closed, listening to the silence. She had imagined emailing Stefan the address and him ringing the bell one afternoon, lifting her off her feet and spinning her round and round until she was dizzy.

Bet took the keys out of her pocket and handed them to Marinela. Two silver and one brass. A plastic tag with space for a label hanging from the ring. There was no label.

'I don't want to write anything down.' Bet held up her hand. 'This is just between us. You come, what? Two times a week. Three?'

Marinela nodded.

'Mornings are best, when Jack's out. You can give the place a hoover. Make something for dinner.'

'I only know Romanian food.'

Bet shrugged. 'Maybe we'll like it. If not I've got some books. Cooking's just following instructions, isn't it? You can move whenever you like.' She gestured to the flat. 'Make yourself at home.'

JACK

Jack opened the front door to the sound of voices. The Romanian girl again. She had been coming round two or three times a week for almost a month now. He'd come home from the shopping centre and the kitchen would be spotless, the bathroom sparkling clean, the floors hoovered. He worried there had been some misunderstanding, that she would want paying, but when he brought it up with Bet she batted his words away. It's all organized, is all she would say. And Marinela seemed happy enough, greeting him now with a 'Hello, Jack!' as he stepped into the hallway.

'Bet says I can do the boxes.' She stood in the doorway of the living room, a scarf tied around her hair. 'I will start next week. It will make everything feel better. Lighter. Did you have a nice walk?'

Jack smiled weakly, nodded his head. It was bitter out and it had started to rain on his way home, a fine, seeping rain that had found its way through his clothes and into his bones.

'I make tea.' Marinela squeezed past him and headed for the kitchen. 'You look tired. Sit down.'

He stepped into the living room. Bet was sitting in the chair nearest the window.

'Put the light on, would you?' she said. 'It's so dark in here.'

They tried not to put the lights on during the day but he pressed the switch anyway. The big paper globe glowed feebly.

'You look nice,' he said. Bet wore a long plum-coloured skirt and a cream blouse. She looked like she'd had her hair done.

'What news from the outside?' Bet said, looking towards him. She never usually asked.

He wanted to tell her about the estate – how there was nothing left of it. Even the piles of rubble had been cleared away. He wanted to say he'd been wondering what had happened to all of that stuff, but he didn't want to spoil her mood. 'Same old,' he said. 'Same old.'

'Tea.' Marinela appeared behind him. 'Sit, Jack.'

Jack sat on the nearest chair. It wasn't right, this girl waiting on them hand and foot. She'd been cooking meals too, leaving them in the fridge for them to heat up. Bet must have told her what they liked – shepherd's pie, chicken casserole, beef stew.

Marinela handed him a cup of tea and put another on the low table for Bet.

'Now, Marinela was telling me about her friend. What's his name?' Bet turned towards the girl.

'Harry.'

'Harry. That's right. He's writing a whole project about the estate.'

People couldn't leave it alone.

'He's interviewed people who lived there, that's right, isn't it?'

Marinela nodded.

'And well, I said he should talk to us.'

Jack lifted his tea to his lips and blew across its surface. Bet had talked to a journalist once. A tall, blonde woman, Jack remembered, with scarlet lips. She had been looking for real-life stories from the estate, but the piece she wrote had nothing real about it. Bet had written to the paper she was so angry, but what was printed was printed.

'I thought you'd want to,' Bet said, sounding deflated. 'Give your side of the story. They write such rubbish about the place.'

Jack coughed. 'I could do that, yes. What does he want it for?'

'He's a student,' Marinela said. 'He's studying,' she gave a vague wave of her hand. 'Cities I think. I know him from a university club – we go walking sometimes, in the hills.'

'What hills?' Jack asked.

Marinela shrugged. 'I have only been once. Somewhere called the Mendips, I think that is it. Very beautiful.'

Jack closed his eyes for a moment, imagined walking up a steep path, fields either side, the sun slipping out from between clouds, the smell of grass and soil and fresh air.

'If you don't want to it is no problem,' Marinela said. 'I haven't told him about you yet.'

Jack opened his eyes and looked at Bet. 'You remember that journalist?' he said.

'She was a fool. Is this boy a fool, Marinela?'

Marinela laughed. 'No, I do not think so. He is good at cooking spaghetti and he wants to have dogs, lots of dogs, when he has enough room for them all. He gets angry about things that he thinks are wrong. He's kind.'

'He won't write nonsense about the place breeding criminals?'

Marinela shook her head.

'You'd like to talk to him, wouldn't you, Jack?'

Jack put his cup onto the table a little quickly, hot tea spilling over the back of his hand. 'Yes.' He tried again, making his voice louder and more positive. 'Yes, why not love? That's a good idea.'

Harry came a couple of days later, with Marinela in tow. Jack opened the door to them. Both in dark coats, drops of rain sitting like tiny glass beads on their shoulders.

'You're Jack? Harry.' The boy gripped Jack's hand and pumped it hard enough for him to feel the tug in his arm muscles. 'Really pleased to meet you. Thank you so much.' He had thick black hair and dark-rimmed glasses, an easy smile.

Jack was no good at this kind of thing. A cold draught poured into the flat through the open door, but he could feel himself getting hot, his heart beating too fast.

'And I can't wait to meet your wife too,' the boy said, still beaming. He was well spoken, posh even, but with a hint of a northern accent. Liverpool, Jack thought, or somewhere nearby. The boy stamped his feet, one then the other, and wrapped his arms around his chest. Outside a car accelerated, its tyres spraying rainwater.

'Come in, come in.' Jack waved them inside, aware as he stepped back of how dim the hallway was; of the grubby paint; the smell of tinned tuna coming from the kitchen.

'Shoes off?' Harry asked and then bent to unlace his – brown leather with slightly pointed toes – before Jack could say he needn't bother.

He led them into the living room. On the television, a man in a suit walked along a street of terraced houses; he stopped in front of one with boarded-up windows, turned to the camera and started talking about property prices and opportunities for investment. Jack watched Harry take Bet's hands – she lifted them towards him as though she was in church.

'It's Bet, isn't it? My nan's called Bet. Best name in the world. And that is a beautiful brooch.'

Jack watched Bet's fingers move over the fussy silverwork. Tommy had given it to her last Christmas, a fairy-tale castle which Jack didn't like much. It wasn't on straight – the spires pointing off to one side.

'A gift from my son,' she said.

'A man of taste.' Harry laughed, a full, generous laugh, and Jack saw Bet quickly suppress her smile. She had always warmed to attention. He should have paid her more.

Harry straightened and looked towards Marinela. He was besotted – it was written across his face; the kind of besotted that would forgive anything, forget anything. Jack had felt the same about Bet, from that first time he'd seen her at the village fair, wearing a pastel-blue shirtwaist dress and white gloves, her dark hair wrapped into a white turban, like she had stepped straight out of the pages of a fashion magazine.

Marinela smiled. It was not a besotted smile and Jack felt a brief stab of pity for the boy.

Jack retreated to the kitchen to make tea. It was a small room with old fittings: a beige lino floor; white tiles edged with aged grout; white laminate cupboard doors chipped and scratched. A magnet shaped like Big Ben held the list of Bet's medicines to the fridge door. A cactus with ridges of short white spikes sat in a plastic pot on the windowsill. He pushed the window open to let in some air. The rain had got harder and he could hear it dripping from the gutters onto the paved area at the back.

He boiled the kettle; filled the pot; transferred Custard Creams – a little worse for wear – from the big white tin onto a plate.

'Can I help?' The boy stood in the doorway. Tall. Grinning. Jack felt a sharp flash of regret for his own, younger self.

Harry pushed the trolley into the living room. 'This is brilliant,' he said. 'I feel like a butler in one of those period dramas. Tea, madams?' He distributed the cups, passed around the plate of biscuits, and then there they all were, sitting in a semi-circle facing the electric fire. The man on the television was in a different house now. It was a mess: rubbish all over the floor, damp stains up the walls and across the carpet. Jack found the remote and turned it off.

Harry took his cue. 'Shall we get going?' He took a small metal device from his bag and pressed a button so a red light came on. 'Are you OK for me to record?'

Jack glanced at Bet, watched her lower her cup carefully onto the table. She had the slightest of curves in her spine, but still managed to sit pretty straight, her legs stretched out in front, her stockings pulled up tight, not sagging at the ankles. He wanted to tell her she was beautiful, but she wouldn't be pleased about it, not with visitors there.

'That's fine,' he said.

'Marinela told you about the project? I'm studying the estate. Its story. How it got built; what it was like to live in; the impact of the demolition on the people who used to live there.'

It made him sad, that's all Jack could think of to say. Every day he walked past it and it made him sad.

'So I want to know about life on the estate. Normal things. Making a brew. Hoovering. Looking out of the window. Shopping.'

Jack wondered what the point of that was.

'And then I'm interested in what it was like to have to move out, and to see it coming down.'

'You want to talk to Jack about all those meetings,' Bet said. 'He wasn't home till gone ten some nights, arguing with the bloody council, and at his age.'

'I have a form for you first.' Harry put a piece of paper on the table. 'To sign. To say it's OK for me to interview you. Nothing serious, just university paperwork. You're happy for me to use the interview in my project. That kind of thing.'

Bet had wanted Jack to go to college once he was back from

the war. Learn something new, she'd said, better yourself. But he'd never liked school much. He'd rather get a proper job, he told her, and she'd looked at him with one of those hopeless, you're-not-who-I-thought-you-were looks that gave him a familiar lurching sense of panic.

'So, maybe you could start by telling me about the estate,' Harry said. 'Anything you can think of.'

Jack glanced at Marinela, who was massaging her lips together, pressing down, releasing, over and again, like a cow, Jack thought, chewing the cud. What he had wanted to do, back from the war, was move to the countryside and rent a little farm. He wanted fields and sky, he told Bet, not the grey dreary grind of London. Half the city still in ruins. He wanted a fresh start. She'd been horrified. Furious. He wondered now if that had been the start of it all – Nell. Bertie's. That bloody American.

'When did you move in?' Harry asked.

'1974. Just when it was built. They knocked down the places that were there before. Slums, they called them. We were down the road in Larcom Street – there was no hot water, no bathroom. We used to go up to Manor Place for a bath.'

Him and Bet in adjoining cubicles, the shouts for more hot water, or time's up, echoing off the tiles. He used to lie and stare at the ceiling and imagine a farm up in Yorkshire, where Bet was from – the fresh clean air on his skin in the morning; long, silent days with the sheep; coming back into a low-ceilinged cottage, a fire lit in the grate, Bet wearing an apron making bread or a stew, or biscuits; the kids running to greet him.

'It was concrete. People don't like that now, do they, but we didn't mind. It was clean. We had big windows. Is this the kind of thing you're looking for?' he said.

'Spot on,' said Harry.

'We liked it,' Jack said. What more was there to say? From the dark cramped flat on Larcom Street to a large, bright place with a view across the whole of London.

They'd lived on the eighth floor and they'd loved it. The light streaming through the windows in the morning. It was a different kind of light up there. From the living room they could look out towards the river, St Paul's, all across the city, which stretched to the very edges of the horizon. Even when Bet's legs got bad, she could sit up there and feel as though she was somewhere, was part of something bigger.

'We were older by then of course. Tommy was just married, moved in with his missus. But there were lots of younger ones, with kids. They'd play out till they were called for their dinner. You knew it was five o'clock when you heard Mary shouting for her Daniel to come in.'

Harry and Marinela were both watching him intently. Bet had picked up her teacup and was holding it to her lips, her head turned towards the blank television. Jack cast about for something else to say.

'There was a man in the maisonettes who made a Jacuzzi,' he blurted. 'Got a great big paddling pool, and then a hose and some kind of lining he put holes into. Used to sit out there with it bubbling away, drinking his beer and watching the TV inside his house. And there was another man kept pigeons. He had little houses for them up on the top of the block. He'd fly them after work. Go up there and let them out for a spin. They're incredible, homing pigeons. Never get lost.'

'That man was an idiot,' Bet said. 'Beat his wife, and his kids too I don't doubt.'

Jack blinked.

'We were most excited about the bathrooms,' Bet said. 'I had a bath every night that first week.'

Both of them together, their heads either end of the tub,

perfumed bubbles puffing up from the water when they moved. They were fifty, but they felt young again. A new home. Just the two of them. Jack remembered sitting in that bath, taking hold of Bet's foot and massaging the tight smooth pads of skin at the base of each of her toes, then making his way up her leg, leaning forward until he was on his knees, leaning over her, his lips on hers.

'And the view,' Jack said. 'You should have seen it. That was difficult, moving to this place. We missed being able to look out over everything.'

'Do you remember that woman?' Bet said. 'The one on our floor who used to draw the view on her window with a felt-tip pen, or maybe a special kind of pen, I don't know. She'd put it all on. The trees and the buildings. And then it would wear off after a bit and she'd do it again. You could see it from the walkway, all the wrong way around and kind of small-looking.' Bet paused. 'I don't know why she did that.'

'They said we'd be able to move back,' Jack said. 'They promised us. Sat there in meetings and promised us.'

'They called it the footprint,' Bet cut in. 'Isn't that right, Jack? We all signed this form – right-to-return.' She laughed. 'That was two years before we left and it lasted seven years, so there's no risk of us going back now, is there?'

They had started out so hopeful. New buildings. Better facilities. They'd gone to a meeting about what the new flats would look like – they could choose the colour of the walls, even the layout, they were told.

'It wasn't a bad place,' Bet said. 'Not like they say it was. They were big flats. Hot water. All those trees as well. And now they're knocking it down.' She gestured towards the window. 'Like it was never anything worth bothering about. Jack, there are photos aren't there? Show them the photos.'

They'd had a Kodak Instamatic. Bet had a better eye than

him for a picture, something to do with the light, and where she positioned the edges of the photo. In the ones he took, the image never quite came out the way he'd thought it would. They had boxes of old albums. Bet used to buy the paper corners from Smith's. She'd spend hours hunched over at the table, the photos spread out in front of her, choosing which ones to include and which ones to put back in their packets.

It took Jack a good while to find the right photos. He went through two boxes, pulling out albums, opening them, putting them back again and trying another. It was like taking an out-of-order tour of their lives, their ages fluctuating erratically. Eventually he found the one Bet wanted and placed it onto the coffee table.

Harry leant forward and started to turn the pages.

The album spanned their first few months in the flat. They'd been excited enough to take photos of everything – each room, usually with one of them sitting on the edge of the sofa or bed; one he'd forgotten of Bet lying, fully clothed, in the empty bath and laughing. The view from the landing outside their front door towards the river. The view from the back room across the estate. The gardens down below – Bet standing next to the statue of a cloth-draped woman amongst the roses. The photos were small, two by three inches or so, the colours matt and a little faded.

Jack watched Harry and wondered if he had got what he wanted. He wondered why he wanted it anyway. There was nothing special about their life. They were just Jack and Bet who lived in a place that didn't exist any more. When their block came down, he'd stood on Elephant Road with his back to the station, trying to keep out of the way of the taxis and bicycles. He'd stared at where the flat used to be, but he couldn't pinpoint exactly where that was. There was nothing but air, nothing but sky and a view up the Walworth Road, with its mishmash of Victorian grandeur and modern utility, shops and cafes, buses and hurrying pedestrians.

'Well, he's soft on her, isn't he?' Jack said when Harry and Marinela had left and he and Bet were sitting in the kitchen eating cheese and pickle sandwiches. 'Poor lad.'

Bet looked up and frowned.

'Because she's not keen,' Jack explained.

'There's someone in Romania,' Bet said and then took a bite of sandwich, chewed steadily. 'Someone unsuitable,' she continued. 'She told me she'd finished it but you can tell she's just waiting for him to turn up and beg her to go back home.' Bet coughed and got to her feet. 'I'd like more tea. Do you want more tea?'

'Do you remember Frank?' Jack said to her back.

'Frank?' She turned, stared at him.

'I don't know why I just thought of him. He was soft on you, mind.'

'Frank.' Bet lifted the kettle and refilled the teapot. 'I can't believe he died.'

Jack had been right next to him in that damned jungle – the mud thick on their boots, the mosquitos taking chunks out of them. He'd seen a shimmer of movement amongst the green, then a bird taking flight in a flash of yellow and blue. He should have fired right then, but he'd waited, let whoever it was get a little closer, and then it was too late and there was Frank lying on his back, blood dripping down his neck into his collar.

'I always felt bad about Frank,' Jack said.

'Nonsense.'

'I bet he wished he'd never invited me home, never taken me to that fair.'

Bet waved a hand to one side as if batting his words away.

'Because it's chance, isn't it? If he hadn't invited me, if I hadn't gone, then we'd never have met.' And who knows what his life would have been.

Bet carried the pot to the table, set it down and then pressed the back of her hand against Jack's forehead. 'You feeling all right?'

'I'm fine.' Jack moved to take her hand but she had already stepped away.

'Well, I'm glad he invited you,' she said, settling herself in her chair again.

Jack felt a quick flood of happiness.

'You're having more tea?' Bet asked.

'Yes, thank you.' He smiled at her but she wasn't looking. 'I will.'

BET

Jack was at the shopping centre. The roast was in the oven. Bet sat by the living-room window waiting for Tommy. He usually arrived just as Jack got home but she had asked him to come for ten – I need to talk to you about something in private, she'd said. He'd done curious, irritated, resigned, and now there he was, a familiar shadow behind the net curtains, his knock on the front door. Bet didn't get up and after a moment she heard his key in the lock.

'Mum?'

'In here.'

He was wearing one of those tops again. Red, with a white zipper, like he was some kind of sports person. There was a glimmer of grey at his roots. Bet had her hair done every fortnight. Just a tidy up, keeping on top of the colour – there was no point using a dye if everyone could see that's what you were doing. Maureen came to the flat. It was like the old days on the estate: Bet sitting on a chair in the kitchen with a tea towel around her shoulders; Maureen filling her in on the gossip; the snip of scissors at Bet's neck. Except they were both old now. Maureen's breathing always sounded a struggle, and Bet could feel the slight hesitation in her hands. And there was no gossip to speak of. Maureen had lost all those customers when the

estate was emptied. She'd kept on going to the ones who hadn't moved too far away, but then she'd pretty much given it all up a couple of years back.

Tommy sat on the chair nearest to Bet and reached for her hand. 'What is it, Mum?'

He thought she was ill. Of course. Bet squeezed his hand. 'Don't panic. I'm not dying.' She smiled, but Tommy was frowning.

'I've been worried sick.'

'You've got better things to do than worry about me. Now. Tea?'

Tommy sat back in his chair. 'I'd rather we just talked about whatever it is.'

'I was waiting until you got here.' Bet had brought in an extra cup and already added milk. Now she lifted the teapot and poured.

'Have you noticed anything?' she asked, raising her own cup to her lips.

'What? You *are* ill? Is that what you're saying?'

Bet gestured to the wall behind him. He turned and then looked back at her.

'Is this a game?'

'They've gone.'

'What's gone?'

'The boxes. You've been going on about them so long I thought you'd at least notice.'

The trick, Marinela had declared, was to do one box at a time. And so every time she came, she would choose one and they would sit together deciding what to keep and what to send to the charity shop. It had been fun. Marinela holding up books, photos, ornaments Bet had forgotten they had – the clock they'd rescued from Jack's parents' bombed-out house; the ugly ceramic rose her mother had given them as a wedding present. Old hats and scarves. Shoes, some without their other halves. Dried-up moisturizers. An unopened tin of beans, three years out of date – they had laughed so hard about that tin of beans.

'Ha.' Tommy rubbed his fingers against his chin, the way he did when he wasn't sure how to react to something. 'You're right.'

'And you should go into the kitchen.'

She wasn't sure what Marinela had used, it didn't smell like bleach, but everything was brighter and cleaner than it had ever been.

'Go on.' She waved Tommy out of the room, listened to him walk along the hallway and stop in the kitchen. 'So?' she shouted. 'What do you think?'

Marinela had re-organized. Cleared the surfaces. Thrown away anything cracked or chipped. You have so much stuff, she had told Bet, you do not need it. If Jack knew how many boxes Marinela had sneaked off with to the charity shop he'd have a fit, but the truth was that with every pile of things they threw away Bet could feel herself getting lighter, happier, younger even.

Tommy reappeared in the doorway. 'You've been busy,' he said, warily.

'I've found a solution,' Bet said.

Tommy tapped his fingers against the door frame.

'I have a helper. You said we needed to move into a home because we can't manage here on our own, and, well, I've fixed it.'

Tommy rubbed his chin. Stared at her. 'I'm not sure I understand.' He walked towards a chair but stopped before he reached it, stood looking at the wall where the boxes used to be.

They had found some old pictures and Marinela had hung them up. A painting of Barden Moor, above Rylstone. Another of a dog – it had been their neighbour's when they lived on the estate. Bet couldn't think how they had ended up with it but she liked the dog's bright, hopeful eyes and had told Marinela to keep it. A handful of framed photographs: Tommy graduating from college, Bet standing next to him wearing a blue hat she had loved at the time but now thought looked a bit cheap; Jack with Tommy on his shoulders standing on Westminster Bridge. Marinela had framed one of the photos from the party too – the one with the three of them, Jack and Tommy standing behind Bet's chair, looking at each other. Not her favourite, but she hadn't liked to say.

'You remember the Romanian girl?' Bet had looked up Romania on a map. It was surrounded by Hungary, Serbia, Bulgaria, and some other countries she couldn't remember now. Marinela was from a place in the south, not too far from the country's tiny stretch of coastline. In the flat bit, she had said, not where the tourists went.

'The photographer?' she prompted, pointing towards the photo. 'Marinela.'

Tommy nodded slowly.

'She comes two or three times a week. Cleans. Cooks. Sorts us out.' She tried a little laugh but it came out sounding nervous. 'So you don't need to worry any more.'

Tommy finally sat down next to her. 'You're paying her?'

Bet moved her head to one side. 'More or less. It isn't important. What is important is that I've found a solution, so you can stop with this home business.'

Outside, a car revved loudly and someone started shouting, a staccato of obscenities.

'We don't know her,' Tommy said.

'She's a very nice girl.'

'She's a photography student, Mum, not a carer.'

Bet shrugged. 'It's working.' She waved towards the wall of

photos again. 'She's getting us in order. Isn't that what you want?'

When she'd taken Marinela to the Islington flat, the walls had been bare where there used to be pictures. There definitely had been pictures, but now she tried to recall them, she couldn't say what they had been. It didn't matter, she told herself, yet she could feel the anxiety reach up towards her throat. That things could be lost so easily. Perhaps she should be trying harder to retain them, and yet the thought exhausted her – to hold so many years, so many things, so many people, inside her head.

Bet turned her palms to the ceiling. 'You can't say you're not pleased.'

'This girl could be anyone, Mum. Care agencies check people out, do those police certificates, they have training.'

'And pay people peanuts. And the checks don't weed out all the bad ones either. I watch the news.'

Tommy rubbed his hands through his hair.

'Well, I just wanted to let you know,' Bet said. 'So you're in the picture.'

'And why all the secrecy?'

Bet looked at him.

'Getting me here when Dad's out.'

'Well,' Bet said, 'that's the thing. I don't want you talking to Jack about this.' She paused. 'He's very sensitive.'

Tommy barked a laugh. 'Dad?'

'You don't know him like I do. He doesn't want to be seen to be accepting help.' She turned her head so she could see his expression properly. She couldn't have him asking Jack about Marinela, confusing things. 'It's working perfectly,' she said. 'That's all you need to know.'

Tommy sat back in his chair and folded his arms. 'I'll need to talk to her,' he said after a long pause.

'We aren't your children, Tommy.'

'Still. I want to meet her.'

'Fine.' Bet waved his words away, tired now. 'Fine.'

'You'll arrange something?'

Bet nodded. 'I might have a lie down before lunch. You'll keep an eye on the roast, won't you?'

'Sure.'

Bet pulled herself to her feet, leaning heavily on the arm-rest. Tommy moved to help her. She waved him away, but he held out his arm and in the end she took it, let him walk with her down the hallway to the bedroom, let him help her onto the bed and off with her shoes. She lay back on the pillows and closed her eyes.

'Everything is working perfectly,' she said.

'Have a nice sleep, Mum, I'll wake you when Dad gets home.'

'Perfectly,' Bet murmured as the bedroom door clicked shut. 'Absolutely perfectly.'

MARINELA

Since moving, Marinela had started waking early. Lying on the high bed watching the sky lighten behind the curtains, listening to the almost-silence – a bird, a car, a child crying. She had been in Bet's flat just over a month, and yet it felt like for ever.

She had cleaned the place until it shone; bought two plates, two cups, two glasses, two sets of cutlery, a sharp knife, a thin plastic chopping board, two saucepans – one big, one small – a kettle, a duvet and a large red cushion. She had worked out that by February she could save enough money from the club to set up a darkroom in the little space off the bedroom.

Her mother would call her naive. Good things don't just happen, she'd say, there is a reason for everything – a price for everything. Marinela rehearsed conversations with her in her head. If it doesn't work out, I'll move. They are good, kind people. The past is the past. Would you have said no?

And the truth was she enjoyed her visits to Bet, enjoyed sitting with her, emptying out boxes and deciding what to keep and what to let go – asking for each object's story. Enjoyed her English cookery lessons – Bet sitting at the kitchen table barking instructions, Marinela rubbing butter into flour, browning beef, measuring stock. Enjoyed making Jack a cup of tea when he got back from his walk – he always looked so tired, and more often than not fell asleep whilst it was still hot.

Today she was meeting Harry in Soho and then going to Bet's birthday tea. Harry had invited her to some protest about the council closing down a club that sounded not so different from the one she worked in. Get dolled up, he'd said, it's going to be a party. Dolled up? she'd asked and he'd laughed, told her to wear something nice. She'd looked up the word in the dictionary Stefan had given her. Doll. A model, a toy – but it had started life as a term for a man's mistress, hundreds of years ago.

She had been Stefan's mistress, she supposed. Making love in his office, in cheap hotels, even in the park one summer evening – and then he would go back to his wife, and she would return to her shared student house, and maybe none of it was as real as she had believed it to be. But then she thought about that night he'd taken her dancing. Some basement nightclub, its walls thick with graffiti, the music pounding deep into her bones. It was packed, but it had felt as though they were the only ones there, locked into each other's gaze. And then, when it was over, they had walked through the city. Early morning quiet. The buildings holding themselves still and silent, reflecting Marinela and Stefan's voices back to them. On the bridge over the Dâmbovița he had stopped short and taken her in his arms, kissed her long and slow – a bedroom kiss; a film kiss. And she had felt so completely and intensely happy. That was what she remembered now, the way the joy filled her up as though someone had found an opening and poured it straight in.

She had decided to wear the green dress for the protest and then change into something simpler for Bet's birthday tea. It was heavier than she remembered, and when she threaded in her arms and let it drop over her head she felt the weight of it, like water, tugging down from her shoulders. The neck was low and loose. It fitted close to her stomach, tight across her hips – a touch too tight, it was like being squeezed – and then fell in soft wide lines to the floor.

There was no mirror in the bedroom, but she knew from the club how an outfit could change a person, each girl sitting at the dressing-room mirror, slowly turning herself into someone else. And this was someone new to her – this woman in the green dress. She walked towards the window, just to feel the shift of the material against her skin.

There were gloves too, tied onto the hanger – silk, almost white, each with a line of tiny pearl-like buttons stretching from wrist to elbow. They smelt, very faintly, of dust, like a room left empty for too long, but nothing more than that. She pulled them on, left then right, the silk uncomfortably tight around her fingers.

The square was tucked back from the long streets of Soho's cafes and restaurants. A patch of grass and trees surrounded by black railings, circled by a patchwork of tall buildings which seemed to want nothing to do with each other – a stubborn mix of red brick, brown brick, white render, columns, arches, windows wide and narrow.

Marinela walked through the open gate, past tall, nearly bare trees, and a squat black and white building. Dried-up leaves littered the grass. Men sat in twos and threes on the benches, with cans of beer and faces that were older than they should have been. On one, a man lay stretched out on his back, swathed in a dirty sleeping bag.

On the far side of the square, a coffin sat on a block of concrete meant for table tennis. A handful of people stood around it. Men in flamboyant suits – with wide sleeves and frilled shirts. Beautiful women, corseted, high-heeled, their hair dyed and styled, their faces painted into flawless masks. There was a man in a tight red dress and heels, with a black feather boa around his neck.

And there was Harry, wearing a fitted brown corduroy suit and holding a brown hat by its brim, turning it one way and then the other and then back again. Marinela stopped, felt something tug at her chest and stomach. Except she didn't think of him in that way. He was just a guy from the walking club, a little over-enthusiastic in his politics, prone to getting drunk and talking too much. Even so, looking at him standing there as if he owned the place, his dark hair ruffled by the wind, she could imagine putting her arms around his neck and kissing him.

But now two other women were approaching him – one in a tight blue dress cut off just below the knees, the other in jeans and trainers and a dark jacket that looked like a man's. They both kissed Harry on each cheek and then fell into conversation, laughing, gesturing. Marinela felt a moment's disappointment, but dismissed it, took off her jacket and straightened Bet's dress over her hips. The cool air drew tiny bumps across the tops of her arms. She walked towards the group, her head high. A boyfriend was the last thing she needed anyway.

'Hi.' She aimed the word just above their heads, stood for a moment, feeling cold and exposed and somehow angry.

Harry lifted his head and a smile flashed across his face. 'Marinela.' He turned to the other women. 'This is the photographer I told you about. Marinela, this is Lane and Aini, they're on my course.'

Lane, the woman wearing jeans, flicked an unfriendly glance in Marinela's direction. 'The *photographer*,' she drawled. 'It's true – we've heard all about you.'

'I'm glad you came,' Harry said. 'And you look great.'

'You said it was a party, not a funeral,' Marinela said.

Harry laughed. 'It's both. A funeral for a burlesque club – pretty cool, eh?'

'Burlesque?'

'Striptease,' Lane said, 'but a bit more liberated than your usual titty bar, or at least that's what they like to think.'

Titty bar. Marinela looked at Lane. Short hair. No make-up. Angry-looking. She did not like her, she decided.

'This dress is amazing.' Aini was next to her now, pawing at the green silk. 'It's original, right?'

Marinela thought of Bet, her dyed brown hair with her scalp showing pink and age-spotted beneath it. The way the skin puckered at the edges of her eyes and mouth.

'Just a shop,' she said. 'I got in shop.'

Aini nodded thoughtfully. 'Well, welcome. Harry's sulking because he left his placard on the Tube.'

'It was a good placard,' Harry said. 'S.O.S. Save Our Soho. I stuck bloody gold stars on it.'

'Harry takes placards very seriously,' Aini said. 'Gold stars indicate a certain commitment to the cause.'

Harry play-punched her on the arm.

More people were arriving. A scattering of hand-painted banners: *Stand up for Soho. Stop the gentrification.* Eventually, a tall man wearing a dark suit lifted the coffin lid and took out a megaphone. We are here to mourn, he said. We are here to protest. We are here to fight for our city. His words blasted out of the megaphone but then dissipated almost immediately, lost in the late November air, the traffic, the trees. Marinela turned to look at the men sitting on the nearby benches. They were paying no attention.

Four men lifted the coffin onto their shoulders and led the way. The group fanned out to cross the road; congealed again at the top of Greek Street, and then stretched into a long line along the narrow pavement, past outdoor cafe tables and chairs, sometimes stepping into the road to get past people walking in the opposite direction.

'What shop?' Aini asked at Marinela's shoulder.

'Shop?'

'The dress.'

The group had slowed to a stop outside a white arched doorway, Christmas lights glittering on the other side of the glass. The offices of the property developers who owned half of Soho, Harry declared. It was positioned in between a cafe, thick with tinsel, whose blue awning was streaked with mould, and a food store with multi-coloured graffiti across its shutters. The man in the suit and a woman in a red corset and black-lace skirt laid a wreath by the door and then he spoke again through the megaphone about gentrification; about closing down venues because new residents didn't think they were appropriate; about pushing people out; about denying diversity. There was applause, people took photos, and they started off again. Marinela had been distracted when she left the flat and hadn't thought about her camera until she was already halfway into town. It wasn't what a professional would do. A professional would take it everywhere.

'The dress, it actually belongs to the woman who owns my flat. I didn't buy it,' Marinela said to Aini, whose skirt was forcing her to take tiny steps like a horse on a short rein.

'I thought you were in that house owned by the Spaniard?' Harry's voice came from behind her.

Marinela hesitated. Bet hadn't wanted her to mention it to Jack, but there was no harm in telling people who had nothing to do with her – she needn't even say her name. And there was something in Marinela that wanted to tell, wanted to measure someone else's reaction to it.

'I moved,' she said, speaking loudly enough for Harry to hear. 'There's a woman. She had affair a long time ago and the man, the one she has the affair with, gave her the flat they used when he died.'

'Used?' Harry asked.

'Don't be such a bloody innocent,' Aini laughed. 'Go on. Did he die young then?'

'No. The woman was old.'

'That must have upset a few people. And you live in the flat?'

'I clean for her, do cooking. She gives me flat.'

Harry whistled out a breath. 'No rent?'

Marinela shook her head.

'Sweet,' Aini said.

'What does she want?' Lane butted in, coming up beside Marinela so there was barely enough room on the pavement for them both to walk. In front of them someone had started playing the trumpet, a meandering, mournful tune.

'Want?' Marinela asked.

'No one gives someone a flat rent-free without wanting something.'

'The cleaning.'

'Cleaners get minimum wage.'

'Well, that is how it is,' Marinela said.

Lane dropped back and Marinela turned to Aini. 'This woman, she worked in nightclub. But you would not know it looking at her now.'

'And the dress is from then? It's probably worth a fortune.' Aini touched the green silk again and Marinela wished she hadn't said anything, wished she hadn't worn the dress.

They stopped to cross another road, a sex shop with red neon lights on the other side. Marinela looked towards Harry. 'What do you think?' she asked.

'It's a nice dress.'

'Is it wrong to be in the flat?'

Harry frowned. 'No more wrong than anyone else trying to afford somewhere to live in this city.'

Lane caught up with them. 'Would you look at this? This place used to be real.' She gestured towards a Japanese restaurant with huge pearlescent lights hanging in the windows. 'Now look at it.'

'It looks nice,' Marinela said.

Lane snorted. 'You should take some of our courses, read about what's happening to this city. All this bollocks, all this money, all this development, it's destroying it. You'll see. If you stick around. Are you staying?'

Marinela blinked. 'I do not know.'

'You're from where? Hungary? Estonia?'

'Romania.'

Lane nodded, pursed her lips. 'Ceauşescu.'

'He died the year I was born.'

'So you're a post-socialist Romanian.'

Marinela shrugged. 'Things don't just stop straight away, do they?'

'And how is capitalism treating your country?'

Marinela wanted her to go away. She wanted to talk to Harry, or just look into the shop fronts as they passed. Cafes. Sex shops. Book shops. Restaurants. She wanted to ask the man with the feather boa how he found high heels big enough for his man's feet.

'Bucharest used to be very poor, very run down, now they are rebuilding, renovating. We have more tourists, more money,' she said.

'Gentrification,' Lane snorted.

'And they killed the dogs,' Marinela said, just to annoy the woman.

'What?'

'There were dogs everywhere. No one could afford to feed

them so they let them go. Thousands of strays on the streets. And then they killed them all. It is better for the city.'

'So why are you here then?' Lane demanded.

'In London? I come to study.'

'No, here. Soho. Now.'

'Harry invited me.'

Lane barked a laugh. 'Harry invited you.'

'You called?' Harry popped up between them and Marinela wanted to take hold of his hand and kiss it.

'We were discussing gentrification,' Lane said.

'Right.' He grinned at Marinela. 'It's pretty shitty, all that.'

They were outside a large glass-fronted cafe, with plants hanging upside down in the window.

'But sometimes it makes places nicer,' Marinela said, gesturing at the building. 'People like it.'

'Rich people like it,' Lane said. 'What about everybody else? People shouldn't be forced out of their homes by idiots with too much money and no fucking imagination. Home's home – it's sacred. I believe that.'

Marinela thought about the flat – the red cushion she had bought for the old sofa in the living room; the handful of books propped on the mantelpiece; her grandmother's wedding photo and the pictures of Jack and Bet and Tommy tacked to the wall by the window. She had been thinking about getting a plant, a fern or a cactus, something easy to look after. In the shared house in Kennington she had glanced into the rooms of her housemates and seen posters on the walls, colourful throws over the furniture, piles of books and clothes – they had looked so lived-in.

'You must miss home,' Harry said to Marinela and she was grateful to him for changing the subject. She thought of her grandmother's house: the smell of baking; the rows of vegetables in the garden; the sound of rain on the roof.

'A little,' she said.

Harry reached out a hand and squeezed Marinela's arm. She turned, frowning and he let go, pushed his hands into his trouser pockets and walked a little faster, catching up with Aini and saying something Marinela couldn't make out.

The group stalled and bunched again at the end of the street; negotiated a clutch of hire bikes and an endless dribble of taxis to get across the road and down another smaller street. They came to a halt outside a black-painted door with a neon sign above, the pavement in front stained and grubby. The coffin-bearers propped their burden up against the door and people piled bunches of flowers around it. The man spoke into his megaphone again. This was the burlesque club. The coffin symbolized the death of both the club and Soho itself. The developers should know that the people of London wouldn't stand for what they were doing to the city. The trumpeter – a small woman wearing an electric-blue jumpsuit – played a tune that sent a shiver down Marinela's spine. The group clapped, and then milled around for a while, talking. Marinela, Harry, Lane and Aini stood huddled to the left of the coffin.

'Does it help?' Marinela said.

Harry frowned and Marinela waved a hand to indicate the group of people who had started to drift apart now, an odd, awkward breaking-up.

'If no one does anything, then there's no bloody hope,' Lane said. 'Someone has to stand up and say, enough, absolutely enough.'

They retraced their steps towards Soho Square, Lane and Aini up ahead, Harry lagging behind with Marinela.

'So where's the new flat?' he asked.

'Angel.'

'Not so far from me.' He paused but she said nothing.

'Maybe we could meet up some night?' He coughed, hurried on. 'Dinner, or just a drink. Only if you want to.'

'I have job,' she said.

'Every night?' Harry laughed but sounded uncomfortable.

'No.'

'If you don't want to, it's fine,' Harry said. 'I just meant as friends, anyway.'

'A drink would be nice.'

Harry did a little skip next to her. 'Great. I'll text you about a date then.'

Marinela nodded, tried to smile, but all she could think about was Stefan – the smell of his skin; the way he lit a cigarette like he was a French movie star; his lips on hers.

'I don't think your friend likes me,' Marinela said, gesturing towards Lane, who was walking in front of them, hands in pockets, head bent.

'Lane? Oh, she's just got a bit of a chip, that's all. She's a sweetheart once you get past all the prickles.'

Marinela kicked a drinks can so it clattered across the pavement and dropped into the gutter. 'Do you like everyone?' she asked.

Harry laughed. 'I don't like my dad.'

Marinela turned to look at him. 'Really?'

'Maybe it's fairer to say my dad doesn't like me. With my leftie politics and funny ideas about equality.'

'But he still loves you.'

Harry raised his eyebrows. 'Well, he's got a funny way of showing it, let's say that. Change the subject now, please, I was having a nice time.'

'The woman is Bet,' Marinela said.

'Sorry?'

'Bet owns the flat. I clean for her and Jack. She lets me stay in her flat.'

'What?' Harry pulled up short and Marinela stopped a few paces ahead, turned.

'Bet had an affair with some rich guy?' Harry said.

Marinela nodded.

Harry blinked, rubbed his hand across his mouth. 'Jesus. You can't second-guess people, can you?'

'You think it's wrong?'

'Having an affair? Bloody hell, I don't know. People do it all the time, don't they?'

'Me staying in the flat. She doesn't want me to tell Jack. He doesn't know.'

'You don't feel it's right?'

'I love it,' Marinela said quietly. 'I love living there.'

'So don't worry about it,' Harry said. 'If it ain't broke, don't fix it.' He started walking again, hands in his pockets. 'You want to get a coffee?' he asked after a while. 'With those guys,' gesturing towards Lane and Aini.

'I have to go. It is Bet's birthday and I meet them for tea. Here, I turn here for the station.'

Harry pursed his lips. 'Give her my love then.' He leant in, kissed her on one cheek and then the other. A faint whiff of musky aftershave. Marinela closed her eyes and breathed it in. 'Enjoy.'

Marinela called a goodbye to Lane and Aini, then crossed the road and headed for the station. After a moment, she stopped and looked back, but Harry was no longer in sight and there was nothing to see but a street full of strangers.

JACK

Claridge's. It was nonsense, them coming here. Just Tommy showing off. Jack reached for Bet's arm as she stepped from the minicab onto the road. She was wearing a dark red dress he couldn't remember seeing before. Perhaps Marinela had bought it – the two of them seemed so chummy, the girl at their flat two or three times a week at least.

Jack and Bet stood, stranded on the narrow pavement, waiting for Tommy to pay the driver.

'Oh, look!' Bet said, lifting her head towards the vast red-brick front of the hotel, bay windows and balconies layered up on top of each other. 'I've never seen it done up for Christmas.'

It wasn't even December yet, but identical cone-shaped Christmas trees sat above the main entrance, each of them wrapped in white fairy lights. More lights tumbled across the front of the building, surrounding the windows and doors and winking back at their reflections in the glass. Gold baubles hung from the underside of the porch and clustered together in wreaths along the fence. Around the doors, gold branches, hung with more baubles, rose up from either side to make an archway.

Bet gave a sigh of pleasure. This was her idea of heaven. She should have been born into a different family, Jack thought. She should have married a different man.

Tommy approached, smiling. Perhaps this Internet dating was a good thing. Their son looked happier than he had in a while.

A man dressed in a long navy coat and a hat trimmed with grey ribbon ushered them through the revolving glass doors into a hallway that was smaller than Jack had expected, more like a house than a hotel – a grand house mind you, like something off the telly. Orange and green geometric carpet. Buttercream walls. A heavy chandelier above them, and to each side mirrors reaching up to the ceiling. There were two narrow sofas pushed against the walls. Jack would have liked to sit down, but they did not look like they were meant for sitting on.

He could feel the sweat pushing its way to the surface of his skin, and the slightest of tremors in his bones, as though his skeleton was not quite steady, as though he might fall. He pictured it for a moment – collapsing onto the floor, bringing Bet down with him. People would rush to help, but all they would want would be for him to not be there, for none of it to have happened.

They made their way up two shallow steps to a square of polished black and white tiles.

'Look at that tree,' Bet said.

It stood to their right, positioned in the lee of a wide, sweeping staircase. Tiny white lights and little paper flags covered its branches. The thing would take up the whole of Jack and Bet's living room back home.

Bet clung to Jack's arm, tilting her head left to right, up and back down again, breathing in the smell of pine and money. Jack had tried to change Tommy's mind. It was too expensive, too much of a fuss. This was not their kind of place. But she'll love it, Tommy had said, and he was right. Even so, Jack wished they had just gone for a pub lunch somewhere out in Surrey.

A woman, dressed in a red jacket and matching skirt, stood by what looked like a church lectern at the entrance to the restaurant.

'May I help you?' she asked.

'We're here for tea,' Bet said in her posh voice.

Jack let himself close his eyes for a moment, just for the quick release of darkness before the woman, with her neat blonde hair and too white teeth, would ask them to leave.

'You have a reservation, madame?'

'Thomas Chalmers,' Tommy said.

That was all it took for them to be led, without the slightest hint of hurry, into the glittering, green-carpeted room, at the centre of which another Christmas tree rose up almost high enough to meet another chandelier.

Their table was in the far right-hand corner, covered with a white cloth and set with gilt-edged, green and cream striped cups and saucers. Just in front of them, a woman dressed in black sat at a grand piano, her fingers whispering across the keys. Another, younger woman, stood at her side with a violin, swaying as she played.

They sat down, Jack facing towards the door, Bet to his left, Tommy to his right. Bet settled herself into her chair, fussing at her dress, patting at the pearl earrings clipped to her lobes. They looked uncomfortable: he could see where the skin was pinched and weighted.

'Jack?' She put her hand on the table, finding a place in between the cups.

'Love?' He placed his own hand over hers.

'Isn't this something?'

He glanced at Tommy and saw him smile.

'Happy birthday, Mum,' Tommy said.

Bet took Tommy's hand and Jack felt himself relax.

A waiter glided towards them. 'A glass of champagne to start?' he said in an accent Jack thought might be French.

'Well,' Jack hesitated. Was it extra, he wondered.

'Thank you,' said Bet.

'Brut or rosé?'

'Rosé, please. Jack?'

A glass of champagne must cost a fortune in this place. 'Oh, I'm—'

'My husband will have the brut.'

'Same for me,' Tommy said.

The waiter nodded and retreated, returned a minute later with two bottles of champagne, filled their waiting flutes.

'To Mum,' Tommy said, raising his glass. 'Ninety years.'

'Don't go on about it, Tommy,' Bet muttered.

Jack saw a flicker of irritation cross Tommy's face, but then he lifted his arm higher and said, 'To your birthday, then. To your good health.'

'To Bet,' Jack said and took a sip. He'd never really understood the fuss about champagne, but this didn't taste too bad.

He looked around the room. It was square, with a central recessed ceiling space where the chandelier hung. Each wall had three tall arches with delicate ironwork frames, the spaces in between covered in mirrors. There were four heavy pillars, structural, he supposed, towards each corner of the room. Maybe twenty or thirty tables – none too close to another. The place was perhaps three-quarters full, mainly women, lifting teacups and glasses of champagne to their mouths, biting into sandwiches, talking and laughing, though the carpet and furnishings soaked up most of the sound, leaving a pleasant burble underneath the music. The whole place sparkled like an overpriced shop.

He took another mouthful of champagne and glanced towards the door.

What he saw made him gulp in his breath so fast he ended up coughing.

It was Bet. Of course it wasn't Bet – she was sitting next to him admiring the silver tea stand. But at the same time there was no one else it could be. Short, slim, straight-backed, with cropped dark hair. And that dress. Green silk falling from shoulder to floor. The woman walked quickly across the black and white tiles of the foyer, and before he could stand, or call out, she was out of sight.

'Dad? Are you OK?'

He was breathing like a horse, fast and heavy. He shook his head side to side, as though he could loosen the image he'd just seen.

'I've just – I'm just—' He dug his hand hard into the arm of his chair and pushed himself to standing. 'Be. Back.' He couldn't get the words into a sentence, and now Bet was fretting too, asking him what was wrong. Did he feel unwell?'

Bet was here. Bet was talking to him. Sitting small and old in the vast chair, her face caught into a frown, her fingers worrying at the tablecloth. Jack hesitated for a moment, looking at his wife, and then he turned and walked as quickly as he was able, past the chattering tables and silent waiters, through the light-festooned archway, back into the foyer.

She wasn't there. Of course she wasn't. He walked past the reception desks, through one arch of golden branches and then another, but she wasn't there. He retraced his steps, back towards the Christmas tree. Close up, he saw that the glass baubles were painted with flags, and at the base of the tree sat model rabbits, a deer, foxes, mice, all of them mechanized – nodding and pawing gently amongst the fake snow. He walked along another, shorter, wood-panelled corridor, but she was not there. Of course she wasn't.

He could feel his heart smashing itself, pointlessly, against his chest, and the sweat starting to cool on his skin. Maybe he should go and see a doctor. He wouldn't. He never did. But maybe he should think about taking things a little easier. The anniversary; Bet's birthday; maybe he was over-tired and it was playing with his mind, making him see things that weren't there.

'Jack?'

It took him a moment to place her. Marinela. The Romanian girl. She wore a black jersey dress that stopped above her knees, flat red shoes, no jewellery. She held a black rucksack at her side as though it was a handbag.

'It is still OK that I come?' She frowned at him. When she touched his arm he felt himself flinch.

'Jack? You are OK? Your face is white.'

Jack swallowed and shook his head, patted down his suit jacket. 'You're joining us?'

She looked surprised for a moment, and then laughed. 'She did not tell you.'

He could feel her watching him, her eyes quick and bright, but he couldn't focus on her, kept moving his gaze left then right, as though Bet – the woman who couldn't be Bet – might reappear.

Marinela followed him through the restaurant to where Bet and Tommy sat – Bet's glass already empty.

'Look who I found,' Jack said, bracing himself.

Bet turned her head, her face lighting into a smile. 'You came!'

'It is still OK?' the girl asked.

'Of course, of course. Tommy, ask the waiter for another chair.'

Tommy looked at Marinela, his eyes wide, a flush on his cheeks.

'This is Marinela,' Jack said. 'You met her at the party. She took the photographs.' He turned to Marinela. 'Tommy thought they were very good.' He had taken one of the prints – said he'd frame it, but Jack had no idea if he had or not.

'Good afternoon,' Tommy said, stiffly, standing and offering his hand to Marinela. She shook it and then bent towards Bet, kissed her on both cheeks.

'Your birthday!' she said.

'Don't even say the number.' Bet held up her hand. 'Now, you need champagne, and a chair.'

'Another place?' The French waiter appeared behind Marinela.

'Yes. Yes please. And another glass of champagne.' Bet laughed, a girlish laugh, and Jack saw Tommy tense. He would take him aside later, tell him that this friendship between Bet and Marinela seemed a good thing. Bet was happier, she was up and about more, she'd unpacked all those boxes that had sat around for so long, she had started singing again – in the bath. He'd been so worried about her eyes but she'd hardly mentioned them for weeks. He wasn't entirely sure about the girl's motivations, but how could they be anything other than kind? There was no money to speak of, no inheritance to steal.

There was a flurry of muted activity, a fourth chair slotted into place. Cups and plates, napkins and cutlery rearranged. Another glass of pink champagne poured. Marinela sat down.

Tommy leaned over to Bet and whispered something Jack couldn't hear. She whispered something back and then turned to Marinela.

'Isn't the entrance divine?' she said, loudly. 'Those tiles, like a chessboard. I'll be the Queen, you be the King, that's what I used say. I always wanted to take my shoes off and slide across it in my stockings.'

Jack looked towards the foyer, expecting to see the woman again, dressed in green silk, gliding across the polished surface and laughing, Bet's laugh.

'Now isn't this nice, all of us here together?' Bet said. 'And Tommy, you were saying you wanted to meet Marinela, so this is just perfect, isn't it?'

Tommy looked at Jack, who just shrugged and allowed himself a small lift of his eyebrows.

'It is an honour,' Marinela said, her voice uncertain. 'To be here. With family.'

Tommy folded his arms, sulking, and Jack remembered all those years of arguments between his wife and son. He'd been born after all the fuss with the American – their new start. And yet it sometimes felt as though he was trying to punish Bet for something. Nothing she could do was ever good enough. Jack sighed. She gave as good as she'd got, and he'd done what he could over the years to keep the peace.

A different waiter approached, soft-footed. 'Are you ready to choose your tea?'

Menus were distributed. Jack liked a good cup of tea, but he didn't like it when people messed about with it – all this orange blossom and smoke. Plus he couldn't concentrate on the descriptions once he'd clocked the price of the whole damn thing. Tommy was a fool. Chucking around money he didn't have.

'Just normal tea,' he said when it was his turn.

'Dad!' Tommy laughed and Jack winced. 'He'll have the Claridge's Blend. OK, Dad?'

Jack handed back the menu and said nothing.

'What would you recommend?' Tommy asked the waiter. He held the menu at arm's length, running his finger over the choices, in his element.

Bet was turned towards Marinela, their heads together, talking softly now so Jack couldn't make out what they were saying. He closed his eyes for a moment. He would like to be at home, he thought, with the TV on and a pot of PG Tips on the coffee table.

When he opened his eyes the tea had arrived in four green and cream striped teapots.

'Yours is best without the milk,' the waiter said, pouring Jack's tea through a silver strainer.

He wasn't having that, but he waited until the man had turned his back before adding it to his cup. He discovered the silver box in the centre of the table held a pile of sugar cubes, the misshapen, rough-sided kind, and a miniature pair of silver tongs. He dropped two lumps into his tea and stirred.

'Bet, I bought you a present,' Marinela said. 'Just something small.' She took a gold-wrapped package from her bag.

Bet pulled off the wrapping paper a little clumsily and held the box up to the side of her face.

'It is Chanel,' Marinela said. 'They say it is a woman's best friend, I think.'

Bet put the box back on the table and patted it with her fingertips, her face flushed with pleasure. 'Thank you.' She took Marinela's hand and kissed it.

Tommy cleared his throat. 'So, obviously, this is your birthday present.' He swept his hand around the table. 'Unexpected guests included.' He gave a short laugh. 'But I got you this too.'

A gold necklace with a pendant in the shape of a bird, its eyes picked out with flecks of diamond, or glass Jack thought, and then told himself to be more generous.

Jack had bought what he always bought: Je Reviens perfume. Bet had worn it as long as he could remember. It looked cheap sitting next to the bottle of Chanel. Usually he'd get chocolates as well, something nice from Tesco's – Thornton's or Milk Tray – but this year he'd chosen a scarf from one of the stalls in the shopping centre instead. It was turquoise with gold stitching travelling in great swoops and curls around the edge. Garish, maybe, but he had stood at the stall with the African woman in her brown and yellow headwrap, pulling out scarf after scarf; this one sir? Or this one? This is beautiful, very special. And it had been the turquoise one which had made him think of Bet.

She pulled it from the wrapping paper and ran it through her fingers, held it to her eyes, then her cheek, before looping it around her neck. It clashed with her dress, he could see that, but he could also tell she liked it and the knowledge settled his heart a little.

BET

In truth, she hadn't wanted to come. She'd done her best to persuade Tommy to take them somewhere else – the Dorchester or Fortnum and Mason's – but he had done his research, he said, Claridge's was the best; she wasn't to worry about the cost. And so there they were, the same black and white tiles in the entrance hall, the same sweeping staircase, and all she could think about was Kit.

He'd been a show-off, she could see that now but back then she'd hardly noticed, let alone cared. She'd been happy to just be with him – his American confidence, his delight in what he called 'the good things': caviar, champagne, fillet steak. There were never awkward, brooding silences, just his endless easy chatter – telling her about New York, Boston, San Francisco; about his parents, his childhood in rural Massachusetts, their old dog, Buddy; about a man he met on the Tube who played a cornet mouthpiece and begged for money, who'd lost a leg and a family in the war. That was Kit all over – he'd talk to anyone.

'So I've got the Malawi Antler tea,' Tommy declared. 'Did you hear what the waiter said? They cut the stem not the leaves so they can't make much of it. Claridge's buy up the whole harvest. It's not bad. How's yours, Mum?'

'It's very nice, Tommy.'

He looked at her, expectantly, as though he wanted something more.

Bet lifted her cup and took a sip. 'Very nice.'

Claridge's had changed. She didn't remember the green carpet, or that great swirl of smoky glass up in the centre of the room. But it felt the same. Pure luxury. She had been beside herself the first time Kit brought her there. The mirrors, the lights, the black and white tiles like a huge polished chessboard. It was like nothing she had ever seen. I feel like a Yorkshire bumpkin, she'd whispered in his ear, and he had guffawed so loudly she thought they'd be thrown out. You are perfect, he had whispered back, and don't let anyone ever tell you any different.

The sandwiches arrived, lined up on thin ceramic platters, crustless rectangles of soft bread with generous fillings. Ham and orange chutney; turkey and cranberry, crisp cucumber steeped in camomile. Bet watched Jack choose one and eye it before taking a bite. He would be thinking about how much everything cost. He would be wishing they were back at home. She lifted a turkey sandwich to her mouth and looked at the glittering Christmas tree in the centre of the room.

Those years with Kit, he'd always gone back to America for Christmas, leaving some small, expensive gift for her in the flat. She'd make the journey up to Angel when she could get away; sit by the window, holding whatever it was – a necklace, a pair of gloves, perfume – in her lap and trying not to think of him with his wife and daughter. When he was in London with her, the future didn't seem to matter, but when he was gone everything felt fragile and she moved through the days with a dark, sick feeling in her stomach.

'Why did you invite her?' Tommy leaned close to Bet.

'These sandwiches are really very good. Have you tried the ham?' Bet took a large bite and chewed slowly.

'It's hardly appropriate, Mum,' Tommy whispered.

'I thought it would be nice,' Bet said flatly. 'And you said you wanted to meet her.'

Tommy snorted. 'Eighty-five-quid nice. And I meant a meeting, not a social.'

'Oh don't be—' Bet waved a hand towards him. 'You said it's my treat, my birthday. Well she's my friend.'

'You've known her for five minutes.'

'Two months.'

'What about Maureen, or Ivy or Joan? You've known them for years.'

But they're so old, is what she wanted to say but didn't. They don't make me feel alive the way Marinela does. There was something about the girl, which reminded her of herself. But Tommy would laugh if she told him that.

'Don't spoil it,' she said, and turned to Marinela. 'Now, how's that nice young man?' she asked.

Marinela looked at her quizzically.

'The one—' Bet couldn't think of his name. 'The one with all the questions.'

'Harry?' The slightest blush on her cheeks. 'He's good. Fine. I just saw him actually. At a protest.'

'A protest?' Tommy's voice veered upwards.

'In Soho. They closed a place. A burlesque club.' She pronounced burlesque with too many syllables.

Tommy's eyebrows shot up. 'And that's bad?'

Marinela shrugged. 'I think it is that they close the old places to make way for development, new flats, people who don't like the burlesque.'

'Nothing wrong with a bit of progress,' Tommy declared. 'Keeps everything going. Keeps everyone on their toes.'

'Means you can't afford a flat,' Jack cut in. 'Means places like ours get flattened.'

'They should have knocked that place down years ago if you ask me,' Tommy said. 'Should never have built the bloody thing.'

'It was only up forty years,' Jack said. 'That's a waste. And we lived there. That counts for something, or it should do.'

Bet was grateful to the waiters who suddenly appeared with fresh pots of tea and plates of cake. There were tiny scones with clotted cream and jam. Then Yorkshire parkin with what looked like a piece of gold on top; a layered chocolate cake with tiny pieces of orange in the sponge; a miniature mince pie, dusted with bronze powder; and a hazelnut macaroon sat on its narrow edge. They looked so good it felt almost wrong to eat them.

'I mean, this,' Jack gestured around the restaurant. 'This isn't right, is it? All this money?'

'It's just a bit of luxury, Jack.' Bet touched his arm. 'Nothing wrong with a bit of luxury on your birthday.'

In Jack's world, everything was supposed to be fair. No one richer or happier or cleverer or luckier than anyone else. Bet remembered telling Kit about it once and him laughing and calling Jack a card-carrying Commie. She'd felt terrible for the rest of the evening, sworn she'd never tell Kit another thing about Jack. That was the only way she'd managed to make it work for so long – putting each version of her life into its own compartment and not letting the two touch each other.

'So, Marinela,' Tommy said loudly. 'Mum said you're behind the great clear-out?'

Bet frowned at him, but he carried on. At least Jack was concentrating on piling cream and jam onto his scone. He would be full already – she felt she could hardly eat another thing – but he was a man who despised waste.

'You must have a magic touch. I've been trying for five years to get them to sort all of that out,' Tommy went on.

Marinela sipped her champagne. 'It was fun, do you think, Bet?'

'She's a godsend.' Bet smiled at Tommy but he was staring at Marinela as though trying to see through her.

'It's working for you?' he asked.

Bet glanced at Jack, but he was looking towards the foyer with a distant expression, a smudge of cream on his upper lip.

'Your arrangement?' Tommy persisted when Marinela didn't reply.

Marinela glanced at Bet who gave her most neutral smile.

'Tommy, I told you, it's all working perfectly. Now, tell us about your new girlfriend. What did you say, you met her on the computer?'

Jack got to his feet, leaning on the table so everyone's tea swayed in their cups and one of the macaroons toppled over. 'Just going to pay a visit,' he said, and set off towards the door.

'There's no issue with payment, any of that?' Tommy asked Marinela.

Marinela widened her eyes. 'No, of course not. It is—' She laughed. 'It's very generous.'

'How do you meet people on the computer?' Bet raised her voice, willed Marinela to stop talking.

'The flat is beautiful,' Marinela said, and Bet closed her eyes for a moment, felt a heavy swill of panic in her stomach. 'I am not sure I deserve it.'

Tommy was staring at Bet but she wouldn't meet his eye. She'd done her best over the years not to think about the Islington flat, because whenever she did it was as though the earth lost its solidity; the ground moving like a wave beneath her feet. Ever since Kit's letter she'd tried so hard to pretend it wasn't there that she sometimes wondered if it might have vanished somehow – bricks and mortar dissolved into air. And yet, if she closed her eyes and concentrated, she could remember it as clearly as if she'd been there yesterday. The yellow kitchen cabinets; the blue lino and the tiny fold-out table with two matching, chrome-legged chairs. The iron-framed bed in the room at the back, with a view onto trees, and more houses. The black, spiked clock with its golden hands that ticked away the time.

'Did you hear about Mr Tooley?' she said. 'Stuart at the party was saying, they moved him out to Morden or somewhere like that and he just died of loneliness. People can die of loneliness – I didn't think that was true, but turns out it is.'

'What flat?' Tommy said, drawing out each word.

She should have got rid of it years ago. She should have sold it and given the money to Tommy, or to some charity – wasn't that what old ladies did? Left their fortunes to cats and donkeys and battery chickens.

Marinela looked flustered. 'I thought—'

'We can discuss this later,' Bet said firmly. 'Tommy. Don't make a fuss. Now, who wants that parkin?'

She kept on chattering – talked about her mother's parkin, how really she preferred gingerbread because it was sweeter; commented on the waiters' accents, wondered if they kept the pretty young men for the old ladies taking afternoon tea and put all the pretty young women in the cocktail bar. She could feel Tommy tensed up next to her. Well bugger him, she thought. It was none of his business.

Tommy waited until they were in the foyer, by the Christmas tree with little animals sitting around its base. Marinela had gone. Jack had shuffled off to the bathroom again. Bet stood very still and waited.

'So, are you going to explain?' Tommy said, his voice low, his hand tight on her arm as if she might be about to run off into the street.

Bet let out a breath. 'I'd rather not,' she said. 'It's been a lovely afternoon, Tommy, don't spoil it.'

'A flat?'

She should have known this would happen. She should have left the keys at the back of the drawer, but she'd wanted to help Marinela, that was all.

'It's a long story,' she said.

'I'm listening.'

What could she say? 'I have a flat.' Four small words, none of them incendiary on their own. 'Someone gave it to me.'

Tommy moved his hand from her arm to his mouth. 'That isn't true,' he said through his fingers.

Bet shrugged.

'Mum?'

'I won't have you saying anything to Jack about it.' She paused. 'I don't want a fuss.'

Tommy raised his eyebrows, waited.

'You have to promise me.'

'A flat? Where?'

'Your dad will be here any minute and I'm not saying another word until you promise.'

'How can *you* have a *flat*? I don't understand.'

'Promise me.'

'Fine.'

Bet took a breath. 'I had an affair,' she said, keeping her voice as steady as she could. She held up a hand to stop Tommy's reaction. 'Just listen, Tommy. It was a long time ago. Before you were born. I'm sorry it happened but it did. He left me the flat in his will, six years ago maybe. I didn't want it. I didn't ask for it.'

'What? You lived there with him? When was this?' Tommy spluttered.

Bet shook her head. 'He gave it to me when he knew he was dying. It was a stupid thing to do. I told your dad everything and he asked me to give it back. I tried, but I didn't manage to do it. It's been empty for a long time and I thought someone might as well get some use out of it.'

Tommy opened his mouth and then closed it again.

'That's it,' Bet said. 'End of story.'

'I don't bloody think so,' Tommy snapped.

And there was Jack, walking slowly towards them over the black and white tiles.

'You promised,' Bet whispered.

'Ready for off, Dad?' Tommy said, too loudly, his voice sounding like a caricature of itself. Bet let herself breathe again.

'We'll talk about this,' Tommy whispered in her ear.

Bet felt strangely blank. She'd have to listen to all his questions, let him shout a bit. But it would all blow over soon enough. It was nothing, really, nothing of any importance.

MARINELA

Marinela was on the edge of being late, and so already a little hurried, a little annoyed. When she opened the door into the dressing room she saw a group of girls clustered at the back. Jess – who had the slot before her – sat on the dirty blue office chair with her head in her hands. The other girls stood around, as though protecting her. One of them looked up as Marinela entered; she was very white, very blonde, very thin, in a black thong and skeletal bra. She mimed the curve of a pregnant stomach with one hand, and then lifted the same hand and sliced it across her throat.

Marinela looked at Jess. She wore a black hoody over her outfit. Bare legs. Bare feet. Her make-up was a mess.

'Who will dance her slot?' she asked, already knowing it would be her. The other girls shrugged.

'We've just done ours,' the blonde girl said.

Marinela glared at Jess, but she was staring at the floor.

The room was a mess of bags and jackets, make-up, stained cotton wool, magazines, half empty glasses. Marinela made a space for herself by moving her forearm flat against the counter so that everything shunted along. One of the girls pulled in an annoyed breath but Marinela didn't look up.

She leant towards the mirror and painted a steady black line around her right eye, then her left, making a flick out from the corner of each. She thought, idly, about Harry. He'd texted saying he was suddenly swamped with work for his project about the estate – something to do with a presentation and then an essay deadline. When he was done, he'd said, he'd love to buy her that drink. She'd messaged back saying sure, whenever, and there'd been nothing since. He wasn't interested, not really; but then neither was she. Marinela rubbed concealer over a spot on her chin, and drew on red lipstick. Jess had stopped crying and was sitting back in her chair, dabbing at her eyes with a tissue.

'Maybe I can just get rid of it. What do you think? Do you think it hurts?'

'Not so much as having the baby,' a girl standing next to her said in a sad, flat voice. Marinela glanced at her and then looked away. They did not talk about their past lives. They talked about tomorrow and the day after. They talked about what they would spend their hard-earned cash on.

'Oh, God.' Jess put her hands up to her face and started to cry again.

Marinela pulled on her outfit – the black one. The shoes took time to do up, and she could already hear the music from the speakers in the corner of the room slowing down towards the end of the song.

'Here.' The girl who had spoken knelt in front of Marinela and took one of her feet. She wrapped the black straps quickly and neatly around her leg, almost up to her knee. 'Go.' The girl looked up and smiled, pushed her palm against Marinela's shin. 'You look good.'

Marinela stood, and felt for a moment unsteady on her heels. Jess's song had started. A single repeated line on the piano, the snare drum starting to snap the beat. Thirty seconds more and Paul would be buzzing into the tannoy system, cursing them all. She hurried along the corridor to the stage, and felt, as she opened the door, the slight fizz of her nerves. No, she told herself, this was a transaction. No one out there knew or cared a thing about her.

She draped herself around the pole – hold, hold, then slide down towards the floor. It always took a while to adjust to the lights, so she kept her eyes half-closed, didn't try to focus yet. She uncurled herself, and then she was climbing. It was all in the thighs and the tops of the arms. Up. Up. You had to get the grip right before you could let go with your hands and lean all the way back.

Down. Down. Careful not to drop onto her head. Stop concentrating and you break your neck. Don't daydream. Concentrate. They thought you were being sexy, but you knew it was work.

The room was busy – most of the upside-down tables filled with upside-down people. Suits. Some dresses too. Someone had strung huge gold and silver baubles from the ceiling. Now she was on her hands and knees, crawling towards the edge of the stage. A mobile phone flashed on the table nearest to her and a man picked it up and gazed at the screen. Marinela rotated her hips, feeling the stretch along her spine; she sat back on her heels, and it was only then that she saw him. Bet's son. He was sitting with a group of men – five in total, the table crowded with champagne flutes and shot glasses. He had his tie loose around his neck and his top shirt button undone. He was staring at her, his mouth a little open.

Ca pula. Fuck.

She lost her place in the music. Her arms felt wrong, like someone had turned them into wood. This was the point she ran her hand from her cheek, down her breasts, across her stomach, held it over the place they were all thinking about. Hold. Hold. Then along her thigh.

She glanced at Tommy; it was definitely him. It had only been a week since they'd met at Bet's birthday tea – he definitely recognized her.

Fuck.

She tried to get back into the music, back into the space where she was just a body, just an idea, where her life was nobody else's business.

The only thing to do was ignore him. She glanced around the room and imagined taking photographs of the men she saw – their flushed faces and styled hair, their lips glistening with beer and champagne. She rested her attention on a younger man, clean shaven, his shirt buttoned tight against his throat, his cheeks red with booze and excitement. She smiled at him and he smiled back. That was better. She was at work; she was paying her way; she was doing nothing wrong.

Once she was done she couldn't get off the stage fast enough. She almost crashed into the girl who had helped with her shoes. She took Marinela's arm to steady her and smiled. It was a distant smile; Marinela recognized it – it helped to empty yourself out before going on stage.

Jess was still sitting on the old blue chair, her knees tucked up towards her chest, twisting one way then the other. She had a glass of vodka in one hand, and when she saw Marinela she lifted the bottle and waved it towards her. Marinela nodded.

'You don't usually drink at work,' Jess said.

Marinela sat on a scratched black stool. 'I see someone I know.'

'Ouch.' Jess poured a full glass and handed it over.

The vodka was warm and cheap and made Marinela think of Stefan pouring from an almost frozen bottle into tiny, chilled glasses, holding one out to her.

'There was a girl last year whose dad turned up. I mean as

a punter, not to drag her away, he was out there watching.' Jess pulled a face. 'Is this guy family?'

Marinela shook her head.

'Well that's something, isn't it?' Jess took a slurp. 'Fuck. My dad would have the mother of all fits if he knew I did this. If he walked in here.' She stared at the vodka, sloshed it around the sides of the glass and then drank again. 'I mean he wouldn't. He wouldn't set foot in a place like this.'

'You don't know that,' said another girl who was painting her eyelids dark green.

'Trust me. He wouldn't. Shit, he is going to kill me if he finds out I'm pregnant. I'm on the fucking pill. How can you get pregnant on the pill?'

Marinela thought about Tommy with his tie pulled loose, the sharp pink point of his tongue darting out from between his lips and then back in again. She should go home. But she had another stage slot in two hours, and Paul was never sympathetic. If she said she was ill he'd just shrug and tell her to take a paracetamol and get the fuck out there and do her job. If she told him there was a man she knew, he'd just laugh and say tough shit. Paul fired his dancers without asking questions. There are so many of you girls, he'd say, rolling the r of girls. I click my fingers – here he would click his fingers – and here's another one. Oh – another click – and another.

She sat a while longer, sipping her drink and listening to Jess, trying to clear her mind. Eventually she stood up. She wasn't going to lose an evening's earnings because of that man. Her corset dug into the tops of her breasts – she tugged it up, smoothed down her hair, and stepped into the corridor, trailing her fingers over the white-painted breeze-block wall all the way to the bar. It was quiet back there, and she stopped to breathe it in for a moment. Would Tommy tell Jack and Bet? What would they would think? She had thought about stopping, but then there was no harm in having savings, and she wasn't sure how long the arrangement with Bet would last.

On the other side of the door it was hot and dark and loud. Paul kept the place like a sauna so the girls weren't shivering and the punters kept on buying drinks. When she left at the end of a night it was always a shock to step outside – like diving into cold water.

There was a crowd at the bar, a bunch of young men just arrived, wearing Santa hats, shouting to each other at the tops of their voices and laughing more than they needed to. She kept her head down and walked in between the tables, away from where she'd seen Tommy.

'Hey! Sexy!' A table of men in their thirties, wearing matching T-shirts sporting photos of the man who was currently decked out in a bride's veil, a plastic penis hung around his neck like a dummy, his face blurred with drink.

Marinela fixed a smile to her face and approached them. 'Table dance, sirs?' She forced her smile wider. 'Twenty house pounds.'

One of the men – who looked a bit like Harry, she noticed – slapped the notes down on the table. Marinela turned away and started to move her pelvis, side and forward and side and back, hands on her hips, sliding them down towards her backside. That was what they called it here: backside, bum, arse, buttocks, bottom. In Romanian it was *fund, şezut, fese*. It was just skin, she told herself, it was just a body. Who cared? It got easier each time she did it.

She turned and put one leg up on the tabletop. She saw the groom-to-be glance at her crotch. He caught her eye and blushed, knocked back a shot of vodka and looked down at his phone.

Marinela ran her fingertips from her ankle along her calf,

across her knee, up her inner thigh. She stretched out her leg and felt the muscles tug tight along the whole length of it.

'Could you help me?' She turned to the man nearest her – ginger-haired, bleary-eyed – and offered the untied lace of her corset. He blinked at her.

'Pull, you tosser,' another man said.

The ginger-haired man pulled and the lace slid through the rows of plastic eyes, letting the corset gape and then fall to the floor. She could feel the men's eyes on her breasts. It didn't matter. They were just breasts. She put her hands to them, pushing them together, fixing her gaze on the shimmering glasses behind the bar.

'Excuse me, gentlemen.'

Tommy's hand on her arm. She turned, saw him glance down at her chest and then back at her face.

'I'm working,' she hissed.

'Hey, old man, hands off,' the ginger-haired man shouted.

'Me and this young lady need to have a conversation.'

'I'm working.' Marinela pulled away from him. 'Sorry, gentlemen.' She flashed a smile at the table. 'Where was I?'

She carried on dancing, aware of Tommy still standing behind her, watching. When she'd finished, she scooped up her corset and retied it, turning away towards the back of the club.

'Marinela, isn't it?' His hand on her arm again.

If she struggled, a bouncer would be there in seconds. I pride myself on that, Paul was always saying. My girls are the safest girls in the business. No one fucks around with my girls.

She turned towards Tommy. He looked hot and flustered, beads of sweat on his upper lip and forehead.

'You're looking for a dance?' she said, folding her arms across her chest.

Tommy reddened even more. 'No. I'm just with colleagues. Stan's birthday. I don't usually—'

'Then I can't help you.' Marinela turned, but he was there behind her, his breath coming ragged into his chest.

'We need to talk.'

'I do not need.'

'Don't they have rooms?'

Marinela stopped. 'VIP rooms. Fifty pounds, five minutes.' She held his gaze. 'That is why I am here. To make money.'

Tommy rubbed his hand across his mouth. 'All right, fine.'

'You want VIP dance?'

'Not a dance, just to talk.'

She shrugged and started to walk towards the private rooms.

'Here.' She gestured for him to go in ahead of her.

They were in the fish room. The circular table had a shallow aquarium built into the middle of it, where tiny brightly coloured fish flitted about amongst fronds of seaweed and models of naked women touching each other's breasts. There was a blue-leather semicircular seat and another, larger aquarium behind that. Opposite the seat was a window onto the main bar, with strings of tiny silver beads hanging over it. There were bouncers outside – to stop people staring in and to come and rescue any girl who knocked on the glass or pressed the emergency button underneath the table, or just shouted.

Tommy sat with his arms folded, chewing at his bottom lip. Marinela leaned her back against the window.

'You know this isn't right, don't you?' he said at last. 'You living in the flat. I've tried to talk to Mum about it, but she's just blocking me. Says it'll kill Dad if he finds out.' Tommy rubbed a hand over his eyes and Marinela felt almost sorry for him.

'I think she doesn't want to have it,' she tried.

Tommy looked at her, bleakly. 'Where is it?'

'Angel.'

'One bed?'

She nodded.

'It'll be worth a fortune. You know you can't live there.'

Marinela looked at the fish in the tank behind him – a bright yellow one kept butting its head against the glass. They're feeding when they do that, one of the bouncers had told her, there's stuff on the glass they like to eat. It looked to her as though it was trying to get out.

'I like it there,' she said.

Tommy laughed. 'I'm sure you do. Did Mum tell you about their old place? Having to move out? Having to bid for properties? It nearly finished us all off, and the whole time she was sitting on a goldmine?' He shook his head. 'I can't believe it.'

'I don't think she knew what to do.'

Tommy reared his head, eyes flashing. She wondered how much he'd had to drink.

'Don't,' he said, shaking his head. 'Don't think for a moment you can stand there, in your—' He flung out an arm. 'Underwear, and tell me about my own parents.'

Marinela lowered her head, waited. 'We're nearly out of time, Mr Chalmers,' she said.

Tommy slammed his fist on the table. 'I won't have them taken advantage of.' He glared at her. 'I won't have some stripper, some Romanian stripper, wheedling her way into their lives, stirring stuff up. You're out for yourself. Mum might not be able to see that, but you can't pull a fast one on me. I bet you found out about this bloody flat and thought you'd get your sticky mitts on it, well I won't have it.'

Marinela thought about Bet – tiny, birdlike Bet with her pink lipstick and her bright eyes. And Jack – quiet and calm, his neat shirts, his remaining hair carefully combed. 'I like them,' she said. 'I don't want to—'

'I want you out of that flat.'

She had been right not to quit her job. She knew it had been too good to be true.

'A week. OK? I'm not a monster – you'll need to find somewhere else, but if you're not out in a week I'm going to have to get people involved. Police. Officials.'

She would speak with Bet. Maybe she could talk Tommy around.

'Five minutes is up, Mr Chalmers,' Marinela said.

Tommy leaned forward, peering at her. 'I'm wondering now,' he said. His voice had changed. 'I'm wondering about your visa.'

She walked to the door. 'I am a student. Romania is in the EU.'

'That so?'

She opened the door.

Tommy stayed where he was.

'I can call security.'

He stood then, his face pale and tired. 'Fifty pounds?'

She nodded.

Tommy reached into his top pocket and pulled out a crumpled house note. 'I've got twenty.'

Marinela shrugged. 'It's fine.'

'I want you out in a week.'

She said nothing.

As he reached the door he stopped, close enough for her to smell his aftershave, and beneath that a sharp tang of sweat. She wondered if he was about to take hold of her throat, or slap her across the face, or kiss her, but instead he turned and walked quickly away. Marinela slunk back through the club to the dressing room, where Jess was redoing her make-up.

'It's probably just a scare,' she said, when Marinela walked in. 'It was a cheap test. I'm going to buy a different one tomorrow.' She was drunk, her movements wild. There wasn't much left in the bottle of vodka. Maybe that would be enough to see off the threat of a baby.

'Thanks for switching,' she said.

Marinela shrugged. 'Is OK.'

'Yeah, but you didn't have to.'

Sometimes Marinela felt as though she was stuck inside too small a space. It could happen anywhere – in a field, or next to a river, or in a room like this one. She poured herself a shot of vodka and drank it in one go, felt it burn down her throat and chest into her stomach.

Jess drew mascara over her lashes. Marinela watched her wiggle the brush, the quick sure movement of her wrist.

'When I came to England I opened a bank account,' Marinela said. Jess glanced at her but said nothing. 'And the woman said there had been someone else with the exact same name as me who'd opened an account just the week before.'

'Weird.'

The woman in the bank had laughed, called over a colleague to tell him about the coincidence. Marinela had tried to laugh too, but it had unsettled her – knowing that there was another woman in the same city with her name, a woman she wouldn't recognize if they passed each other on the street.

'Did you see the guy?' Jess asked.

Marinela pulled a face and nodded.

Jess dragged a blood-red lipstick over her mouth. 'They're all the same,' she said. 'They're all bastards. Trust me.' She took a blusher brush from her make-up bag and gestured with it towards Marinela. 'We should set up some kind of a commune. Strippers' Village.' She cackled. 'Strippers' fucking Village. We can be the founders, you and me.'

BET

'You can't just pretend none of this is happening.' Tommy had pulled up a chair close to hers and sat, leaning forwards, his chin propped in his hands.

Bet was tired, and the dark smudge in the centre of her vision seemed to have got bigger overnight. 'Tommy, it's nothing.'

'It's a one-bed flat in Angel.'

Bet turned her head, tried to make out his expression. 'Have you been snooping?'

Tommy massaged his fingertips over his mouth. 'I spoke to Marinela last night.'

'No!'

He held up a hand to stop her. 'I told her she needs to be out in a week.'

Bet folded her arms across her chest. 'You have no bloody right.'

'She's taking advantage.'

'She cleans, she cooks. This whole flat is a different place since she got here, you've said so yourself.'

'It's not a fair exchange.'

'It is if I say it is.'

Tommy shook his head. Outside, a child started crying, a steady insistent wail.

'You were worried about your dad and me on our own, now we're not on our own. I did this for you, Tommy. I was listening to you.'

He was shaking his head again. 'You had an—' He hesitated. 'An affair.'

Bet laughed. 'And that's what this is about? You're kicking a girl out of her home because of something I did nearly seventy years ago?'

A car's horn blared, so loudly Bet felt herself jolt in surprise. Sometimes she would sit there on her own, with the television off and her eyes closed, and listen to what was going on outside – little snatches of conversation as people walked past the window, shouts and car engines, dogs, even foxes sometimes.

'It's not her home,' Tommy said.

'She lives there.'

'Not the same thing.'

'What I did is what I did. I told you, I'm sorry. I didn't ask for this mess.'

They sank into silence. Bet looked towards the window. She could hear her son biting his nails, a thin tap each time his teeth slid off to meet each other. His last wife had made him wear some kind of nail varnish that was supposed to taste bad enough to stop him, but it hadn't worked.

'How much do you know about her?' Tommy said after a long pause.

'I'm not having this conversation again. Now, did you say you brought mince pies?'

Tommy sighed and turned his attention to the box on the table. He handed Bet a mince pie. She prised off its foil container and took a bite. 'I like her,' she said. 'And it's my flat, I can do what I want with it.' She took another bite and the pie disintegrated between her fingers, half of it falling onto her lap.

'She's a stripper,' Tommy said quietly, and then let out a long breath, as if he was a balloon someone had blown up and then let go of before tying the end.

Bet knew exactly what he meant, but for a moment all she could think of were their old neighbours on the estate, the ones who'd bought their flat off the council. The great DIY-ers, they called them. She was always stripping off one lot of wallpaper and hanging another. And every weekend he'd have the electric drill out, or some kind of saw, or he'd be banging something into the walls.

'Did you hear what I said, Mum?'

One time the woman – Bet couldn't remember her name now – had papered the hallway with black and green striped paper. Do you think it's a bit cheap-looking? she'd asked, the two of them standing at the front door, looking down towards the kitchen. I think it's fabulous, Bet said, and she did. Jack wasn't one for changing things.

'You can't go around accusing people you don't know,' Bet said.

'I saw her,' Tommy said in a low, flat voice. 'Dancing.'

'Nothing wrong with dancing.' Bet felt around in her lap for the stray pieces of mince pie, slotted the ones she found into her mouth.

'In a strip club,' Tommy said.

The neighbour was called Annabel, that was it. She had an electric machine that boiled up water and then spewed out great puffs of steam. Gets the paper right off, no fuss, she'd say, you just have to be careful you don't burn yourself.

Bet opened her mouth to speak, but Tommy hurried on.

'I don't want you to think I go to places like that. It was Stan's birthday. I've told you about Stan – he's a good client.'

'I'm sure you mistook her for someone else.'

'No. No, I didn't.'

Bet's breath seemed to have got itself into some kind of a muddle, she couldn't think how she usually did it. She thought of the men sitting in the dark booths at Bertie's, talking shop. Nothing changed, it seemed.

'What Marinela chooses to do in her spare time is none of my business. Or yours,' she said.

'Are you serious?'

'Absolutely.'

'You're quite happy hanging around with a stripper? A Romanian stripper?'

'That's racist.'

'No, that's a fact.'

'If you'll excuse me.' Bet got slowly to her feet. 'Call of nature.'

Tommy didn't move to help her. Bet brushed the rest of the crumbs from her skirt and walked as quickly as she could to the bathroom, locked the door, lowered the toilet seat and sat down.

A stripper. Part of her didn't believe a word of it. But then perhaps it was true. A student and a stripper. Bet listened to the news. Tuition fees. House prices. Women had done it for centuries. They sold the one thing they had. The one thing that was always wanted.

Bet drummed her fingertips against her knee and thought about Bertie's: the dancers with their immaculate faces and feathered costumes; the curved flesh beneath their sheer stockings; the way they would walk onto the stage as if they owned the place, when ten minutes earlier they'd been bitching and slouching in the dressing room. The dancers were a different breed from the hostesses. Bet used to watch them out of the corner of her eye. Teasing. Flirting. Taking off a feather boa.

Unbuttoning. Moving their hips and their breasts as though they were liquid rather than flesh. They were looked down upon, of course, and yet there was something about them which triggered a kind of yearning in Bet.

Nothing wrong with any of it, she told herself. A bit of fun, maybe. But then she thought about Marinela on a grubby stage, unhooking her bra, and Tommy watching her, and it made her feel quite wretched.

Maybe Marinela sent what she earned back home. Bet had noticed that her coat felt old – the cuffs worn, the fabric softened almost to the point of fraying. Romania wasn't a rich country, she was sure about that. Or maybe she'd started it so she could pay her rent, though wouldn't she have stopped now she was living in the Islington flat?

She allowed herself to sit a while longer. If she was there too long Tommy would be banging on the door, asking if she was okay. Eventually she got to her feet, flushed the toilet, ran the tap and returned to the living room. Tommy was sitting with his head tipped against the back of the chair, his eyes closed. He looked tired.

'When do we get to meet your girlfriend?' she said.

Tommy's eyes snapped open. 'Huh?'

'Your girlfriend? The computer one.'

'Oh.' Tommy shrugged.

They had split up, she could see it in the set of his jaw. She wanted to touch his arm, or say something kind, but before she could he had started again,

'I told her she had a week. I'm guessing she'll come crying to you, so I want you to know I'm serious.'

Bet sat down, smoothed her skirt, placed her hands in her lap. 'I might be old,' she said slowly. 'I might be a woman – though I'd hoped I'd brought you up better than to think that was a disability. I might not be particularly good with money or business or any of that kind of thing, but it is my flat, Marinela is my friend, and you will stay out of it.'

Tommy put his hand on hers. She pulled away.

'Mum, it's wrong for her to stay there. You've got to see that.'

'I'm tired now.'

'You're always tired when I'm trying to talk to you.'

Bet raised her eyebrows.

'I don't want to get the police involved, Mum.'

'So don't.'

'I'll tell Dad, then.'

Bet sniffed in a breath, squeezed her hands into fists. 'You promised.'

'Before I realized what a mess you'd got yourself into.'

There were tears, Bet was surprised to find, at the bridge of her nose, poised to make it into her eyes. 'You can't,' she whispered. 'Tommy, this is working. Can't you see this is working?'

'If she isn't out in a week,' Tommy said, 'I'm going to have to tell him.'

'You can go now,' Bet said flatly.

Tommy sighed, stood. 'I'm doing this because I care. I'm trying to help.'

Bet kept her gaze lowered, and eventually Tommy turned and walked towards the door.

'I could have gone to New York, you know,' she called after him.

He turned. 'Sorry?'

'I could have gone, but I didn't.'

Tommy walked back to her chair, bent down and kissed her cheek. 'I'm sorry to upset you, Mum, but it's for the best, I promise.'

Bet pulled away from him.

'I'll call you. I'll come over on Friday maybe? We'll sort this out. You don't need to worry about it.'

And then he was gone, and it was just Bet in the empty flat, the rain starting outside, a draught sneaking through the single-glazed windows.

MARINELA

She didn't know what she'd been thinking. She had never thrown a party in her life. Though it was hardly a party, she told herself. A handful of people. Wine, vodka, mince pies, music on her laptop. She'd asked a couple of girls from her course, then a couple more, then she'd messaged Harry and told him to bring a friend so he wouldn't be the only man there. And then last night she'd invited Jess without really meaning to. She'd gone out and bought cheap wine glasses, strips of tinsel, fairy lights.

Maybe it was because she hadn't felt quite at ease in the flat since that evening with Tommy and just wanted some company. She'd talked to Bet, who had assured her Tommy had no idea where the flat was, and so wasn't about to turn up and turf her out. Turf, which Marinela's dictionary said meant grass and also territory. Tommy had given her a week and there was only one day of that week left. So maybe this was actually a farewell party rather than the Christmas drinks she'd described it as.

The girls from her course arrived first, glossed lips, perfumed, clutching bottles of wine. Marinela ushered them up the striped stairs, remembering that first time, Bet moving glacier-slow in front of her, the keys gripped in her palm. It was only six or seven weeks ago, but it felt like a year.

'Is this Romanian?' One of the girls gestured towards Marinela's laptop.

Marinela nodded. 'They're called Vama. The title means, "Perfect Without You".'

The girl lifted her chin into a half nod, and then drifted away.

'Nice flat.' Another girl from her course – Susie, long dark hair, a round, almost ugly face, who took photos through microscopes: pollen, bee's wings, bacteria.

Marinela smiled. 'I have to leave soon.'

'No?'

Marinela shrugged.

'Landlords, man.' Susie shook her head. 'They can do what they want, can't they? Where are you going to go?'

She had no idea.

'Well, shout if you're stuck,' Susie said, drinking her wine too fast so it spilt down her jumper – red, oversized, with a picture of a reindeer taking up most of the front. 'I've got a friend who might be looking for someone.'

Marinela smiled stiffly. What was wrong with her? Why couldn't she relax? Instead there she was wishing she'd invited Bet instead, cooked her a nice beef casserole and cake for afterwards – just the two of them sitting together at the table.

The doorbell rang and Marinela excused herself. There was no intercom, so she had to run down to the front door. Before she opened it, she stood for a moment in the hallway, thinking about the people in her flat, which wasn't her flat, which had never been her flat, for all her pretending. She could just leave. She could just walk out of the front door and not go back. Someone would probably notice eventually, but she suspected it would take a while.

A knock on the glass. For a moment she had the ridiculous

thought that it might be Stefan, holding a huge bouquet of flowers, telling her he'd been a fool to let her go.

She opened the door to see Harry and Jess standing next to each other. They looked like a couple. Both of them skinny and dark-haired, wearing black jackets and thick-framed glasses. She glanced down, almost expecting to see them holding hands.

'My friend stood me up,' Harry said, 'but I found one of yours on the doorstep.'

Jess laughed. Her face looked washed-out in the porch light, dark smudges beneath her eyes.

Marinela just stood there.

'The party's in the porch?' Harry said.

'Sorry. I am sorry. Come in. Come in.' She stepped back, ushered them inside. 'It's upstairs, number seven.'

She let them go first, followed behind, thinking again about turning around and walking out into the night.

'He is cute.' Jess took hold of Marinela's arm and steered her away from Harry. 'Are you two—'

'No.' Marinela shook her head.

Jess peered into her face. 'But you want to.'

'No.' Marinela pulled her arm away. 'He is a friend.'

'I didn't tell him,' Jess whispered. 'Our dirty secret, and all that. Boys tend to get a bit confused about strippers, I find.'

'Are you not well?'

Jess blinked, pulled her arms across her front.

'You do not look well.'

Jess shrugged. 'I got rid of it.'

For a moment Marinela didn't know what she was talking about.

'The baby,' Jess said, the word baby coming out too loud, too fast.

Marinela reached for Jess's arm.

'What else was I going to do?'

'It hurt?'

Jess shrugged again. 'Let's find this sexy man of yours,' she said, brightening her voice. 'Let's find out what he's got to say for himself.'

At one point in the evening, Marinela stood by the window and looked into the flat – a group in the kitchen, another in the living space – Harry on the sofa with three girls sat on the floor at his feet. The music weaved in and out of voices and laughter. It was a good party, she realized. She had had a good party. And yet she still felt as though she was only half there, as though she was waiting for something to happen.

Once the first person left, the flat emptied quickly until it was just Jess and Harry.

'Marinela, I want to help clear up, but I've got to get my train,' Jess said, giving her a brief wink.

'Go,' Harry said. 'I'll help.'

Jess grinned. 'See you at work, missy.' She leant towards Marinela and planted a kiss on her cheek. 'Don't let him get away,' she whispered, then drew away. 'Lovely party,' she declared, and was gone.

'She's nice,' Harry said.

'Yes.'

'You work together?'

'Yes.'

'Where's that?'

Marinela blinked. 'Just a bar.'

Harry was carrying glasses into the kitchen.

'You don't need to clean.'

'No, I want to.'

Marinela went to the sink and turned on the hot tap. 'Thanks,' she said over the sound of water hitting steel.

Harry set the glasses carefully onto the counter. 'I'm sorry I still haven't sorted that drink.'

'It's fine. Really.'

'They just piled a whole load of stuff on us in one go.'

'I have assignments too. It's fine.' Marinela squeezed washing-up liquid into the water and watched the bubbles form. 'I have to leave,' she said.

'London?'

'The flat. Bet's son – he, well, he told me I had to leave.'

Harry pursed his lips. 'Bad luck.'

'Bet says to stay. Tommy says he will call the police.'

'You aren't doing anything wrong.'

'He thinks I am.' She gestured towards the now empty flat, the tinsel looped above the window, the paper plates scattered with crumbs. 'What is the phrase? Too good to be true?'

Harry collected up the plates and tipped them into the kitchen bin. 'Do you miss Romania?' he asked.

She thought about Galaţi. The bus ride from the station to her parents' flat: wide streets and tall trees; the buildings that had been done up and the ones that had been left to crumble and rot; her old school with its red and white frontage; the tangle of tramlines and electricity lines. Past the cinema, past the water fountain that looked like the seed head of a dandelion, towards Micro 20, the road lined with shops, and above them, apartments, the blocks sitting one next to the other with barely a breath of sky in between them. Her parents lived on the seventh floor, a corner flat with a small balcony and view of the factory – its curved cooling towers, tall skinny chimneys, funnel-shaped water towers, angled chutes.

'Sometimes.' She placed each glass carefully into the hot water. 'But it has only been three months, a little more. Maybe that is too soon to miss home?'

'You'll go back for Christmas?'

She shook her head. 'My mother is crying every day, but.' She shrugged. 'It is too expensive at Christmas time. And I have work. I tell her I will be home in the summer, it is not long away, but.' She smiled. 'There is only me. No brothers or sisters.'

'And you've no boyfriend back there or anything?' Harry asked. 'I'm sorry, that's not my business.'

'No.' Marinela shook her head. 'No. Well, not really.'

'Not really?'

'It is . . .' She hesitated, cursing herself for starting this. 'Complicated – you say that?'

'Sure.'

The flat felt suddenly quiet and empty. Marinela washed each glass and arranged them neatly on the draining board. It had been stupid to buy glasses – she would never need so many again.

Harry coughed and she glanced over. His cheeks were red, with wine or embarrassment she didn't know. 'Do you know,' he started. 'I was just thinking. Well, if you wanted to come to Liverpool.'

'Sorry?'

'For Christmas.' He held up both hands. 'I don't know, maybe you'd like to experience an English Christmas?'

'That's very—'

'Though I can't guarantee peace and harmony on earth at my folks' place. To be honest, you'd be doing me a favour. You'd be a distraction. I mean that nicely.'

'You said you don't like your dad?'

Harry rubbed his fingers through his hair. 'The thing is, my brother is the golden child: works in the City, owns a flat in Clapham, engaged to a nice girl from the Home Counties. I'm the proverbial black sheep. Maybe inviting you is a terrible idea, I'm sorry, I don't know why you'd want to spend your Christmas watching me argue with my family.'

She wanted to reach out and smooth his hair where he had

ruffled it, but she kept her hands under the water, though there was nothing left to wash. 'Do you go home much?'

Harry shrugged. 'Twice a year, maybe. For Christmas and then my mum's birthday. Mum's not so bad, but she always goes along with whatever he says. She never backs me up.' He took the tea towel from its hook and started drying the glasses. 'I have to shut up. Tell me about your family.'

Marinela looked down at the water, the bubbles almost gone. 'It's just me and my parents,' she said. 'And then there was my grandmother, who I loved. Bet reminds me of her sometimes. But she died. Three years ago.'

Harry said nothing – waiting.

'She lived in a little town called Tuluçesti, in this tiny house. A poor house.'

Her grandmother's street followed a curve from the church down to the railway: a dirt road, criss-crossed by power lines, fruit trees leaning their branches over tall metal fences, dogs basking in the sun or huddling together for warmth. She used to run down that road as a child, not a care in the world except whether Bunica had made cherry cake, or Snow White cake.

'After she died, we emptied it out.' Marinela shook her head. 'I hated that. It was like we were killing her, like we were pretending she'd never been there. All those things she'd cared about. And then no one would buy it, and it started falling apart. I thought maybe I should move there, but there is nothing there for me to do. No jobs.'

A scattering of houses. A couple of shops, the railway line. She used to cross the tracks behind her grandmother's house, walk out past the low block of flats, past the big grain shed, past the cluster of electricity pylons, along the track to the concrete bridge over the slow river. In winter a layer of ice would form across its surface and she would stand and watch the water moving, sluggish and reluctant, underneath.

'I went there before I came to London,' Marinela said. 'I went to light a candle for her in the churchyard.' The sun bright in her eyes; the flowers a riot of red and pink and white. 'The house—' She stopped. 'It's just a house. It's just wood and plaster, and whatever. I know that.'

She hadn't seen what had happened until she had drawn level with the gate in front of the house. And even when she saw it, it took a moment for her brain to understand what she was looking at.

The right half of the house's front wall had collapsed. Inwards, it seemed, because the room that had been revealed was full of rubble. Her grandmother's sitting room. The walls painted turquoise, the tall wooden dresser still standing in the corner. On the back wall, now exposed, was the wooden door through to the kitchen.

She'd stood and stared, her fingers reaching for the wire mesh of the gate.

Ruined. The low roof was still on, but the wooden fretworked edge had slipped and now hung from one corner, half buried in a woody clump of ivy, which was taking over the right-hand side of the house. The remaining front wall had lost its render and was riven with cracks, the window smashed and the frame rotting. The ceiling of the exposed room was starting to sag. Marinela had stared at the dresser, at the turquoise walls and the wooden door, and felt a surge of anger sweep up from her stomach. It was an insult. Her grandmother – a quiet, private woman – would be horrified.

'You think houses last for ever, don't you?' Harry said. 'We all think that.' He leant forwards and touched her arm, a brief pat of his palm against her jumper. She wondered what it would be like to kiss him. Gentle, she imagined. He would be gentle. And then she thought of Stefan – his mouth hot and urgent on hers; telling her to put on a dress when it was already gone midnight because he just had to take her dancing, right this minute.

'I should go.' Harry folded the tea towel in half and then half again, laid it on the counter. 'Have a think about Christmas,' he said. 'I'd love to have you there if you want to come.'

Marinela stepped towards him, thinking she'd kiss his cheek at least, but he'd turned away, looking for his coat and she ended up almost kissing the back of his head, like an idiot. When he turned towards her she'd already moved away.

'Thanks for coming,' she said, brightly.

'Thanks for inviting me.' He hesitated for a moment as if deciding whether to say something else, but instead he threaded his arms into his coat and pulled a woollen hat almost down to his eyes. 'Text me about Christmas?' he said. 'No pressure.'

She let him go. And once he had left, she sat for a long time on the sofa, hugging the red cushion in her lap. She made herself wait an hour before she picked up her phone, went to Harry's number and wrote, *Yes please. Thank you. M x.*

JACK

Wednesday. Early December. The sky flat and grey with clouds. The air pinched cold. Jack had had to force himself out of bed that morning. He'd avoided his eyes in the bathroom mirror as he gargled with sharp mint mouthwash and got his teeth in, then washed his face, splashing water up from the cupped palms of his hands. Every day, he thought. Every bloody day. Which was no way to think. He wasn't someone who dwelt on things. He was a practical, straightforward kind of a man and he prided himself on it. Except these last few weeks he'd found himself doing this: washing his face and wondering what the point was, really, and indeed how many more times he would hold his hands under the tap before bringing them up to his cheeks. It was winter, and he had some kind of virus coming on, something low-level and grotty, the kind of thing that took all your energy and turned you in on yourself. But he knew it had more to do with Bet than the weather or any illness. She wasn't herself. Fidgety. Irritable. Distracted. Drifting off half-way through a conversation, looking up at the slightest of noises. He might ask her, of course, what was happening, if she needed some help, but it was not his way; it was not their way. Things passed eventually. They had both learnt that.

And so he continued his slow ritual of getting ready, and at just after ten o'clock he walked out of the front door, his coat buttoned, a woollen scarf tight around his neck.

He was tired. It was as though somehow his very bones were tired, right the way through. It was harder than usual to lift one leg and then the other, to find enough energy to propel himself forward. He kept thinking about the past, memories floating up to the surface of his mind like bloated fish. Bet in the flat on Larcom Street, wearing that green dress and turning her face away from him – don't kiss me, you'll ruin my make-up. Bet's friend Nell standing on the street, saying, I had to tell you Jack, I just felt I couldn't let it go. And then her lips on his – the smell of her cigarettes and perfume and the bitter-sweet taste of gin as her tongue moved against his. He had pulled away. Of course he had. And if there was a fraction of a pause before he did, then it was simply due to the shock of it all. Bet and an American – a customer. His Bet. And if he'd felt something when she kissed him, then it was just instinct. There was nothing more to be said about it.

He paused before the bridge, next to the new flats with their beige and orange and brown balconies. A train rushed by above him and he glanced up at the rows of carriages and felt the hurry and thud of the wheels on the rails echo somewhere around his heart.

He'd sent Nell away, said he wouldn't listen to her nonsense. She had shrugged, hurt he thought by his rejection, but as she turned, the light from the hallway catching her features, it was pity that he saw. After she'd gone, he hadn't known what to do. Even lies and nonsense have a way of getting under your skin.

He would ask Bet, he decided, get it out in the open. If it was true, they would sort it out together. But when she got home that night, she had put her hands either side of his face and kissed him, a long, soft, Martini-laced kiss. And when she finally pulled away she had smiled the smile he loved and said, 'You're the best, Jack Chalmers. I have spent all night missing you.' And so he said nothing.

Jack resumed his walk – under the bridge, which was stained with years of rain and the moss and mould that followed its tracks across the bricks; past the hotel, to the pub on the corner with its Tudor upper storey and leaded windows. He had never drunk there, but thought, now, about stepping inside and ordering a pint. How many years had it been since he'd done that? After a day on the buses – the cool relief of it.

He didn't stop, but carried on across Walworth Road by the sexual health clinic, past the boarded-up museum, and there, again, the estate. Which was no longer the estate; which was nothing but emptiness and dust, machines and men in fluorescent jackets and hard hats. On the hoardings, he read the words *an inspiring place to call home* in neat white text across a green background. He stared at it. Sometimes he had a sense of another version of himself: a person who would get angry at a sentence like that, written just there. A person who would march to the site office, knock on the door and ask how dare they? But that was not how he was. He was Jack. He took things as they came. He did not look back. He knew when he was beat.

The shopping centre was quiet, only a handful of people moving through the wide corridors under the stark lights. One man sitting on the red benches outside Barclays; only three or four drinking coffee in the cafes. The Christmas decorations were the same as last year's – oversized silver baubles taped to the ceiling; tinsel wrapped around the pillars. Jack stopped where the two corridors crossed and examined the gumball machine, which shone as though someone polished it every night. The sweets were of every colour: lime green; yellow; bright blue; silver. They were twenty pence each. You put a coin in the slot and turned a little lever and one popped out into the tray.

Jack stared at the coloured sweets and imagined eating one – the hard ball in his mouth letting go of its dye and whatever flavour it was supposed to be. He couldn't quite shake the thought that maybe there was no point him being there – he had nothing to do, no one to see.

Rubbish. Every time Bet got in a mood like that it was Jack who would snap her out of it. No use worrying about things you can't control, he'd say. Best just to get on with it; think about what to eat for dinner; watch something good on the TV. No use in dwelling, he'd say, nothing good ever comes of it.

The escalators were only wide enough for one. He remembered when the centre first opened and kids would come and spend hours going up, coming down, trying to beat them by running in the wrong direction, laughing and squealing as though it was unbelievable – these stairways that moved. Now he was just grateful not to have to make the effort of getting his body down to the ground floor, step by step.

Once he was settled in the Sundial he found himself thinking about Marinela. She'd looked tired the last time he saw her – her face white and pinched. Homesick, maybe. He sipped his coffee and traced a pattern in a patch of spilt sugar on the tabletop. A circle. A square. A circle. The radio was on, loud enough for him to hear. Christmas carols. The one about the chestnuts roasting. Maybe they should ask her if she wanted to come over for Christmas. She'd have something better to do, he was sure, but it would be nice to offer. He'd suggest it to Bet when he got home. And then he'd ask whether everything was OK with her, and was there anything he could do?

There were fewer people in the cafe than usual too. Another old man sitting alone. Two women wearing Tesco's uniforms. It happened sometimes, places were quiet or busy for no obvious reason. Except he couldn't help thinking it was more than that. The estate gone. The shopping centre dying. They'd talked for years of knocking it down, so maybe it would happen. More cranes, more rubble, the whole place turned into somewhere unrecognizable.

He should have stayed at home. The cold – he was sure he was getting a cold – was starting to build up behind his nose and across the rugged expanse of his forehead, as though something inside his skull was being slowly tightened. His whole body ached, and then his mind, dwelling, thinking about things long gone and forgotten. Bet turning away from him; Nell shifting from one heeled foot to the other, looking him full in the face and saying: It's not right, Jack. You're a good man. You don't deserve this.

Except maybe he did. Maybe he deserved all of it. Bertie's. The American. Because if Bet had been happy, she wouldn't have done it, he was certain of that. And if he couldn't make her happy – and he couldn't, for all his trying – then what could he expect?

Jack drank the last of his coffee and used his teaspoon to scoop out the slug of undissolved sugar from the bottom of the cup. Then he got himself to his feet, leaning heavily onto the tabletop to lever himself up. For a moment he wondered about trying to find a taxi, or getting a bus along the Walworth Road at least, but when he reached the shopping centre entrance, the wintry air braced him a little. He sniffed and drew back his shoulders. The walking kept him going, kept him fit. He would feel better once he'd started.

He fell on the street, at the bus stop by the museum, just past the estate. It might have been the lip of a raised paving slab, catching at the sole of his shoe. It might have been ice – it was cold enough, a few flecks of snow in the air, melting as soon as they met the ground. Or it might have been nothing.

Either way, he fell, quickly and gracelessly, twisting to his left and landing hard on the jut of his hip bone, his arm bent beneath him, his cheek grazing the pavement. For a moment he lay, quite still and alone, looking towards the road – car wheel, scratched hub cap, cyclist with orange shoes. The pain was so complete he almost couldn't feel it, as though his body had been taken over by someone or something else and all he could do was try to remember how to breathe, try not to register the heat of it shooting through his body.

And then the people came, their faces looming, their hands touching his arm, their voices asking questions. He waited for himself to answer them, to get up and brush himself off, let someone walk with him to a cafe and buy him a cup of tea to calm his nerves. But instead, he stayed where he was. The pain was settling in now, tendrilling up from his hip and arm into the rest of his body, forcing out his breath in short hard gasps.

This is it, he found himself thinking. This is it. And his next thought was of Bet, sitting in the flat with an empty pot of tea on the table next to her armchair, waiting for him to get home, fix her some lunch, tell her about his morning.

'Don't move. Best to stay still.' A woman's voice, her grip firm on his arm, pushing him towards the ground.

He tried to push back, to get himself up, but he had no strength in him and when he moved the pain found new routes through his body so that every cell seemed to pulse with it.

'We've called an ambulance,' the woman said.

Jack closed his eyes. An ambulance. Blue lights, polished white, stretchers and machines. How would he tell Bet? How would he say, Bet, I'm in hospital. Bet, the pain's so bad I'd rather everything just stopped. Because what would she do?

The woman kept her hand on his arm. She didn't pat him, which he was glad of. He concentrated on the heat of her touch through his coat and realized that he was shaking.

People passed on either side, stopping sometimes so they could look and wonder at this old man, lying on the ground. The cars and lorries and buses kept on going, and just behind him he could hear the noises from the building site – a hard drilling sound, and then a high-pitched metallic whine. Jack could feel himself drifting. Stay awake. Don't let yourself go. Stay with me. He forced his eyes open. A dirty piece of chewing gum glued to the concrete. A bit of grass reaching up between two slabs. The kerb dipping down to the dark tarmac road. The woman's hand on his arm.

And then the ambulance. Blue lights bouncing. Soft voices and gentle hands. More questions. Does this hurt? This? It did. All of it. And he needed to get home. Make Bet a fresh cup of tea. Put some washing on. Think about lunch.

A scratch, someone said, just a scratch. A needle in his arm and then, there, a new kind of drifting, as though he was being lifted up above himself, and the cold, the pavement, the stabbing, throbbing pain, were getting further and further away.

Bet. He tried to say it. But the word got lost somewhere between his brain and his mouth. They put him onto a stretcher and hoisted him into the back of the ambulance. The high-pitched whine started again from the estate, and even when they closed the ambulance doors, he could still hear it, ripping through the air outside.

BET

She couldn't bear the thought of it: Jack in hospital, wearing a thin cotton gown, lying on one of those awful beds, surrounded by masked doctors and machines. Someone had called her – a nice, softly spoken man, who had laid everything out quite clearly and calmly. Jack had fallen, broken his hip, was in theatre being operated on as they spoke. Theatre. The word lodged in her head as the man kept on talking. Costumes and lights. Drama.

'He's doing just fine,' the man said. 'A bit bruised, a bit shocked and tired, but he's doing just fine.'

Jack.

People talked about falls as the beginning of the end. He had a fall, and then it was all downhill from there. She had a fall and was never quite the same again.

Bet told the man that she, too, was quite all right. No, she didn't need him to call anyone. Yes, she was quite sure. She would get in touch with her son straight away. No, no need to involve social services or any of that nonsense. She was perfectly fine. Thank you.

She'd ended the call and sat with the phone in her lap. She would ring Tommy, but not just yet. There was a pain lodged somewhere in her chest. She would just wait for it to go.

In the end she ordered a taxi. The driver got out to help her inside. She had to stop herself from leaning on him too heavily.

'Very cold,' he said, once Bet was settled and he was pulling out onto the road, shouting over the music – something foreign with a wailing female singer.

'Yes.' Bet nodded, and then didn't know what else to say. Cold as a witch's tit – that's what Nell would have said. Bet wished, for a moment, for a gin sling, burning down her throat, across her chest and into her stomach, and for Nell, her wide, lipsticked mouth, her too-loud laugh. Her way of running at the world head first, and fuck the consequences. The way she could say that: fuck the consequences, when Bet could barely bring herself to think the word.

'You are brave woman.'

She laughed in surprise. 'Some would say stupid,' she shouted back. She wrapped her arms across her chest, but couldn't stop herself from shivering.

'No, no.' Bet could make out the movement of his head, a vigorous shake. 'On your own, in cold. Very brave.' He drove slowly, carefully. The car smelt of air freshener – sweet and appley. The heater was on full and she felt the warmth seep into her. 'It is difficult to be old in this country, no?'

Bet pulled her shoulders back and patted at her hair.

'In my country, all old people live with the family.'

For all he knew, she lived with hers. Tommy had never offered and she wouldn't accept even if he did, but this man did not know that.

'Not out on own.' The driver shook his head again. He drove for a while in silence, then said, 'My country is Iran,' as though Bet had asked him the question. 'Very beautiful country.'

Bet angled her head towards the window. She should have called Tommy. She should call him now. Except she didn't want to. Didn't want to say it out loud. Didn't want him asking questions, fussing, making everything worse than it already was.

'My children do better here,' the taxi driver said.

Bet turned her attention back to the man in front of her. 'Will they look after you?'

He moved his head so she knew he was looking at her in his mirror. He did not think he would ever be old.

'My son wants to put me into a home,' she said. She did not know why she had told him that.

The driver sucked in his breath. 'You must say no.'

'I have.'

'Home,' the driver said, with his accent. Different to Marinela's, thicker and more rounded where hers was sharp. 'Home, home, home.'

Bet closed her eyes and rested her head back on the seat. The driver started telling her about his children. Three girls. Very clever. Very beautiful. She let his words drift over her and he carried on talking, all the way to the hospital.

Just finding Jack's ward exhausted her. Endless brightly lit corridors. Everyone hurrying along as though they knew exactly where they were going. The place smelt of cleaning fluid and stale coffee. So far to walk and her legs hurt. Her head hurt. Her eyes felt dimmer than ever. There was a part of her that felt like just stopping, lying down in the corridor and waiting until someone picked her up.

But then she was there, Jack's name written up on a whiteboard near the nurses' station, a woman taking her arm and leading her to a line of chairs.

'He's still in surgery, darling.' She was black, tight plaits against her skull, a lilt in her voice. 'Shall I make you a cup of tea? You can sit and wait if you'd like.'

Bet lowered herself into the chair. The ward was hot, she could feel sweat on her upper lip, under her arms, and yet she was still cold inside. The woman disappeared and Bet sat and waited, but no tea appeared, no Jack appeared. She fidgeted one shoe off and then the other. There'd been a time she'd walked in shoes with three-inch heels. There'd been a time her feet were smooth and soft and beautiful. I want your foot carved out of marble, Kit said once. Jack wouldn't have thought to say such a thing. She wiggled her toes inside her stockings and tried to remember the last time she'd painted her toenails. There must have been a point at which she'd stopped, when she'd decided to let the varnish flake off until it was gone and then not paint them again, but she couldn't imagine herself doing such a thing.

She sat listening to the bleep of machines, the low chunter of a television, a man talking loudly into his phone. Her eyes were heavy, tired. She blinked hard, gripped the chair's arms with her hands. She would be here, awake, when Jack got back. It was the least she could do.

Bet woke, disorientated, her neck cricked. For a moment she had no idea where she was. Polished floors. Fluorescent lights. And then she did know and she wished she could close her eyes and fall back asleep.

If Tommy was there he would have asked questions, he'd still be asking questions – how was Jack doing? When would he be out of surgery? How long would he be in hospital for? But the thought of even standing up made Bet feel exhausted. So she just sat there, watching the nurses walk back and forth, the patients shuffling to the bathroom, visitors arriving with flowers and chocolates. Waiting.

When Jack did appear, he was paper-white, exhausted from the anaesthetic. He looked so thin, so old, under the hospital blankets, it made Bet want to weep. The nurses hustled and bustled around him, pressing buttons on machines, fiddling with the tube attached to Jack's hand. And then they were gone and it was just the two of them.

'Jack?' Bet touched her finger against his. 'Love?'

His breathing sounded difficult.

'You know what Tommy will say, don't you? What were you doing, out walking on your own, Dad, I told you something like this would happen.' Bet laughed, but it sounded more like she was crying. 'He's bloody right too.' She stroked Jack's little finger from knuckle to nail. 'He's bloody right, isn't he? Maybe we should go into one of those homes. Jack?' She leant forward, looking at his closed eyes. 'Maybe we should be somewhere a bit,' she hesitated, 'safer.' She would do it. She would move tomorrow, if doing so would make Jack open his eyes, look at her and grin; make his mouth move and say, Bet Chalmers, are you crying? Not my Bet?

MARINELA

It was three days since Jack had fallen on the street and ended up in hospital. Marinela was at Bet's, baking. I'm not hungry, Bet had insisted, but Marinela had carried on regardless and now a tray of sweet *cornuletes*, stuffed with walnuts and dates, sat on the kitchen counter next to a plate of *saratele*, dotted with fennel seeds. She bit into a *cornulete* – the filling so hot she almost had to spit it out again. Her head felt thick from the wine the previous night. She had met Harry in a bar on Upper Street, all stripped floorboards and bare light bulbs. They had talked – about his family, his university debts, his plans to set up a charity to find solutions to the housing crisis; about her family, Galați, her photography, Jack and Bet. They had drunk a bottle of wine and eaten over-priced wasabi peanuts that came in a glass tumbler. And then they had said goodbye, and he had kissed her cheek, and paused, so that she could have kissed him on the lips if she'd chosen to, asked him back to her flat, started all of that. But the feel of his stubble had made her think about Stefan, and before she had told herself to stop being an idiot Harry had stepped away, and it was too late.

'Do you like it?' Bet said, walking into the kitchen and lowering herself onto a chair.

Marinela looked up. 'Baking? It reminds me of my grand-mother.'

'Being on stage? Having them all look at you?'

Marinela blinked. She had heard nothing more from Tommy and had thought maybe he'd decided to let it go, with Jack in hospital and Bet on her own. She hadn't thought he'd tell Bet about the club.

'I was never brave enough,' Bet said before she could answer.

Marinela looked at her, the skin loose at her neck and chin; her remaining teeth shipwrecked along her gums; her scalp shining through her dyed brown hair.

'I used to watch them,' Bet said. 'Up on stage in their feathers and glitter, all that flesh. And I'd watch the men watching them – well, men and women I suppose. I used to wish I was brave enough to do it.' She laughed. 'They were the dancers; we were hostesses. Very different.' She held up one finger and moved it from side to side. 'They're just words, though, aren't they?'

Marinela started to move the *cornuletes*, one by one, onto a wire cooling rack. 'Did you like it?' she asked. 'Being a hostess?'

'We wore such beautiful dresses. We made conversation. We made the men feel at home – that was our job, Bert used to say. Bertie's was comfortable, safe, somewhere to hide away from your troubles. Bertie's was what a home should be like, without the wife and the kids and the things that were broken, and the smells of cooking, and the bills and the neighbours fighting next door. It was our job to pretend, and to help everyone else pretend too.' She let out a sigh. 'I loved it. It was like living on a film set: everything brighter and more beautiful than it was in real life.' She smiled. 'My mother always said I was a dreamer, couldn't keep my two feet on the ground. She used to say, Bet, if you aim too high, you'll just end up flat on your face, and who do you think is going to come and pick you up? Nobody, that's who.'

Marinela dropped the last *cornulete* onto the rack and turned towards Bet.

'The place I work is not so glamorous,' she said at last. 'It's a job. I don't like it much, but it earns more than working in a cafe, so.' She shrugged.

'He was there?' Bet asked.

'Tommy?' Marinela thought of him sitting in the VIP room, the yellow fish butting its head against the glass.

'He tried to make out he doesn't go to those places, but I don't believe him.' Bet sniffed.

'A friend of mine worked there,' Marinela said. 'She taught me the dances, gave me Paul's phone number – he's the man who runs it.'

Bet smiled. 'Just like Nell. She's the one who persuaded me to work at Bertie's. Do you know, if it wasn't for Nell I sometimes think it would all have been different. And then I think, that's ridiculous, Bet. You can't blame your whole life on someone else. You are who you are. You do what you do. I never set out to hurt anyone, though. I'm not like that.'

'You think I should stop?' Marinela said. 'Is that why you ask?'

Bet smiled again. 'What you do is none of my business, love. As long as you're happy, that's what matters, isn't it? Now, you're not to worry about Tommy and his ultimatums – I've told him to leave you alone. And don't you worry about Jack either, he's strong as an ox, that man. Survived the war, didn't he? So he can survive a little fall.'

Marinela walked to Waterloo Bridge and took the bus back to Angel. She sat on the top floor, raised up above the city, looking down at the traffic, the cyclists in their bright yellow jackets and the people stopping and starting along the pavements. The bus moved north across the river, then turned right, past high white buildings – hotels and offices – the road choked with cars. As they reached a pale, sombre-looking church with a tall clock tower, she heard someone crying behind her. It was a man, on the opposite side of the aisle, sitting close up against the window, both hands gripping the metal bar of the seat in front of him. He was in his forties, maybe, wearing an old green jacket, black hair thinning, a scratch of dark stubble across his cheeks. He was crying hard – his face streaked with tears and snot – and noisily too, great gasping sobs coming up from his stomach. Further down the bus two girls stared at him and laughed to each other.

For a moment, Marinela sat and looked, then she glanced at the girls and they smirked, as though she shared their amusement. It was this that made her stand up and go to sit next to the man. He lowered his head onto his arms and continued crying. She had no tissues. She had nothing to say to him.

When they reached the Barbican, Marinela lifted her left hand and placed it over the man's right. He froze – a dart of tension the whole way along his body. He raised his head a fraction, but only to look at her hand, not her face. Neither of them spoke. She glanced sideways at him and saw a tattooed word written in fussy, curlicued letters across his neck. She could not work out what it said. It would be the name of a girl-friend or a child. Maybe that was what he was crying about. Except he had stopped now. He sniffed, wiped his face against the sleeve of his coat and then lifted his head. They sat, staring forwards, the heat of his hand transferring into Marinela's. At her stop she didn't get up until the bus had braked, and then she did it quickly, hurrying down the stairs with her head lowered.

Marinela stood on the pavement, shaking. She fancied she could hear Bunica's voice – you did a good thing, a kind thing, angel – but then she lost it amongst the noise of Upper Street. Someone knocked into her and swore, not at her, it seemed, but at London, at the crowded pavements and the failing sunshine, the scratty pigeons and the people with their dark coats and shopping bags and hurrying strides.

Sometimes she missed her grandmother so much her insides hurt. She closed her eyes and kept herself still, let the people buffet around her. She thought of her grandmother's house, the way it was when she was still alive: its stone floors and handmade rugs; the painted icons hanging above the fireplace and the beds; the embroidered mats on the kitchen table and the plates carefully arranged in the dresser; the low ceilings and squat window at the back with its view of the railway line and the fields stretching out into nothingness beyond. And then she thought of her grandmother – how Marinela had had to bend a little to hug her; how her clothes always smelt of woodsmoke; how her hair – so thin and soft – would tickle Marinela's cheek like a spider's web caught on her skin.

The walk from the bus stop to the flat felt slow and arduous, though it took barely ten minutes. She passed Christmas tree after Christmas tree shimmering in bay windows. In Elephant and Castle, the lights were more colourful, Father Christmases and snowmen made out of plastic piping and flashing red and green lights. Here, they seemed to prefer white lights and silver decorations, transparent glass baubles, fake snow sprayed onto the bottoms of the windowpanes as though it had piled up there overnight. She turned onto her street, feeling the tug in her calves from the gradient. There was a man standing on the doorstep of her flat, but she didn't notice until she was almost upon him.

Stefan. Tall. Thin. Blue-eyed. His dark hair specked with grey. Pale, with dark patches under his eyes. Wearing jeans, white shirt, a dark jacket. A bulging sports bag at his feet.

'Mari! Sparrow!' He opened his arms and stepped towards her, took her by the shoulders and kissed one cheek then the other. 'My darling.'

Marinela stared at him.

'You are surprised! I have surprised you.' He laughed, gleeful as a child. 'I am an early Christmas present.'

Marinela swallowed. She wanted to reach out and touch his face. She wanted to slap him.

'How did I find you, you are thinking?' He laughed again. 'I am a detective, am I not?'

She had thought about sending him her address but had stopped herself. He'd never come, she'd told herself, and yet here he was. Stefan, standing on her doorstep, his hands dancing as he spoke. She wanted him to put his arms around her.

'I have missed you, Sparrow. We have so much to talk about. So much to say.'

He was not wearing his wedding ring.

'Stefan—'

'This is where you live?' He turned towards the front door. 'It is nice. I want to see everything. I want to know everything.'

Marinela thought about the man on the bus. She wished for a moment she was still sitting next to him, her hand on his, moving through the city, saying nothing.

'You've left her?'

Stefan waved a hand in a vague gesture. 'Let's go inside!' he said. 'I have țuică, I have Eugenia biscuits. We must celebrate. Come, come!' He gestured at the door, and Marinela stepped forwards to put her key in the lock, like a woman in a trance.

'It's upstairs. Third floor.' She went first, could hear him behind her, knew he was looking up at her as she walked. The stairs seemed endless, the striped carpet made her head spin. When they eventually reached number seven she stopped for a moment, her breath sharp in her chest. Stefan. A tremor of happiness rose in her chest; she couldn't stop herself from smiling.

Stefan dropped his bag in the hallway, turned and put his hands on Marinela's hips, pulled her towards him.

'Beautiful Mari. I missed you,' he said, and lowered his mouth to hers.

It was like melting. It was like stepping out of the cold into a warm room.

But he had cheated on her, she knew it. With that girl in the boat. And when she'd said she was leaving he had cried and sulked, but he hadn't stopped her. Marinela pulled away from him. 'You never called,' she said.

'I thought about you every day.' His fingers on her cheek.

'You never wrote.'

'Every day, Sparrow. You left and I was heartbroken, you know that.' He kissed her again.

She drew back, her heart thumping against her ribs. She thought about Harry, his easy laugh, his kind eyes, his hair springing in every which direction.

'You are not happy to see me, Sparrow?'

She wanted to lean her head against Stefan's chest and breathe in the smell of him. She wanted to lift her face to his and let him kiss her again.

'Have you left her?' she asked.

Stefan walked through the kitchen to the small table by the window and sat down. 'I love you,' he said, his voice low and sad. 'I've always loved you, Mari.'

'She left you?'

He shook his head. 'None of it matters. I am here, in London. For you.'

She tried to stay strong, but there she was, walking towards him, putting her hand on his shoulder, letting him pull her onto his knee and kiss her, his hands moving over her body. She felt a surge of desire pulse through her. Was this how Bet had felt, she wondered, with the American man? Knowing she should say no but saying yes all the same. She let Stefan lift her up and carry her to the bedroom; let him lie her down and stroke her hair, tell her how much he'd missed her, how much he loved her, how right it was that they were together again; let him kiss her until she could think about nothing else; let him put himself inside her and move until she came, hard, crying out with it.

Afterwards, she lay next to Stefan, her eyes fixed on the ceiling as the light gradually dimmed outside. She didn't feel right. A bubbling anxiety in her throat. A heaviness in her limbs. She turned onto her side and closed her eyes, willed herself to sleep, but her brain wouldn't let her. It was hurrying, wheeling, separating itself from her body. She was lost again.

Stefan's breathing sounded wrong – a warped, rushing noise that made her feel sick. There he was, next to her in the bed, eyes closed, one arm thrown up next to his face. There she was, half naked, lying next to him. But it felt as though she was far away, so far away she might never get back to him.

Close your eyes. Take a minute. It will pass.

She wanted to pummel Stefan's bare chest with her fists and cry and cry and cry. But all she could do was lie as still as she could – her hands gripped around the duvet as though she was holding on to a ledge – and wait.

She must have slept, because she woke, with a start, to find herself alone in bed, the shower running next door. She lay very still and listened. Running water. Just running water. It was dark outside, the neighbours' windows lit like yellow advent squares – a plant, a table, a tall, arched lamp. Marinela turned onto her back and waited. Her head hurt, but everything else seemed the same as it always was. She ran her hands over her arms, down her legs to her knees and ankles. All there. All connected.

'Sparrow, where are your things?' Stefan stood in the bedroom doorway, a towel wrapped around his waist.

'Things?'

He waved a hand towards the room. 'Pictures. Rugs. Books. Stuff. Where is your stuff?'

Marinela blinked.

'You threw it all away? It's some art project where you throw everything away?'

She nearly laughed.

Stefan gave an exaggerated shiver. 'I will buy you things. Pretty things.'

She had only once visited his flat, in an old, unassuming building near the hospital. The stairwell had been dull and worn, but the flat had been recently decorated. Pine laminate floorboards; a gold and white chandelier in the hallway, and another, dripping with cut-glass beads in the living room. The walls were white, except for a single stretch of bubble-gum pink glimpsed through one door, and another, yellow, in the living room. It was not the kind of apartment she had expected him to live in. She would have guessed at wooden floorboards, mismatched furniture, something more stylishly down at heel. And there were things everywhere: a row of ceramic cats on a shelf above the electric fire, a large print of Audrey Hepburn clutching her cigarette holder; bowls of potpourri interspersed with plants on the windowsills; scented candles and a box of tissues covered with a red and gold embroidered case on the coffee table. She had assumed they were chosen by his wife. She had assumed he hated them as much as she did. But perhaps she'd been wrong.

'It's fine,' she shook her head, feeling the ache at her temples. 'I don't need anything.'

'No, no.' Stefan shook his head. 'It is too empty. Like you just moved in, or you are just leaving.'

'I have to leave. I thought I would already be gone, but—'
Tommy hadn't done anything to make her go and so she'd
stayed, though it was an uneasy staying. She would wake sometimes in the middle of the night with a start, sure the doorbell
had just rung.

Stefan shrugged. 'So, for the next place. We will go shopping and buy things for you.'

Harry would never say such a thing. Marinela thought of
him standing in her kitchen, drying wine glasses.

'Why are you here?' she asked.

Stefan tipped back his head and laughed. 'You crazy girl.'

'I'm serious.'

'To see you.'

'And Anca? The children?'

Stefan flicked his palm towards her, but then said, 'There is
no me and Anca any more. It is over. Finished with.' She saw
something – regret, sadness, she wasn't sure – flicker across his
face, but only for a moment. Then he was smiling, saying, 'And
now I am here, with you. And now is the only thing that matters.' He let his towel fall to the floor. 'My beautiful Sparrow.'

JACK

The ceiling was moving. As though Jack was at the bottom of the sea with waves passing above him. The plastic tiles rippled, and the strip lights too. He could not steady himself on the bed, which was too narrow and too high, the sheets twisted and hot between his limbs.

A boat. He must be on a boat. The slip slide of water underneath him, his whole body out of sync, the bile rising in his throat. But he wouldn't set foot on a boat, hadn't done since 1947. He'd waited for months and months to get a place on the damn thing out of Burma and then vomited the whole way home – feeling as though his insides wanted to be on the outside; feeling as though he was going to die.

Bet had wanted a holiday in France, but he wouldn't go. There were things he'd change if he could go back and do it all again.

Why was the ceiling doing that? He rolled onto his side so he could see the floor. It was the same: ripples pulsing across it, moving the chair legs, the laminate cabinet, the yellow bin.

Ah! Frank. How did he get here? Blond hair. A smile to lift your day. But he was wearing a nurse's uniform. Jack laughed. You're not a nurse, Frank. You're a soldier.

Frank was dead. 1945. A bullet in the back of the head. Jack could still see him, splayed out in the mud, muttering words

Jack couldn't make out however hard he tried. Once he was quiet, Jack had looked in his pockets. He couldn't have said why, except maybe he knew what he would find – a photo of Bet, her head tipped back, laughing. He had kept it – dog-eared, soft with Frank's sweat – still had it somewhere, he guessed; at least he'd never thrown it away.

Had he ever said sorry to Frank? I'm not his girl, Bet had insisted. I'm not anybody's girl. But only a fool wouldn't have noticed the way Frank looked at her. He couldn't remember if he'd apologized, and what good would it have done anyway?

He looked up again, the ceiling had stopped moving. He stared, but it did nothing. Made out like it never had and he was some crazy man, wandering along the Walworth Road, muttering to himself. Stinking.

He didn't feel right – his body hot and aching; a needling below his guts. Nothing a good kip wouldn't sort out – except that when he slept he dreamt of the jungle, too hot to sweat; too hot to breathe; his skin bitten red raw by mosquitos, and the mud – everywhere, the mud.

'Dad?'

Jack started awake, flailed a hand in front of his face to get rid of whatever was there – an insect, he thought, there were so many insects.

'Dad. How are you doing?'

Tommy's face loomed above him. Why was he there? He'd never liked the shopping centre – cheap, he said, shoddy. You and Mum should move to the country, he said. Ha! Bet would rather step in front of a bus than live in the country. Had enough of that as a girl, she said. He'd have gone. He'd have gone in a heartbeat.

Bet. He looked around, rearing up out of bed and moving his head from side to side. Bet in the flat with no eyes. He had to get home. Wires. Tube in his hand. Damn tube.

'Dad? He's saying not to pull at the tube. You've got an infection. They need to keep you hydrated. Dad? They're trying to help.'

Jack closed his eyes. Nothing a good sleep wouldn't sort out, he told himself.

When he opened his eyes again, Tommy was still there.

'Bet,' Jack said, feeling panic grip at his insides.

'Mum's fine.' Tommy lifted his hand to his jaw. Lying.

'Bet.' Jack tried again to sit up, but it made his head swim and the sweat start to trickle down his back.

'You need to rest.' Tommy's hand on his arm.

'She won't—She can't—'

'We're working on it,' Tommy said, hand to his jaw again, nodding as though trying to convince himself.

This body of his. Jack cursed it – useless skin and bones. If he could just stand up, just call a taxi and get himself home.

'Don't upset yourself, Dad. It's OK.' Tommy danced his fingertips against the top of his thumbs, as though he was playing an instrument, or trying to wipe something away.

'I nearly lost her,' Jack told him. 'Your mother. I nearly lost her.'

More than once. She must have loved the American, he supposed. Enough to think she'd fly halfway across the world for him. He had found her passport tucked inside a cookery book on the kitchen shelf. He'd stood with it in his hands for a long time before he opened it: Bet's face staring out at him, her eyes serious, her jaw set; a visa for America.

He'd nearly lost her then – and still couldn't say for sure how he hadn't – and then again, when that letter came about a flat in Islington. She'd come to him white as milk, telling him everything as though he didn't already know it. He'd told her to give it back – hadn't known what else to say. It doesn't matter, none of it matters – that's what he'd say now, if she was here. Jack closed his eyes. Tiny specks of blue and purple danced together on the backs of his eyelids. What was done was done.

'We'll sort something out, Dad. I'm looking at some options – care packages, meals on wheels. She won't want to do any of it, but we'll get there. You're not to worry.'

It was just a flat. A jumble of windows and doors, beds and coffee cups. He had got up early one morning, while Bet was still sleeping, and opened the envelope thick with papers she had hidden at the bottom of the desk drawer. The address was on the front of the deeds. Just a number, a street name and a postcode. Nothing momentous.

He coughed. 'I can't help thinking I've been a bad example to you.'

'What?'

'With women.'

So many divorces. So many false starts. Surely some of it had to be his fault.

'Dad, don't tire yourself.'

'I mustn't have been a good role model.'

Tommy rubbed at his jaw again. 'Dad, my marriages have nothing to do with you. Seriously, we've talked about this. I've made some bad decisions. But you and Mum—' He hesitated. 'Well, I guess you did something right, didn't you? Seventy years together and all that. And let's face it, if anyone set a bad example—' He stopped.

'Yes?'

'Nothing. It doesn't matter. What matters is you getting some rest.'

'I'm nothing without your mother,' Jack said. 'You have to understand that. Nothing.'

'Sleep.' Tommy stood up. 'Sleep, eat, get yourself better. I'll bring Mum to see you tomorrow. OK?' He touched Jack on the shoulder, a gentle squeeze. 'You get yourself some rest.'

BET

Bet just wanted Jack to come home. It had been over a week and she wasn't coping. She'd told Tommy that she was fine – insisted on it – but he was no more convinced than she was. The flat felt as though it had turned against her – furniture jabbed at her shins and elbows. Cups and plates slipped from her grasp and broke themselves into pieces on the floor. The boiler woke her in the night with its groaning. Taps wouldn't turn on, and then wouldn't turn off again. She couldn't find the things she needed.

Marinela was still coming every couple of days but Bet told Tommy he could organize the meals if he wanted to. If it distracted him from trying to get Marinela out of the flat, then it was no bad thing. She even agreed to him putting the keys in a safe outside the front door so the meal people could let themselves in. You're the one who thinks we'll be murdered in our beds living here, she'd said and shrugged.

There were always two of them, sometimes the same, sometimes different. Always cheery, talking in raised voices as though she was deaf. They were involved with some church it seemed. Bet had had a dalliance with the church when she and Jack moved onto the estate – spent a couple of years trying her best, but it never stuck. Coffee mornings and cake bakes and visiting the elderly – it didn't suit her. At least they weren't from one of those agencies Tommy kept talking about. A care package – that was what he wanted her to have, as though it would arrive in a bundle, wrapped in brown paper and string.

'Steak and kidney pie, a bit of mash, and carrots. Make you see in the dark they will.' The man, Brian she thought his name was, had one of those high-pitched, sing-song voices. 'And then a little pot of lemon syllabub for your pudding. Syllabub. Ha!' He laughed. 'What kind of a word is syllabub?'

Bet wondered if he said the same thing to every old lady he visited, or whether he changed his patter each time, just to keep himself entertained. There was a woman with him who didn't say much. Bet listened to her jangling her car keys as she moved around the room, snooping.

'Just get all this set out for you. And whisk these empties away. There you go, love.'

They put everything onto the trolley Jack used to bring in the tea, with the cutlery and a glass of water. They did not wait while she ate; they left the food and then went. That was the arrangement.

But before they left, the woman bent down towards Bet. 'Now, you've just got a teensy bit of mascara, just here.'

Before Bet could say anything the woman was rubbing her finger across the skin underneath Bet's left eye. Bet tried to move away but there was nowhere to go.

'And then. Oops! Just a bit of lipstick.' The woman put her finger above Bet's top lip and rubbed again. 'There you go.' She stood back up in a waft of perfume. 'Right as rain.'

'We're off and away, love,' Brian said. 'See you tomorrow!' He pulled out the word tomorrow into three bright notes.

Bet listened to them go – footsteps, shuffling coats, the door closing and the key turned, and then more footsteps outside onto the street. The woman said something as they passed the window but Bet couldn't make out the words. She touched her lips, then wiped a finger along the bottom of each eye.

She ate the lemon syllabub first. It had a faintly chemical taste, but she persevered. She used to make it, she realized, recognizing the dense creaminess of each spoonful; the way it popped against her tongue. It had been years since she'd even thought about it.

The flat would smell of pie all day – a heavy brown smell, Worcestershire sauce and dark meat and sweated onions. Bet scraped out the last of the syllabub, tipped her head back against her chair and closed her eyes for a moment. She was not in the least bit hungry. But she would have to eat it all up: the pie, and the potatoes, and the carrots. There would be two more people tomorrow and if she had not eaten it they would see. They would talk to her as though she was a child who did not know what was best for her. They would ask if she was unwell. They would call Tommy.

That was how things were. She was being observed. Looked after, Tommy called it. He telephoned her every morning. Eleven o'clock, pretty much on the dot. It was to make sure she had got out of bed. And it worked. There was a phone on the bedside table, so she could have answered it there and pretended she was up and dressed and washed, but she'd always thought that a person could tell if you answered the phone in bed.

She either visited Jack or telephoned him around two in the afternoon. The people came with her dinner at four thirty. And then Marinela came every other day or so, spent a few hours cleaning, baking, or just sitting with Bet, drinking tea and asking about Jack – how did they meet? What was their wedding like? She couldn't imagine the girl really wanted to know the answers but it was kind of her to try.

Bet found herself unable to settle. Unable to sleep properly.

Her mind would not keep itself still. She kept lifting her head to call to Jack and then realizing. Every time she sat down she wanted to stand up again. Which was such a palaver, such a matter of pain and effort that she stayed sitting, but her mind wandered and flitted and she fidgeted her fingers against the chair, her clothes, the cushions. If Jack was there he would have made her a cup of tea, and when he handed it to her he would have rested his palm against the back of her hand and it would have calmed her.

But Jack was not there. They had mended his hip and he had been happily getting himself back on his feet before the infection. It was just urinary, Tommy said. They were giving him antibiotics.

There were plenty of women who lived on their own. Young ones – they got flats and ran about being independent and carefree; and then there were the old ones like her – stuck in their chairs, half-blind, confused. The men tended to go first, that was the way of things, and so there they all were, an army of little old ladies.

Tommy was coming in the morning. There were things they needed to talk about before they went to see Jack, he'd said, and she'd rolled her eyes and sighed, and he'd told her to stop being a drama queen. My husband's in hospital, she'd snapped. He hadn't said anything for so long she thought he hadn't heard, or he'd hung up on her, but then she heard him take a breath and say, he's my dad too.

Tommy arrived before she was ready. She was still in her dressing gown when he knocked, her make-up not done. She'd been putting it off; she didn't want Tommy thinking she couldn't get the line of her lipstick straight when she'd never had any problems before.

'Mum.' He drew her into a hug right there on the doorstep, which was not what they did. He smelt of the outside – rain and soil and car fumes.

She pulled away. 'Don't let all the hot air out.'

He came inside and they moved clumsily around each other while he took off his coat, put down his bags.

'I did some shopping,' he said. 'Bread and cheese, milk, some tins with the pull openers – tuna, baked beans, soup.'

Bet said nothing.

'And then there's some other stuff – toilet rolls and soap, toothpaste, some dishcloths.'

Stocking up for a siege.

'Jack used to get that kind of thing,' she said. 'Milk. Soap.' Not that she used much of anything now it was just her. The milk kept going sour before she could get to the end of it.

'It's no trouble,' Tommy said. She could feel him looking at her. Assessing her. 'Do you want me to wash your hair?' he said, just like that.

Bet's hand went straight to her head. She couldn't say when she had washed it last. It wasn't easy, leaning over the sink with a cup, water and soap in your eyes and all over the floor too.

'I was dark, you know,' she said. 'A natural brunette.'

'It'll only take five minutes.'

It was unthinkable, but she could not seem to say so.

'Go on. It'll feel good. And then you'll look nice for Dad.'

She allowed herself to be manoeuvred into the bathroom. Tommy dragged in a chair from the kitchen and had her sit on it with her head bent over the bath. Water poured down her neck, into her ears, her eyes. She felt how carefully he rubbed her hair against her scalp, as though he might break her head if he pushed too hard. By the time he had finished, and had dried her hair gently with a towel, she found she was crying. She tried to pretend it was just the shampoo in her eyes making them sting. Tommy tugged a comb through her hair and then said he'd give her a moment, make them both a cup of tea.

Bet got herself to the bedroom, dried her hair and put on her blue wool suit, then just a touch of light brown eyeshadow, a little pearly peach lipstick. She walked through to the living room and said, before she could stop herself, 'How do I look?'

'Perfect, Mum, you look perfect,' Tommy said and the damn tears nearly spilt out and ruined everything again.

She sat herself down and took up her tea – nearly cold now, but no matter.

'How are the meals?' Tommy asked.

Bet thought of that woman, her wet finger pressing into the skin below Bet's eye. 'Fine,' she said.

'And the flat looks in order.' He spoke with an odd formality.

'Marinela—' Bet cut herself off but not quickly enough.

Tommy coughed, rubbed his hand over his mouth. 'I've let it slide, Mum, because of everything with Dad, but she needs to leave. You know that?'

Bet folded her arms across her chest.

'We can do it nicely, or—' He left the sentence hanging.

'Or not at all,' Bet said, and when Tommy didn't respond, she carried on. 'It's my business.' Still he said nothing. 'And you don't know where it is. You don't even know if it exists. I could have made the whole thing up.'

Tommy stood and started to pace back and forth in the small space between the armchairs and the fireplace. 'Why didn't you have any more children?' he said after a while.

'What?' Bet turned her face towards him. 'Why are you asking that?' She put her hand to her chest as though to protect herself, and then touched her hair. She could still feel the faint pressure of his fingertips on her scalp.

'Why not? Was I that bad? Or – I mean, am I even Dad's?'

Bet rested her head back on her chair and closed her eyes.

She thought about the bedroom in Islington with the tall window that had to be propped open with a book, or a saucepan; the long white curtains that moved in the breeze like dancers. The iron bed. The photo on the dressing table: Kit with his square jaw and broad shoulders, his arm around her waist, both of them laughing.

'Kit went back to America in 1952. You were born in 1954.'

Tommy said nothing for a long time. Then, 'I followed her.'

Bet kept her eyes closed.

'Marinela. I followed her.'

'You did what?' Bet said, slowly.

'From work.' He paused. 'Did you think she'd stop stripping if you let her live rent-free? Is that what all this is? Some kind of mission? You're trying to make amends?'

'For what?'

'For what you did to Dad.'

Bet took a breath. 'Did she see you?'

Tommy shook his head. 'No. And I thought I'd come and speak with you before I go and talk to her.'

'How thoughtful of you.'

Tommy sat back down next to Bet. 'Mum, I'm serious about this. You are going to need care. Whether that's in the next month or the next year, you cannot get away from it. And that flat—You sell that flat and you have choices.'

'And you can get the rest of the money when I've gone.'

For a moment, Tommy looked lost, and she remembered him as a little boy, tears springing to his eyes when a toy broke, or an ice cream fell from its cone, or another child turned their back on him or spoke unkindly.

'I tell you what,' Bet said. 'How about we do an exchange? A deal.'

'A deal?'

'You want me and your dad to go into one of those homes, yes?'

'I want you to be comfortable.'

'You want us in a home.'

Tommy lifted both hands, palms up. 'I think it could be a good solution.'

'So how's this – I come to look at homes with you. We choose somewhere and then if your dad needs it when he's better, we'll be ready.'

'And in exchange?'

Bet folded her hands in her lap. 'You leave that poor girl alone.'

Tommy gave a half smile. 'It doesn't work like that.'

'So, what? We fight? We spend Christmas on our own? We argue over Jack's hospital bed? Do you want that?'

Tommy blew out a long breath and Bet stopped herself from smiling.

'I knew you'd see reason,' she said.

'It's not going to go away, Mum.'

If only it would. If only she could wish hard enough so the damn place wouldn't exist any more. Sometimes she'd imagine a volcano erupting. There was that place in Italy – the whole town covered in lava and ash. She'd seen a volcano on the television one time. Bright red liquid leaping out of the ground faster than you could think possible. That's from under the crust, Jack had said, as though the earth was some kind of steak and kidney pie. But how was it so hot? she'd asked, and he'd said that was just how it was. The earth was filled with hot molten lava and sometimes it broke through. Not in Islington though, not in Islington.

MARINELA

It felt right having Stefan in the flat. Each time Marinela woke up next to him she felt a little fizz of happiness. There was something calming about speaking her own language, about touching a body she knew so well. He brought her breakfast in bed, on a tray he had bought especially – red flowers across white plastic; he pulled her into the cramped shower, his hands straying across her skin; they went on tourist excursions together – Buckingham Palace, Tower Bridge, The Globe. I have to work, she insisted and he held up both hands and said, of course, Sparrow, of course. I don't want to get in your way.

So she wrote her assignments and went to clean for Bet and visited Jack in hospital and did her usual shifts at the club, shoving her outfits into her rucksack when Stefan was in the bathroom. Stefan shopped for food and 'pretty things' – tiny glasses with gilt edges; a clock in the shape of Big Ben that ticked so loudly she made him take the batteries out; a red and blue rug which he placed in front of the electric fire; a big wooden bowl enamelled yellow on the inside.

She took his photograph. Again and again. In bed. In the kitchen wearing his boxer shorts and socks. By the flat door. On the street. On the Tube. On the bus. She couldn't seem to stop. He was flattered at first. But after a while he started to shake his head, move his hand towards the camera to block the lens. What are you trying to do? he asked, but she couldn't say. You think there is something I don't tell you? Is this it? Stefan demanded, and maybe he was right, maybe she was trying to see something.

He had left Anca, he told her. Something in the way he said it made her wonder if he was lying. But what did it matter, really? Like he said, he was there with Marinela, not in Bucharest with his wife, and didn't that say everything that needed to be said?

She cancelled her Christmas plans with Harry. *Harry, I am sorry but I cannot come. I have friend here from home. M.* He'd written straight back. *Gutted! Maybe you can come for New Year? How long is your friend staying?* She hadn't yet replied.

But maybe she had been too quick to assume everything was going to carry on as smoothly as it had started. Less than a week after he arrived, Stefan grabbed her arm as she went to leave for the club.

'Where are you going?'

'Work.'

'Where is work?'

Marinela held her rucksack against her chest and glared at him.

'A bar?' Stefan said.

'That's right. The same place I went last night.'

Stefan shook his head.

'You said you wouldn't get in my way.' Marinela stepped forward and Stefan matched her. They were close now, close enough for her to see the flecks of stubble on his cheeks and upper lip, close enough to smell the musk of his aftershave.

Marinela drew herself taller. 'I am going to work.'

'Why are you lying to me?'

Marinela narrowed her eyes but said nothing.

'I found these.' He took his hand from behind his back, her red hot pants and strapless leather bra clenched in his fist.

Marinela swallowed. 'And?'

'You are stripper, right?' He stepped closer, brandishing the clothes at her. 'Not you,' he whispered, shaking his head. 'Not my Sparrow.'

She felt the anger rip up from her stomach to her throat. 'Don't you dare,' she hissed, reaching for the bra and pants. She got hold of a corner of red leather and pulled, but Stefan did not let go. 'Don't you dare come here telling me how to live my life.'

'Like a prostitute,' Stefan spat.

'No, not like a prostitute.'

'You let those men look at you.'

'I get paid.'

Stefan loosened his grip and the clothes fell to the ground. Marinela scooped them up and shoved them into her rucksack.

'Are you so naive, Stefan? You think these things don't happen to nice girls?'

'I will give you money. You want money?' He took his wallet from his jeans pocket, started pulling notes from it and throwing them towards her.

'I'm going to be late.'

'How much do you want?' He threw another note and Marinela watched it drift to the floor.

'Let me past.'

'You can't.' He was shaking his head now, his voice cracking with tears. 'Not my Sparrow.'

'Your Sparrow can look after herself.' Marinela stepped to one side and pushed past him towards the door. He did not stop her.

Her anger carried her all the way down the stairs, onto the street, to the bus stop; she sat with it on the top deck, a writhing thing lodged somewhere near her heart. It stayed with her the whole night – crawling on her hands and knees across the rough stage; smiling and laughing with the men at their tables; drinking vodka with Jess in the dressing room. It made her bolder, wilder. If someone had asked her to suck them off in the VIP room she might just have done it.

By the time she got back to the flat, the anger was still there, but she was tired, her ears ringing from the music, her muscles aching, her eyes dry. If she was lucky, Stefan would be asleep. She could make a cup of tea, sit on the sofa for a while and watch something on her laptop.

But he was awake. And drunk. Sitting at the table by the window, the dictionary he had given her open at the page she had ripped out, and a more than half-empty bottle of *țuică* in front of him.

'I brought this for you,' he slurred, lifting the bottle and waving it in her direction. 'For Christmas. I thought we would drink it on Christmas Day.'

Marinela poured a glass of water and drank it standing at the sink.

He fingered the ripped edge of the missing page. 'I've been sitting here all night, thinking about you in that place.'

Marinela walked into the bathroom and locked the door. She turned the shower on, peeled off her clothes and stepped underneath the water.

'Mari?' The door handle turned, once, twice, three times. 'Mari?' Stefan was banging on the door now.

Marinela squeezed shampoo into her palm and rubbed it onto her scalp, feeling it lather between her fingers.

When she finally came out of the bathroom, wrapped in her dressing gown, Stefan was slumped at the table again, two full shot glasses in front of him.

'Will you have a drink with me?' he asked, lifting his head towards her.

Marinela hesitated, then crossed the kitchen and sat on the

chair opposite Stefan. He pushed one of the glasses towards her and she took it, sipped. It reminded her of her father, of the tiny flat in Galaţi – the heavy black sofas, the sideboard crowded with crockery, the purple curtains embroidered with gold stars.

'A boy came to see you,' Stefan said.

'A boy?'

'Dark hair. Skinny. Glasses. He pretended he was just passing, just called in to say hi.'

Harry. Marinela took another mouthful of brandy.

'You two are—?'

'No.' Marinela shook her head and looked towards the window. A plane blinked its wing lights against the dark sky.

'But he likes you?'

Marinela shrugged. 'I have to go to bed, Stefan.'

'I am sorry,' Stefan said. He leaned towards her, his eyes bloodshot. 'I am sorry, Mari. I was upset. You are right. It is your home, your life. I cannot—' He made a helpless gesture with one hand.

Marinela finished her drink and pushed the glass towards Stefan, who filled it to the brim.

'I saw you,' she said. 'On the lake. With some girl, laughing.'

Stefan stared at his own glass, wouldn't look at her.

'Who was she?'

Stefan shook his head. 'I don't understand.'

'I saw you. I was in the park, I don't even remember why now, and there you were on the lake, in one of those little boats. We never did that, you never took me there.'

'I don't remember.' He rubbed his palm over his cheek, still didn't meet her eye. 'It would have been nothing. Maybe a friend. I have a niece.'

'Don't lie.'

'I am not.' He looked up then and Marinela felt her heart give a little. 'I know it was hard for you,' he said. 'With Anca,

176

and the kids.' He stopped then and she saw the bob of his Adam's apple as he swallowed.

'What happened?' Marinela said softly. 'Really?'

He swallowed again, traced a pattern on the table with his forefinger. 'The usual,' he said after a long silence. 'I came home one day and they had gone. Clothes. Toys. Books. Everything. Not even a note, just gone. The flat empty.' He shook his head. 'I cannot be in the flat. It makes me want to die.'

'Don't say that.'

'I went onto the roof. You remember the roof?'

They had climbed up there, out of the kitchen window onto the gravel-topped expanse – looked out across the city.

'I was going to jump. Not even jump – I thought, I can just step off into nothing and then it will all be finished.'

Marinela closed her eyes. Imagined the weight of a body falling through the air.

'And then I thought of you, Sparrow. I thought I couldn't die without seeing you again.' He was on his feet now, stumbling towards her, reaching a hand to cup her face. 'I am sorry,' he said. 'I'm only trying to do things right.' He got onto his knees, lifted his face to her and she leant forwards and kissed him, gently on the lips.

'Come,' she said, standing and taking his hand. She led him into the bedroom, unbuttoned his shirt, his jeans, pulled off his socks and boxer shorts. He was quiet and pliant, and every time she looked up she saw him gazing at her as though she was something worth worshipping. She folded back the duvet and he lay down, still looking at her.

'Stefan,' she whispered, lying on her side next to him and stroking his hair, his chest, his arms, moving down towards his stomach, his cock. 'Stefan.' She manoeuvred herself on top of him, felt the warmth of him along the length of her. There was no harm in it, she told herself.

JACK

The infection subsided. Jack could feel it going, leaving him washed out like an old rag; but cooler, calmer. The hallucinations faded. He was back on a busy geriatrics ward – strip lights and pleated blue curtains, lowered voices and the squeak of rubber soles.

He needed to get out. Needed to get back on his feet. Needed to get home to Bet. But his legs had rusted up and the whole of him ached as though he'd been battered, kicked about. He could just about sit up to eat his lunch, kept in place with piles of pillows.

Tommy arrived after they'd cleared away the plate of overcooked macaroni cheese and pot of yoghurt. He didn't look well. White around the gills. Chewing at his bottom lip the way he did when he was fretting about something.

'Is everything all right?' Jack asked.

Tommy looked startled.

'With the new woman?' Jack tried.

Tommy blinked, shook his head. 'It's fine.' He paused. 'Well, it's finished, but it was mutual. No hard feelings.'

'I'm sorry.' Jack felt on shaky ground – they didn't have conversations like this. Tommy's eyes were a little bloodshot, as though he'd been drinking, or not sleeping enough. 'You look tired.'

Tommy shrugged. 'It's just – you know.'

'Bet?'

'What did she do before I was born?'

'Do?'

'Did she have a job?'

Nightclub hostess. He couldn't say it out loud. Jack had never wanted her to take the job. He'd thought she'd get bored, work whatever it was out of her system. Maybe he'd been a fool. Maybe if he'd said no, he wouldn't allow it – that would have stopped everything going the way it did. But they'd talked about it and she'd been so reasonable. They wanted to save up for a new place and being a hostess paid a lot more than working at Lyon's or the Co-op. She was doing it for them. And then she'd come home with her stories and they'd laugh about the pompous men and the vain, needy women, and he'd tell himself it was all for the best.

'It's not worth going over all that.' Jack concentrated on the ceiling above him. It had moved, he seemed to remember, in his dream. It had been like lying on the bottom of the sea.

Tommy stood and pulled the curtain around the bed, yanking hard at the stubborn plastic rings. He lowered his voice, 'Dad, what did you do when she told you about the affair?'

Jack looked at Tommy. He wanted to say, things come and things go and everything changes. He wanted to say, you've cheated on your wife – your wives – so don't judge. He wanted to say, once you decide to let something go there is such freedom, such lightness. What he said though, was, 'I'm tired.'

'You think you know people, don't you?' Tommy said. 'But actually you never do.'

Jack closed his eyes for a long moment, then opened them and looked at his son. Sixty years old. His hair dyed black but

179

thinning against his scalp. Puffed skin below his eyes. This is what it amounted to, he thought, imperfect people doing their messy, incompetent best.

'You can make too much fuss about the past. It gets you nowhere,' Jack said.

'Did you know? I mean when it was going on?'

Jack moved his head side to side as though trying to shake off the words. 'Things stop being so important after a while – you understand.'

'Dad?'

'It's not important, Tommy, trust me. We're still together, aren't we? Seventy years together – that's what matters. And we always loved you.'

'But you never had any other children.'

Jack shrugged. He had wanted more. He'd have had three, four, five, but Bet had never seemed that keen, and it hadn't happened in any case. 'What's important is that we had you, we loved you, we loved each other.' He waved his hand to one side. 'None of the rest of it matters.'

'She's going to come and look at some homes with me,' Tommy said.

Jack raised his eyebrows.

'She said she'd think about it.'

'Really?'

Jack thought about Bet, feeling her way around the kitchen, twisting her head so she could make out what was where; sitting in the living room with the TV on; lying in bed on her own, her arm stretched out into the space where he should be. Maybe it would be for the best – moving into some place with emergency buttons and wardens, decent heating, handrails.

'I'm coming home, Tommy,' Jack said after a while.

'I know, Dad.'

They sat, saying nothing, until a nurse called out from behind the curtain and came in to check Jack's blood pressure.

'I'll be going,' Tommy said.

'This will only take a sec,' the nurse said, wrapping the sleeve around Jack's upper arm.

'I need to anyway.' Tommy got to his feet, patted at Jack's shoulder and stood for a moment as though trying to find something to say. 'I'll be back in a couple of days, Dad. Okay?'

Jack nodded. 'I'm sorry about your girlfriend.'

Tommy gave a half laugh. 'Plenty more fish in the sea, right? You said that to me once.'

'I did?'

'We'll have you out of here in no time, won't we, Mr Chalmers?' the nurse said, pressing a button which made the sleeve contract, squeezing Jack's arm until it almost hurt.

'That's right,' Jack said, smiling at her. 'That's right.'

BET

She knew something was wrong as soon as the nurse took her arm at the ward entrance and said, in a gentle voice, 'I'll walk you there, shall I, Mrs Chalmers?'

'He's taken a bit of a turn for the worse,' the nurse half-whispered as they moved along the corridor. 'Something on his chest.'

It would kill him. She knew that even before they arrived at Jack's bedside and she heard his fast, shallow breathing and touched the chilled clammy skin of his forearm.

'There are carol singers coming after lunch,' the nurse said. 'They're supposed to be good.'

Neither Bet nor Jack replied. Bet had always liked carols – their familiar sweetness. Jack wasn't a fan.

'I suppose you can't get away,' Bet said, once the nurse had left. 'Captive audience, that's what they call you.'

'Bet?' His hand reaching for her. She could tell by his voice that he knew things had got bad. 'Bet.' He curled his fingers in between hers. 'Love.'

All she could feel was a terrible kind of nothing. It wasn't even panic. Or sadness. It was darker and wilder and bleaker than that.

'Pneumonia, Bet.'

'Are they giving you something?'

'Of course they are.'

His breath was too thin and too fast. Bet felt her own start to hurry, as though to catch up.

'How are you?' Jack said, in a whisper.

'Me?' Bet thought about Tommy washing her hair; the woman leaning in to wipe mascara from her face; the feeling she had when she woke, too early in the mornings, as though her veins had been filled up with concrete.

'You,' Jack said.

Bet opened her mouth to speak, but found tears there instead, overtaking her words.

'Stupid old woman,' she muttered, fishing a tissue out of her handbag. 'Stupid.'

'I just need to get back on my feet.'

He was worn out; she could hear it, feel it. She patted at his hand. The place smelt of cleaning fluid and a deeper, dustier smell of skin and drugs and dying.

'Do you remember the estate, Bet?'

'Course I do.'

'We were happy there, weren't we?'

They were. At the beginning at least. Everything new and clean and modern. Tommy grown up and moved out. That year she did something she'd heard about on the radio – placed each of her mistakes into an imaginary box, turned the key, and put them up on a high, imaginary shelf.

'You carried me over the threshold,' Bet said.

Jack laughed and then started coughing. 'Nearly did my back in,' he managed to say at last. 'But those views, Bet. That light.'

King and Queen of London. Nothing between them and the sky.

'This might be the end, love,' Jack said.

Bet squeezed her eyes shut. Fucking hospitals, she said, inside her head, fucking fucking hospitals. She felt the word ricocheting around her mind, hard-edged, out of control.

'It's just your hip,' she said, but she couldn't get the words to sound convincing. 'And those pills cleared up the other infection, didn't they?'

Jack said nothing.

She took his hand again and squeezed. 'We'll be all right, love,' she said. 'You and me.'

'Do you remember the bathroom?' Jack said. 'Hot water. You filled the bath so high it nearly came over the edge.'

They'd clapped their hands into the bubbles so they shot up in the air. God, they'd laughed.

'We did all right, didn't we?' Jack said.

Bet swallowed.

'I know I didn't always—' He coughed and coughed and then sank back into his shallow breathing. 'I tried my best. And I know—'

'Shush.'

He was staring at her now and she was blushing, she could feel it. She leant as close to Jack as her body would let her. Maybe she could catch pneumonia too – they could go together.

'I wasn't a good wife,' she said.

She heard him reaching for her hand, searching across the stretch of bed between him and her. She wouldn't take it.

'You were the best,' he said.

She sat back in the chair. 'I was selfish.'

'You were unhappy.'

Bet shook her head. She had not been unhappy, up in that flat with Kit, her skin on fire, her heart on fire. She had not been unhappy in the club, with the music snaking through her and the drink softening her insides.

'It's all gone,' Jack said. 'All past.'

'You're ninety in March,' Bet said. 'That's no time.'

'I won't make it.'

'Don't talk like that.'

'I'm being honest, Bet.'

But they had never been honest. Not really. Not in the ways that mattered. Bet brushed the tears from her cheeks. She could hear someone further down the ward humming 'Jingle Bells'.

'I'm worried about Tommy,' Jack said.

'Don't be.' Bet stroked her forefinger over his knuckles. 'He's fine. Just a bit angry.'

'With you?'

'I never got it right with him, did I?'

'You did great.'

'They don't teach you, do they? They just expect you to know what to do.'

'Bet, don't.'

'It's true.'

'No. It isn't.' He reached for her hand again and this time she took it. 'I love you, Betty Harris,' he said.

Oh, her heart did some kind of jump. Betty Harris. Nineteen years old. Pretty as a picture in her blue dress and silver sandals, the band playing, the beer flowing. You're beautiful – Jack had said, leaning so close she could feel his breath hot on her cheek. You are the most beautiful girl I've ever seen.

'I didn't give it back,' Bet said, before she could stop herself. 'The flat. I didn't give it back.'

Jack said nothing. She could hear him running his tongue around his gums.

'I tried. I wrote to them. I kept writing to them but they never answered and I couldn't work out what to do about it.' The words came out fast and jumbled.

Jack shifted in the bed, pulling his hand away from hers.

'Do you hate me?'

He puffed out air, almost a laugh, and she felt a flush of relief.

'I couldn't hate you if I tried.'

'I've made a mess of it, haven't I?'

Jack said nothing for such a long time Bet thought he'd fallen asleep, or died. He was going to die. She wanted to crawl into the bed with him, but it was too narrow and she was too old for such acrobatics. It would have soothed her though, to lie her head next to his, to lay her palm over his chest and feel the thud of his heart, still beating, beneath his ribs.

'Maybe I shouldn't have got involved,' he said at last, his voice faint. 'It's yours, Bet, after all.'

A tall woman with a heavy Nigerian accent stopped at the end of Jack's bed with the drinks trolley. 'You want?' she said. They asked for tea, which came lukewarm and milky in plastic cups, shoved into flimsy plastic holders. Jack left his on the narrow table that reached across his bed. Bet drank hers in tiny sips, hardly pausing for breath.

'I said Marinela could live there,' she said, when she'd finished. 'It just seemed. I don't know. Suddenly it seemed a waste.'

Again, Jack said nothing for a long time. Then, 'She's a nice girl.'

The ward door opened and a blast of music swept in – 'The Holly and the Ivy'.

'You said she reminded you of me?'

Jack nodded. 'Is she happy there?'

'I think so.'

Bet sat in the chair next to his bed, listening to him breathe. He was going to die and there was not a single thing to be done about it.

She didn't know how to say goodbye to him. Just that?

Goodbye, Jack. Was that what people said? Now her own heart was beating fit to burst.

'I'm sorry, Jack,' she said.

A slight pressure on her hand. Had they ever talked about dying? They must have done, over the years – what it would be like to get to the end and then pass over. For all the talk of heaven and the other side and the life after, nobody knew; perhaps there was nothing at all. She didn't know what Jack thought about all that any more. They hadn't been to church for years. She had no idea if he still believed in anything.

'I'm sorry, Jack,' she said again. 'I'm sorry.'

MARINELA

'You are friends with an old woman?' Stefan said, a sneer in his voice. He was sitting at the table, watching Marinela make *prajitura cu visine* for Bet.

'How old?' he asked.

Marinela broke an egg against the side of the bowl and let it drop from its shell. 'Ninety.'

Stefan made a disgusted noise. 'I do not like old people.'

Marinela tapped the next egg too hard and the shell collapsed into the mixture. She took a spoon and scooped it back out.

'People should live to what, seventy-five, and then just get a pill, or an injection or something. Do everybody a favour.'

'You don't mean that.' Marinela stirred the mixture, the egg turning the flour into slick clumps.

'I do.'

Marinela stared into the bowl.

'No one dares talk about it, but they are leaching the world of resources. Getting older and sicker so there's no room in the hospitals. Going into these expensive homes to rot. It's our pensions paying for it, Mari.'

'They are people,' Marinela said softly. 'Same as you and me.'

'They're not useful any more.'

'Are you useful?' She looked up then, raised her voice.

Stefan laughed, smoothed his hair back from his forehead. 'I work.'

'Now?'

'I'm on extended leave. I work. I pay tax. I don't lie around in hospital.'

'Jack broke his hip.'

'Precisely.'

Marinela lifted the bowl and tipped the contents into a cake tin, laid the flour-covered cherries neatly over the surface and bent to open the oven door.

'You shouldn't waste your time with such people,' Stefan said. 'They'll get you down.'

Marinela slammed the oven door closed. 'Shut up,' she said quietly.

'You need to be friends with people your own age,' Stefan went on as though he hadn't heard her.

'I said, shut up.'

Stefan hesitated. Then he stood and came to her, his hands on her waist, in her hair. 'Mari. You are too good. Too kind.'

She pulled away. 'Bet had an affair. A long time ago.'

Stefan raised an eyebrow.

'She nearly left Jack, but then she realized what she had with him was better than what she would have if she left.' Bet had never said as much, but Marinela was sure that was how it had gone.

'Or she was scared,' Stefan said, leaning back against the kitchen counter.

'Why do you think the worst of people?'

He held up both palms. 'Not of you, Sparrow.'

'She realized that what she already had was the thing she needed. And now they have been together for seventy years.'

She turned the taps on, squirted washing-up liquid into the sink. 'Are you getting a divorce?'

Stefan blinked, laughed.

'Are you getting a divorce?'

He opened the cupboard and took out a glass. 'I suppose,' he said.

She took the glass, filled it with water and handed it back. 'You suppose?'

'These things take time, Sparrow. Time and money. So many forms to fill in.'

'And then what?' Marinela asked, turning off the taps and putting the cake bowl and spoon into the hot water. 'You want to stay in England?'

'I want to take you home,' Stefan said. 'That's what I want.'

Except she couldn't say where home was right now. Galați. Bucharest. Islington. She opened her mouth to say as much, but Stefan was talking again.

'I am going shopping today,' he said. 'Some last-minute Christmas presents. And then I will take you for a nice dinner. Eight o'clock?'

Marinela didn't answer.

'We will dress up. Eat good food. Talk about all these things – divorce, Romania.'

'I'm working.'

She saw the dart of tension in his face.

'It's good money, this time of year,' she went on, not knowing why she was pushing it, but wanting some kind of reaction from him. 'Everyone wants a special treat. Everyone's throwing their money around.'

Stefan held up a hand.

'Extra tips. More dances.'

'So I will buy special things for breakfast, tomorrow. I will cook.' He kissed her, lightly, on the cheek, then turned and left the flat.

Marinela stayed where she was, the cake starting to fill the kitchen with its rich, sugary scent. She tried to think what Bet would say – all that about old people? Oh, he was just winding you up. Men, Marinela, are a law unto themselves. Jack, though, Jack wouldn't like Stefan, he'd think he was too full of himself; too quick to judge; that he didn't listen. And Harry? Harry wouldn't like him either.

When she got back from the club, Stefan was asleep, and the next morning she woke late to an empty bed. For a moment she thought he had left and she couldn't rightly tell how she felt about it. But then she heard his voice from the other room, low and intense, the words not quite discernible. She stood, quietly, walked to the door and eased it open.

'Of course I love you,' she heard him say. 'How could you think such a thing? It is just taking a little longer than I thought.' A pause, then he laughed. 'You are such a worrier, my chicken. Do not worry.'

Marinela leant her head against the door frame. She was an idiot. She was an absolute idiot.

'No, I'm having a terrible time,' Stefan said, and laughed again. 'How could I be having a nice time with you not here? Now will you tell those monkeys I miss them?'

Anca. He was just taking a break? A little holiday in England? Marinela stepped out of the bedroom and walked into the kitchen. Stefan stood by the window, looking out at the streets. She folded her arms and waited.

It took a moment. But then he turned, coloured, almost dropped his phone.

'I have to go, I'm sorry, I'll call you later.' He fumbled to hang up. 'Mari.'

'I am Sparrow, she is Chicken?' Marinela said. 'And the girl on the lake, she is what? Dove? Goldfinch? Hummingbird?'

'Mari, I can explain. I was just calling to talk to the children.'

'Of course I love you,' Marinela mimicked.

'You know what she's like. I've told you what she's like.'

'Get out.'

Stefan shook his head and walked towards her. She was wearing pyjama shorts and a T-shirt, no bra. She folded her arms across her chest, wished she'd thought to put a jumper on.

'It is nothing. A misunderstanding.'

'I should never have let you stay.'

'Sparrow.'

'Do not call me that. Never call me that again.'

He was close now, his eyes already filling with tears, his hands reaching for her.

'I'll go out for an hour,' she said. 'Give you time to pack your things. I want you gone by the time I get back.'

'I bought croissants,' he said, waving towards the kitchen counter. 'Blueberries. Mango. Let's have breakfast and talk about it, Mari.'

Marinela backed towards the bedroom, slipped inside and slammed the door hard. She stood for a moment, feeling her heart thump, adrenaline fizzing through her body, then pulled on jeans, a jumper, grabbed her handbag and stepped back into the hallway. Stefan was still standing there.

'I can explain,' he said.

'Give me your keys.' Marinela held out her hand.

Stefan's eyes strayed to the kitchen counter, and she stepped past him to pick up his keys before he could stop her. She dropped them into her bag.

'I will go for one hour. Close the door behind you.'

'Mari.'

'Goodbye.'

He was a liar. She had known he was a liar and yet she had let herself believe him. She'd messed things up with Harry because of him. Marinela thought about Bet deciding to end things with Kit – she'd been ready to go, a plane ticket, a visa, a bag packed, and then she'd not gone. Sometimes, she told Marinela, she'd try to imagine what would have happened if she'd made a different decision, but there was no point to it really. It turned out that there were no bad decisions, she said, just the decisions you made and the things that came afterwards.

Marinela walked to the flat door, stepped outside and closed it without looking back. She walked quickly down the stairs, listening for Stefan behind her, waiting for him to call out. But she reached the front door without hearing a thing and so she stepped into the cool morning and lifted her face to a sky showing patches of blue in between the clouds.

BET

'I want you to have an open mind, Mum, or there's no point.'

Bet folded her arms and stared at the passing streets. Nearly every house seemed to have a Christmas tree in the window. 'We should be at the hospital, shouldn't we?'

'He's doing fine.'

'He isn't, Tommy. Pneumonia. People die from pneumonia.'

'People die from crossing the road. We'll pop in on the way back.' Tommy pulled off the road into a car park and cut the engine. Bet swallowed. This was her own doing, she reminded herself. All she had to do was walk around, nod, smile; she hadn't promised anything more than that.

Tommy helped her from the car, kept a hold of her hand and led her towards a large brown building. Bet moved her head left to right. Ugly, she decided. 1980s architecture. Low roof. Narrow windows. Red railings up a wheelchair ramp to the front door.

The smell hit as soon as she stepped inside. Disinfectant and cooked vegetables, and something else she couldn't put her finger on.

'It smells,' she whispered to Tommy.

'It doesn't.'

He wanted her and Jack to live in a place like this. He

wanted to visit once a week, sit in the armchair next to theirs and drink a cup of tea someone else had made.

Tommy was talking to someone now. Bet turned, just as a woman with a soft Irish accent stepped forward and took her hand.

'Mrs Chalmers, it's lovely to meet you. Welcome to The Willows.'

Bet turned to Tommy. 'That's not the right name.'

Tommy let out a puff of irritation, glanced at the woman. 'We're seeing a couple of different places,' he said, as though he had something to apologize for. 'Mum, this is one of the places I told you about.'

'We've twenty rooms, so we're nice and small, intimate. Everyone gets to know everyone else,' the woman said. 'I'll take you around now and then you can have a cup of tea in the lounge. Are you all right on your feet, Mrs Chalmers?'

Bet waved her stick. 'I'll not win any races.'

The woman laughed more than she needed to. 'We'll take it at your pace. And any questions, just shout.'

They walked along a wide carpeted corridor, handrails either side, silver-framed pictures of flowers on the walls, tinsel looped from one side of the ceiling to the other, a couple of oldies creeping in the opposite direction, hanging on to Zimmer frames.

'My mother's eyesight's not too good,' Tommy said to the woman. Her eyesight was no one else's business. 'Macular degeneration,' Tommy went on and the woman sighed in sympathy.

'It's pretty common,' she said.

'I do fine,' Bet snapped.

'It's impressive, living independently at your age, with your condition.'

Maybe she could get Tommy to take her and Jack somewhere high – a hilltop or a tall building – and they could hold hands and step off the edge and that would be it. Over.

'Are you OK, Mrs Chalmers? You want to take a seat for a moment?' The Irish woman was at her side. Fussing.

Bet shook her head. 'I'm fine.'

'We'll just show you the games room, then one of our bedrooms. We've got a couple empty right now so you're in luck. Most times there's a waiting list.'

Bet followed obediently. Stood in doorways and listened to the woman describe what was inside. A single bed. A wardrobe. An en-suite bathroom. Residents could bring their own furniture if they chose to. There was yoga every Tuesday and Friday – very gentle, great for the circulation. Some of the residents enjoyed chess, backgammon, Connect Four. There was a gardening club, a music-appreciation group – something for everyone.

'Are there double rooms?' Bet asked.

'Sorry?' said the woman.

'My husband,' Bet said.

'Oh. Well. We don't cater for couples, I'm afraid.'

Bet looked at Tommy and raised her eyebrows.

'There isn't a room we could squeeze a double bed into?' Tommy asked.

'Company policy.' The woman shook her head. 'I'm sorry, I thought I'd explained on the phone.'

'Well, we're done then,' Bet said.

'I'll just finish showing you round, why don't I?'

'Thank you,' said Tommy, before Bet could speak.

She followed them back towards the entrance, then left into a large room. Tables and chairs on one side; armchairs on the other. A tall thin Christmas tree laden with cheap baubles. He wasn't dead. Jack wasn't dead.

'This is our lounge,' the woman said. 'Where everything happens.'

Entertainment. Exercise classes. Film nights. Knitting circles.

'How long do people last?' Bet asked.

'I'm sorry?'

'Six months? A year?'

'Mum,' Tommy snapped.

'I'm just asking.'

The woman laughed, nervous. 'We have people who've been here four or five years, Mrs Chalmers. We make sure everyone has the best care. Why don't you take a seat? I'll see if I can find someone to make us a cup of tea. We might even be able to dig out a mince pie or two.'

Bet lowered herself into an armchair. To her right, two old women sat, their heads dropped forward onto their chests, fast asleep.

'Seems nice,' Tommy said.

Bet straightened her skirt across her knees. 'How does that Internet dating work?' she asked.

'What?'

'Where you look for someone on the computer.'

Tommy said nothing for a while, then, 'You make a profile. You look at other people's profiles. If you like the look of them you send them a message. If they like the look of you they send a message back.'

'And it works?'

'Sometimes.'

'Tommy, I'm not living here.'

Tommy drummed his fingers against the arm of his chair. 'It does smell, you're right,' he said.

Bet laughed. A small laugh, but it took hold. She pressed her fingers against her mouth but she couldn't stop it.

'Mum. Don't.' But Tommy was laughing too, she could

hear it bursting from his mouth, and now her shoulders were heaving and there were tears in her eyes.

'You'll wake them up.' She gestured at the sleeping women.

'Stop it.' Tommy slapped his hand onto his knee. 'Stop it.'

They laughed until they couldn't laugh any more, Bet's ribs and stomach aching with it.

'I never meant to hurt your dad.'

She felt Tommy's hand on her arm. 'I know.'

'He'd like this,' Bet said.

'But it smells.'

'Not here. Us. Laughing.'

'Yeah.'

They sat in silence for a while. The Irish woman strode back, said she had to go and take a phone call. Someone called Nadia would be bringing them tea any moment.

'We'll try the other place,' Tommy said. 'It's not far. Let's just look and then we'll go and see Dad.'

Bet shrugged. 'I won't like it.'

'You might.'

The next place was called Springfields. Bet remembered the brochure, the pages so glossy they felt varnished. She'd made Jack throw it away. There was a building with thirty bedrooms, a dining room and lounge. It smelt of air freshener – lavender, she thought. There were self-contained flats too, a distance from the main building, suitable for couples. And large, neatly mown lawns. Trees. Shrubs. Flowerbeds. Benches.

'What do you think?' Tommy asked, in the car on the way back.

Bet shrugged.

'You could take one of the flats.'

It had been so quiet there. The occasional plane overhead. A bird singing.

'I've lived in Elephant and Castle since 1944,' she said.

'Time for a change, then?'

'I don't know, Tommy.'

'I thought it was nice. That last place. Nice gardens.'

She hadn't had a garden since she was twenty years old.

'It's more expensive, but—'

Bet traced the edges of the car seat with her fingertips. 'You think he'll die, don't you?'

Tommy sniffed.

'That's why you took me to that first one. With the single beds. You think he's going to die and then it'll just be me.' She could hear her voice rising as she spoke, a wave of panic washing underneath her skin.

'Let's just wait and see, Mum. You said you'd come and have a look and you have and I think that's a great first step. We don't need to rush into anything.'

'And you're going to keep your side of the bargain?' She turned to look at Tommy, who kept his eyes fixed on the road.

'Tommy?'

'Sure. But we'll have to deal with it sooner or later.'

Jack would get out of hospital and maybe they would move – a little flat with white walls and double-glazing, dinner over in the main house if they couldn't be bothered cooking. There was a bus, the woman who showed them round had said, so maybe Marinela would visit now and again. Maybe they'd be happy there – her and Jack.

JACK

Night-time. Christmas Eve. A light rain on the windows. In the hospital foyer, empty cardboard boxes wrapped in gold paper lay beneath a fat plastic tree. Silver decorations swayed and shimmered on the corridor ceilings. The ward lights were on but dimmed, the patients lumped under sheets and blankets. It reminded Jack of the war – a tent filled with rows of beds, the hustle and hurry of new arrivals and the long, groaning nights.

Not enough oxygen. Not enough air. The nurses had fixed a mask to his face with a strap of yellow elastic and he could hear the pump and sigh of the machine on the floor beside his bed. The problem was his hip, he kept telling himself. He just needed to get back on his feet. But when he tried to sit up, the whole room dipped and swam and he could feel the sweat spring to the surface of his skin, dribbling in icy lines underneath his pyjamas. His bones ached and his chest hurt, a sharp, tight pain like someone was trying to press the life out of him.

He wasn't a fool. He knew a bad situation when he was in one. And yet, he had always thought there must be a reason he hadn't died out in the jungle all those years ago, the way Frank had. There was something he was meant to do, and lying in that bed, listening to the wheeze of the oxygen pump and staring at the white ceiling tiles edged with grubby-looking plastic strips, he was certain that he had not done it.

Too late. Sometimes it was too late.

He reached his right hand across the sheet to take Bet's. But she had gone. Of course. Middle of the night. She'd be in bed, in a nightie, her skin soft with cold cream, an extra blanket maybe to make up for his absence. She talked sometimes, in her sleep – nothing he could ever make any sense of, but often urgent sounding, as if she didn't have enough time, or couldn't find the right words, to say what she needed to.

Had he ever said, in so many words, that he had forgiven her? Years ago. Too many years ago to count. Had he ever actually said it? I forgive you; none of it matters.

Too late. Sometimes it was too late.

For a moment, he let the heavy sadness sweep through him. End of the road, old man, he said to himself. End of the road.

There was no one there to bear witness. They had been and gone: Bet. Tommy. They had sat by his bed and spoken in stilted sentences about nothing very much. There was the flat – the one he'd thought she'd given back – but he couldn't find it in himself to get worked up about it. It was just bricks and mortar, nothing more.

There was no great drama. No cries. No flailing limbs; just his left arm bending up at the elbow, his hand clenching as if to catch hold of something. A quiet shutting down.

The oxygen pump kept up its steady wheeze. The drip continued to release its liquid. Someone would notice soon enough – a nurse walking soft-footed through the ward, checking each bed as she passed.

A mile or so away, his wife slept, fitfully, two extra blankets piled onto the bed. His son sat in his crowded bedroom in a rented one-bed flat in Guildford, the light from his computer screen turning his face an unhealthy shade of white, searching for care agencies, emergency alarms, home help. Soon, their phones would ring and they would have to make space for this new reality, but for now, for a little while at least, no one knew that Jack Chalmers was dead.

MARINELA

Stefan had gone. No note. No broken crockery. Just a space in the drawer where he had stored his clothes and a quiet emptiness to the flat. It had taken her a day or two to get used to it, to stop expecting him to knock on the door holding a bunch of roses and a bag of pastries. There were texts, four or five a day, ranging from pleading to angry, contrite to critical. She read them but did not reply. He would get over it – go back to Anca and his children, or find another girl to adore him, or both. And it would be as though it had never happened. When Marinela was ninety, he would be a distant memory – nothing important.

She had considered calling Harry, asking if she might come for Christmas after all, but the thought of him standing at her front door talking to Stefan stopped her. It was rude, surely, to say yes and then no and then yes again. She had considered calling Bet, suggesting she cooked them an English Christmas lunch, but Bet would be with Tommy and Jack in the hospital – Marinela would just be intruding. Better to spend Christmas on her own.

And so there she was, in a borrowed flat in Islington, standing at the kitchen counter eating cornflakes straight from the packet, listening to some English radio station play carols one after the next.

Harry would be in Liverpool now. A trip home is a matter of survival, he had told her. There were tricks: don't talk about politics, don't talk about history, don't talk about university, don't listen to the news; stick to neutral things – the garden, food, the weather, although even that wasn't a guarantee of success. Escape from the house as often as you can without causing offence. He had shown her pictures of the city's waterfront, old white buildings and new glass apartment blocks, and she imagined him there, sitting by the railings, dipping his toes into the water.

Marinela made herself coffee, curled up on the sofa and called her parents.

'Mamă?'

'Mari? Oh!'

Marinela closed her eyes. 'Don't cry, Mamă.'

'I just. Your voice. And it's Christmas, Mari. You never call.'

'I do.'

'Two, three times. You break our hearts.'

Marinela took a mouthful of coffee. 'Happy Christmas,' she said, wiping the back of her hand across her mouth. 'You got the presents I sent?'

'We did. Yes.'

Marinela's bedroom in her parents' house was still exactly as she'd left it when she moved to Bucharest. Red and silver wallpaper. A photo of her and her parents on holiday in Brasov taped to the wall. A glass bowl of potpourri and plastic starfish, which used to smell of strawberries, or was it grapefruit? The window looking away from the factory, towards identical blocks of flats, a playground just below and next to that a scrubby area with benches and a few spindly trees. Maybe she should have gone home for the holidays. Let her mother fuss over her. Eaten too much.

'Somebody called,' her mother said. 'Your professor – about a job. Here in Bucharest. He wrote to you?'

Which was how Stefan had got her address.

'I'm not sure it's quite what I want, Mamă.'

'You can't afford to be fussy, Marinela. A good job. And your professor asking for you especially.'

'I want to be a photographer. The job, it's—' She cast around for a convincing lie. 'It's administration.'

Her mother sighed. 'How is school?'

'University is fine.' Marinela stared up at the ceiling. The plaster was whipped into low peaks, which cast their own little shadows, a pool of darkness around each tip.

'Fine?'

Marinela took a breath. 'It's good.'

'You have friends?'

'Yes.'

'A boyfriend?'

'Mamă.'

'I hear Gabi's getting married,' her mother said. 'And a baby soon, I'm sure. And then Livia, at number 33, they've just had twins.'

'Mamă, don't.' Marinela got up, walked to the window and opened the curtains. It was a dull day. No one in sight.

'A woman's looks don't last for ever.'

Marinela looked at the house opposite – a Christmas tree positioned in the downstairs bay window, silver tinsel, silver baubles, real candles in silver holders. 'It's 2014. 2015 nearly. It doesn't work like that any more.'

'The breasts sag. The face, the whole body. You don't stay young for ever.'

'There is someone,' Marinela said, and then immediately regretted it.

'Yes?'

'It's nothing really though, he's a friend. He studies cities.'

'Cities? That is a subject?'

'He's nice.' Marinela could feel her own heartbeat. 'You'd like him.'

'Well bring him home, Marinela. Why don't you bring him home?'

Marinela traced an M in the condensation that clouded the bottom half of the window, then an H. 'I'm sorry I'm not there for Christmas, Mamă.'

'Well.'

'I'll come at Easter.'

Her mother sniffed. She'd be smiling, Marinela thought, and smiled herself.

'You'll bring that boy?' her mother said.

'Maybe. You have everyone coming later?' Her aunts and uncles, cousins and associated girlfriends and boyfriends.

'Yes, and so much to do. So much food to make.'

It was her mother's idea of heaven – a house full of people, a list of tasks almost too long to achieve. 'In fact I must go, the *cozonac* will be ready to take out – I've made it with walnuts this year – your favourite. And your dad wants to speak to you.'

Marinela moved into the bedroom, stood by the window and listened to her dad relay his news: more people laid off from the factory; a divorce just down the corridor and an affair on the floor below; a handful of unaffordable mortgages and aggressive evictions; mutterings about the mayor's ability to do his job; the head teacher at Mamă's school diagnosed with cancer. She looked down at the gardens below; watched a pigeon make its clumsy way from fence to grass to fence again, looking for food. There were pigeons that could be driven hundreds of miles away from their homes and always find their way back. This one didn't look so clever.

'You are happy?' her father asked.

Marinela watched the pigeon lift itself into the air and flap gracelessly out of view. A woman with a blue headwrap opened a door onto a paved yard and stepped outside. She looked up towards Marinela, who backed away from the window. 'Yes, Tată, I'm fine.'

'You just ignore your mother, won't you?'

'Tată?'

'You must do what you want to do, Marinela. It's not always easiest, but it is for the best.'

Marinela went back to the window, put her palm flat against the glass, her fingers spread.

'Don't let anyone bully you into anything. You promise me.'

'I promise.'

She eventually hung up but stayed standing at the window, her hand still pressed against the glass. Her dad would be stepping onto the balcony now, lighting a cigarette, looking out across the blocks of flats towards the factory crowding the horizon, its chimneys pumping black smoke up into the sky.

She went out, because she had nothing else to do. The streets were eerily quiet. The shops shut. She had nowhere to go and so she simply walked and walked. After an hour or so, she found herself at Buckingham Palace, staring through the huge gates at the guards in their narrow boxes, wearing their dark grey-blue coats and tall black hats. Stefan had found them hilarious, tried to get them to talk to him, shaking his head at their impassive faces. Marinela looked at them now, like ceramic figures, hardly breathing, and wondered if their mothers were disappointed not to have their sons home for Christmas.

She carried on walking until she reached the river. It was high tide, the water sweeping through the city as if it had somewhere better to go. A handful of gulls bobbed on its surface; empty boats rocked at its edges. Marinela found a bench and sat, looking across at the buildings on the other side. Christmas was just another day, she told herself; it was only important because people had decided it was, and therefore she could decide it was not.

Her phone trilled in her pocket and she pulled it out. If it was Stefan she wouldn't answer.

'Bet?'

Nothing on the other end of the line.

'Bet, are you OK?'

A thin cough, the rustle of someone moving.

'Bet? Do you want me to come round? I am just by the river. I am not far.'

'He's dead.'

She almost asked Bet to say it again, because it couldn't be true, could only be a trick of her hearing, but she stopped herself, said instead, 'Jack? Jack's dead?' She tried to swallow but it felt as though there was something in the way.

'I wasn't good to him, Marinela.'

'No. That is not true.' She couldn't keep her voice steady. Jack. Kind, quiet, calm Jack. 'It isn't true, Bet, you mustn't say that.'

'Pneumonia. It gets in your lungs, doesn't it?'

Marinela cleared her throat. 'I'm sure they helped him, at the hospital. I'm sure they made him comfortable.'

'I wasn't there. Nobody was there.'

An old man on a hospital ward, light leaking in from the corridor, the lowered voices of nurses.

'Bet, I'm sorry.'

Bet sniffed, said nothing.

'Shall I come over? I'll come now.' She had bought Bet chocolates – an expensive box from a shop on Upper Street, wrapped with a thick red ribbon. But they were back in the flat and anyway they felt too celebratory to offer her now.

'I can come,' Marinela tried again, wiping away the tears that had spilled onto her cheeks.

'Tommy's here.'

'Tomorrow, then? I'll come tomorrow. You'll be OK, Bet.' Marinela rolled her eyes. It was a stupid thing to say. 'He loved you,' she tried.

A noise, which might have been a cough, or a sob, she couldn't tell.

'Tommy will make sure you have something to eat?'

'He liked you.'

'Tommy?'

'Jack. He said you were a nice girl.'

Marinela thought of Jack – his slightly stooped frame, sharp cheekbones, his smile. 'I liked him,' she said. 'I really did.'

BET

Bet lay, listening to the high-pitched blip of her alarm clock. It was cold – she could feel it on her face and shoulders – the boiler refusing to fire up again. She could ask Tommy to call someone, sort it out, but she didn't have the energy, because Jack was gone – really gone this time.

I am alone, she told the ceiling. I am alone now.

Don't be such a drama queen, Jack would say, would have said, to that.

It was January already. 2015. She used to love New Year. Drinking fizzy wine and making promises to herself – this year I will be a better person; this year I will get everything right. But this New Year had come and gone with barely a whisper. Tommy had offered to take her out for dinner but she'd put him off, said she didn't feel so good, had lain in bed and listened to the fireworks exploding across South London.

She felt as though someone had cut a hole out of the middle of her body. She'd be making a cup of tea, or turning the television on, and there'd be a falling sensation, a dip somewhere between her breastbone and lungs as if there was nothing here. A black hole. Weren't they the things in space that swallowed everything up? That was what she had – a black hole right in her middle.

She wanted to be cremated when she'd gone – a brief flare of heat and then nothing left but her ashes. Jack, though, wanted burying, so that's what they were going to do. A quiet, plain affair down in Tooting. Bet reached a hand out from the warmth of her blanket and pressed the button on the alarm clock. The blipping noise stopped. She needed to get out of bed and get herself dressed, but she couldn't. She was too heavy, too empty, too tired.

They would bury him next to his parents. Mr and Mrs Chalmers. She'd called them that even when she'd lived with them, those first, dark, bleak months in London when she'd tried so hard, every day, to convince herself she hadn't made a mistake.

1944. Bet had gone from driving tractors to driving ambulances. She'd been on shift that night – had walked home in the early hours of the morning, picking her way over piles of bricks and rubble and burnt timbers, around the holes in what used to be pavement, or road, park, or dwelling place, glass crunching beneath her feet. That was how it went – the city rewritten each night, its inhabitants negotiating a new landscape each morning. As soon as she'd turned the corner into Jack's parents' street, she'd understood what had happened.

It wasn't there. The room at the back, with the narrow bed and the wardrobe with Bet's clothes inside, the table where she had arranged her photos – Jack in uniform; her brothers sitting up on the tractor pulling faces. The dark kitchen where she'd bathed in the tin tub in front of the fire. Gone.

She remembered the harsh morning light on the mess of it. A blue dress – Bet's – ripped and ragged amongst the rubble; the carriage clock from the mantelpiece, its face cracked; a strip of brown flowered wallpaper from the hallway. She'd known they were dead, even before Maureen from down the road spied her and came out to break the news. A V1 launched at just the right angle and with just enough fuel to fall exactly there. And Jack's parents asleep, or half so, he in his blue pyjamas, she in her white nightdress. Bet had been to enough bombsites to know what would have happened to them. Struck by the roof falling in, or glass burst from the window, or furniture slammed across the room; or trapped in amongst the rubble without enough air to breathe; or crushed; or burnt. She'd seen heads that had been severed from necks. She'd seen limbs without bodies attached.

That had been how she'd met Nell, she remembered. At the Rest Centre. She'd made up a bed for Bet to sleep in, found her a nip of brandy to calm her nerves.

Today was Jack's funeral and she needed to get up. Wash. Put on her black dress – it was old and too baggy around her middle, but it was the only one she had. She had to go outside into the world that was so bright and fast and noisy it gave her a headache just to think about it. Tommy had already started on a new campaign, getting Bet out and about – community transport and day centres, activities. She wasn't sure if it was a replacement for the idea of a home, but she was having none of it. She was quite happy just the way she was. As happy as she could be with that black hole, dark and pulsing, right in the middle of her stomach.

She was still in bed when Tommy arrived. She lay and listened to his knock, then the sound of the front door being unlocked. She waited for him to walk to the living room and see she wasn't there, then the kitchen, then a knock on the bedroom door.

'Mum?'

She mumbled a response and the door opened, the draught excluder brushing against the carpet. She must look a mess, lying there in her nightie with her hair all over the place. No matter.

'Mum, we've got to leave in an hour.'

Tommy. Her son. Jack's son. Tall and washed out in a black suit. Both of them in their own tight circle of grief. She suddenly remembered a news report she'd seen years ago, somewhere in the desert, women in black, sitting together and wailing. She couldn't remember what had happened, only that these women sat one next to the other and howled as though there was nothing to be embarrassed about; as though grief was something to be shared.

'Are you ill?' Tommy asked.

She shook her head. 'Cold.'

'Do you not have the heating on?'

'The boiler.' She shrugged.

'I'll have a look. You need to get up, Mum. Can you get up?'

She waited until he'd left the room and then forced herself to sit up, move her legs over the edge of the bed, tip her weight onto her feet so she was standing.

Jack. She glanced back at the empty bed and felt a rush of anger, pure as fire. How could you – she wanted to shout at him – how could you? But he wasn't there to ask. He had gone. And yet, looking around, she couldn't help feeling that he was still there somehow, in the arrangement of the room – the wardrobe, bed, bedside tables, rug; in the blankets which he used to smooth and tuck every morning; in the plain white lampshades either side of the bed; in the pink linen curtains, which he would whisk open every morning declaring 'good morning, day' to the view of a brick wall and a patch of sky up above; in the sound of a tap running in the kitchen; in the smell of tea and toast. If all that was still there, then surely part of Jack was too?

Jack was in a coffin. They would bury him that afternoon. Bet put her hand against the wall to steady herself. She didn't want today to happen – she didn't want any of it.

The chapel was cold – a couple of electric heaters positioned by the door puffing heat up towards the high ceiling. Stone walls. Elegant arched windows. A handful of people in the dark wooden pews. Bet saw Marinela sitting alone, a heavy black shawl wrapped around her thin shoulders.

'You came,' she said, breaking away from Tommy and touching the girl on the arm.

'Of course.' Marinela stood and embraced Bet, who felt she might fall the moment she let go. 'How are you?' Marinela pulled back and looked into Bet's face.

Bet didn't have anything to say. There, at the front of the chapel, with an arrangement of lilies splayed on top, was the coffin. Jack's coffin.

'Mum?' Bet turned to see Tommy, pale-faced, standing in the aisle. He was looking at Marinela rather than at her, a frown creasing his forehead.

'I'm so sorry,' Marinela said. 'About Jack.'

Tommy sniffed, nodded, then held out his hand to Bet. 'Come and sit, Mum.'

Bet let him lead her to the front pew. So close to the coffin she felt she could reach out and touch its varnished surface. Tinny organ music rose from a portable CD player. The electric heaters hummed. She wanted to go back to the flat. At least there she felt as though Jack hadn't completely disappeared.

It was a woman who led the service. Small and birdlike, her head bobbing as she spoke, her hands describing neat circles in the air. She hadn't known Jack, but Tommy must have written some things down because it sounded as though she had. Soldier. Bus driver. Devoted father. Loving husband. She talked about all that campaigning he'd done while they still lived on the estate, the award he'd won for it, which Bet had completely forgotten about, and then how he used to walk to the shopping centre every day for a coffee, how he kept himself active, kept himself connected.

Oh, Jack. Bet stared at the coffin and the black hole pulsed inside her, threatened to swallow her whole. There should be an option to just go if you wanted to, she thought. A button you could press. Or one of those tiny vials of powder people used to carry in spy films. Quick and painless.

Now Tommy was standing, walking towards the coffin, his shoulders stooped as though his head was too heavy to hold. He turned, a piece of paper trembling in one hand, and cleared his throat.

'My dad,' he said.

She couldn't bear it. She couldn't.

'We used to make models together,' Tommy was saying now. They'd spend hours, the two of them, bent over bits of wood, the smell of glue and varnish making Bet's head spin. They made aeroplanes mainly, which they'd take out to Burgess Park and end up flying into a tree – have to come home and spend more hours fixing wings and fuselages in order to repeat the whole process again. She had never seen the point of it.

'He was kind,' Tommy said. 'To a fault, sometimes. Would always go out of his way for people, whether he knew them or not.'

Bet tried to keep her attention on Tommy, but it kept getting drawn away to the coffin with its polished brass handles and the lilies lying open-mouthed on its lid.

And then it was over. Tommy was back in his seat, breathing hard, and six men in suits – men she didn't know – lifted the coffin onto their shoulders and took it away. Everyone stood, fussing with coats and handbags and orders of service.

'You didn't want to do that?' Bet waved towards the departing men.

'I thought I'd stay with you. Come on.' Tommy held out his hand, solicitous. This, it seemed, was what death did: brought out the best in people, distracted from endlessly repeated arguments – it made people cling to each other and forget all the other stuff.

She took his hand, let him lead her down the centre of the chapel, out into the grey day. The graveyard was old, half the stones propped up with bits of wood, grass growing over those that lay flat against the ground. The small group followed a tarmacked path past the chapel and up a shallow incline.

'Do you know, when your dad got back from the war, I was a bit frightened of him?' Bet said.

'Of Dad?'

'I'd read an article about a soldier who'd come home and seemed fine and dandy until he stabbed his wife and kids when they were sleeping, and then slit his own wrists. No one would have suspected, that's what the paper said, it was never the ones you'd expect.'

Tommy said nothing and Bet pressed her lips together, looked at the line of bare trees at the far end of the cemetery.

Jack hadn't told her he was coming home. He'd got stuck in Burma along with everyone else, waiting for a boat, writing her long letters filled with plans for the future – kids, holidays, a place of their own. And then he'd just rung the doorbell one afternoon, and there she was in her old grey dress with two cardigans piled on top of each other, not an ounce of make-up. She could still picture his face, that grin – the way he picked her up and spun her round. I'm never going away again, he told her, from now on, I'm always going to be here.

They came to a halt by a deep hole, fake green grass draped over the edges as though that could hide the reality of it. The woman with the dog collar read from the Bible. The six men Bet didn't know lowered the coffin into the ground. She thought she might be sick, but she was not. She stood and listened. She took a handful of soil from the basket and dropped it onto the coffin, a thin, ringing sound on the wood.

People drifted away but Bet stayed where she was.

'Do you want a minute, Mum?'

Bet didn't answer and Tommy patted her arm. 'I'll just be over there, by the path.'

The coffin lay at the bottom of the hole, littered with dirt. She had seen a small yellow digger at the entrance to the grave-yard. They would wait until they had all left, and then get to work – tip all that earth back onto him.

'I love you,' she whispered. Feeling, for a moment, foolish, standing there talking to no one, to a dead man. 'I love you, Jack Chalmers,' she said, a little louder. A blackbird landed at the far end of the grave and started pecking at the disturbed ground. Up above, a plane lumbered across the sky leaving a white trail in its wake. Bet swallowed, brushed her hands against her coat and pulled herself straight. She turned away from the grave and walked slowly towards Tommy.

'Ready?' he asked, and she gave the slightest of nods, took his arm. 'That girl said she couldn't come for drinks,' he said as they made their way towards the road. 'She said to tell you she was sorry.'

Bet paused. 'Did she say that or did you not tell her about the drinks?'

'Mum.' Tommy squeezed her arm.

'And she's called Marinela.'

'Fine. She said she had some presentation at university or something. She said she would call you.'

'Do we have to do the drinks?'

'Dad would have liked it, everyone together, it'll be nice.'

So she went with him, sat at a corner table with a gin and tonic and listened to the people who came and told her how sorry they were, what a great man Jack had been, how they'd miss him, and Tommy was right – it was as nice as such a thing could be.

MARINELA

Marinela decided to walk home after her presentation, following the route of the Northern line – over the river and up through London Bridge, Bank, Old Street. All the Christmas decorations had been taken down and the city felt colourless, hard and unfriendly. It was getting dark by the time she reached Angel. Her feet ached. Her heart ached. She had tried to think about Jack as she'd walked, but the image of him kept slipping away from her. Letting herself into the empty flat, she stopped for a moment in the hallway and listened to the silence. She missed Stefan more than she'd expected – would find herself standing for minutes at a time holding something he'd bought her: a tiny blue glass bowl; a cactus in a yellow pot.

She locked the door, drew the curtains, turned up the heating. Walked discontentedly from room to room. In the end she turned on the shower and stood under it for a long time, trying to keep her mind blank and calm. In her dressing gown, she went to the kitchen, made tea and toast and took it to the table. She sat, eating without registering the taste.

An hour or so later, the doorbell blared. Whoever it was kept their finger down a long time, released it for a second as though taking a breath, and then pressed again.

Stefan? Harry? Marinela hurried down the stairs to the front door, pulling her dressing gown close around her.

It was Tommy. She heard her own intake of breath.

'You,' she said, and then wished she'd said nothing, wished she'd slammed the door, wished she'd never opened it in the first place.

The outdoor security lamp clicked off then on again, casting its ghoulish light onto his face. He looked tired. Drunk.

'You came to Dad's funeral,' he said, his words slurring into each other.

'Of course.'

Tommy shook his head as though trying to get rid of something.

'Your speech was very nice,' Marinela said.

'You need to leave.' He was staring past her, into the hallway. 'I let it slide it because of Mum, because of Dad. But you need to leave.' He shook a pointed finger as he spoke, like a caricature of a headmaster.

'It is late.'

'This needs to stop.' Tommy leant a hand on the door frame, his eyes still not meeting hers. 'I gave you notice. You need to go. I want my mum somewhere safe where the bloody heating works.'

Marinela glanced behind her at the dim hallway. She loved it, with a sudden and disproportionate passion – the striped carpet, the scuffed walls, the wide black door with its wrinkled glass panes. She thought about her grandmother's house – the front wall collapsed into rubble; the garden choked with weeds. It was pointless getting attached to places – she should have learnt that by now.

Marinela swallowed. 'Tomorrow. I can pack tomorrow and go.'

Tommy swayed a little, righted himself. 'Now.'

'This is my home. My things.' She waved a hand towards the stairwell.

'No.' Tommy shook his head. 'No, it isn't.' He was looking past her, trying to see inside. 'I want you to leave.'

'Where will I go?'

Tommy looked at her and seemed to hesitate for a moment, but then he shook his head again. 'That isn't my problem.' He paused, rubbed at his jaw. 'You can stay in a hotel. It's not like there aren't any hotels in London. You've got money, I'm guessing?'

She had no contract, no tenancy agreement. She'd known it couldn't last.

'I can call the police if you want me to,' Tommy said. 'Do you want me to call the police?'

If she hadn't thrown Stefan out he'd have thought of something – taken Tommy on, or just whisked her off to a hotel and ordered champagne.

'I need to dress, and pack.'

Tommy lowered his eyes and for a moment she wanted to take his hand and lead him upstairs, sit him on the sofa and make him a cup of tea.

'Half an hour,' he said. 'And this door stays open.'

'You don't come upstairs.'

'Fine.'

Marinela took a shaky breath, nodded. 'Do not come up the stairs,' she said again, as she backed down the hallway. 'Or I shout for help.'

'I've started counting. Half an hour.'

There was a game they used to play at school: if your block was on fire, what would you take with you when you ran? Books? Toys? The television? Marinela pulled on jeans and a jumper, then packed her photographs and camera equipment into her suitcase, tucked clothes and shoes around them. She put her laptop and library books into her rucksack.

She thought about calling Bet, but she was an old woman, living on her own, and it was the night of her husband's funeral – it wasn't fair. She texted Jess, *I have problem with my flat. May I sleep at yours? Just one night?* But a few minutes later she got the response, *Hun, I'm in Wales. Don't ask. Is there somewhere else you can go?*

As a child, she used to bid places goodbye. Goodbye house. Goodbye school. Goodbye field. She walked around the flat, trailing her fingertips over the furniture. Goodbye bed. Goodbye kitchen. Goodbye sofa. And then she pulled the door closed behind her and walked downstairs.

Tommy sat in the porch, slumped against the door frame, the smoke from his cigarette curling up into the dark. Marinela walked out of the building with her head held high, her suitcase rattling its wheels on the pavement behind her. A steady rain had started and the air felt cold enough for snow. She did not have anywhere to go.

'Keys.' Tommy was next to her, his hand held out.

She took the keys from her pocket and placed them in his palm, walked away before he could say anything.

Marinela made her way towards the Tube station. By the time she had reached Upper Street, she had decided to go to Harry's. They hadn't been in touch since before Christmas and most likely he would not be pleased to see her, but she couldn't think of anywhere else.

She knew he lived in Kentish Town, in a shared flat above a greengrocer's on the main road. It couldn't be that hard to find. She should call him, she thought, stepping onto the escalator that led down into the station, or text him at least. But instead, she simply took the Tube to Kentish Town, and walked up and down the row of shops until she found a place that matched his description.

She rang the doorbell.

For a long time, there was no response. She rang again, and after a minute or so, the intercom crackled.

'Hello?'

She could not tell if it was his voice.

'Harry?'

'Hello?'

'It's Marinela.'

Silence.

'It's late. I'm sorry.'

The intercom gave a sharp buzz and Marinela pushed at the now open door. The stairs up to the flat were steep and narrow, carpeted a rough industrial blue. When she reached the top he was standing at the open door, bare-footed, his shirt untucked. A smell of frying onions drifted out of the flat.

'Are you OK?'

Marinela swallowed and put down her suitcase. Harry looked at it, then back at her. He would invite her in, make her a cup of tea, or pour her a glass of vodka maybe, and she would tell him everything. About Stefan. About Tommy. About Jack and Bet.

But Harry stayed at the door, looking at her, waiting.

'You had a good Christmas?' Marinela asked. 'New Year?'

Harry shrugged. 'It was nice, thanks.'

'I'm sorry,' Marinela said. 'About not coming to Liverpool.'

Harry waved her words away.

'I should have answered your messages.'

'Doesn't matter.'

'It does. I was brought up properly.'

Harry laughed, shook his head. 'We're about to eat spaghetti. You want some?' He opened the door a little wider and

Marinela saw Lane, sitting at a small table set for two, wearing a short black dress, a chunky yellow necklace and matching earrings.

'Marinela?' Lane raised a hand. 'Hi.'

Marinela felt the blood rush to her face, burning up across her cheeks to her forehead.

'I should go.' She reached for her case.

'Don't be stupid. Come in.' He was looking at her intently but she couldn't return his gaze.

'You're busy,' she said, turning in the narrow space.

'Marinela. Come on. There's loads of food.'

And so she let him hustle her into the flat, sit her at the table while he found extra cutlery, doled out spaghetti and sauce, poured her a glass of wine.

'I'm sorry,' Marinela muttered. 'I do not want to disturb, but I had to leave. I didn't know where to go.'

'Leave where?' Lane asked. She was pretty – Marinela hadn't noticed that when they'd met. Her body neat, her stomach flat, her breasts neither too small nor too large.

'Bet's son said I had to leave the flat, tonight. He just turned up.' She looked at Lane. 'You were right, it was not a good arrangement.'

'He can't just do that,' Lane said. 'He has to give you notice.' A little knot of a frown at her forehead, her fork jabbing at her pasta as she spoke.

Marinela shrugged. 'He had told me to go before, but I didn't think he would make me. I have no tenancy agreement. I was stupid to think—'

'Have some more of this.' Lane filled Marinela's glass. 'There are other places to live. And Harry's sofa is very comfortable.' She laughed, a delicate, kind laugh that made Marinela want to cry.

The flat had low ceilings, dark carpets, a faint whiff of damp

beneath the smells of cooking. The table they sat at was squeezed into the corner of the living room, behind a large blue sofa. A TV sat on a chrome and black stand in the corner; wooden blinds were half-lowered over the windows.

'It is OK to sleep on the sofa, for maybe just one night? Two?' Marinela on the sofa; Harry and Lane in bed behind a closed door. Too close. She swallowed hard.

'Course it is.' Harry still wouldn't meet her eye.

'There is a notice board at university I think. I will look there tomorrow for flats.'

'You could end up with any old crazy person doing that,' Harry said.

Lane tapped him on the arm. 'We can both call some people, ask around. There's always someone needs a flatmate,' she said.

Marinela gave a half smile. 'That would be kind.'

'Great. So forget about it for now. Everything works out. Tell us about your Christmas. You went home?'

Marinela shook her head, glanced at Harry. 'I had a friend staying, but he left.'

Lane raised her eyebrows and Marinela found herself blushing again.

'I told him to go,' she said.

Harry coughed, covering his mouth, turning away from the table for a moment.

'I went for a walk,' Marinela said.

'Christmas on your own,' Lane said, 'sounds ideal.'

'Hear, hear,' Harry said, his voice louder than usual. 'I managed not to kill any of the members of my family, but only thanks to serious amounts of self-control.'

Marinela took a mouthful of spaghetti and sauce. It was good. Tomatoes, garlic, rosemary. She stole another look at Lane. She looked relaxed, happy, a different person to the one

Marinela had met back in November. And Harry? She looked at him too but he had his head down over his plate.

'But then I found out that Jack died,' she said. Harry looked up. 'He died on Christmas Eve. It must be as though Bet has lost half of her body.'

'Oh God, I'm sorry.' Harry put his hand on her arm. It was all Marinela could do not to lean over and kiss him.

'He fell,' she said, focusing on the last strands of spaghetti on her plate. 'Then a problem in his lungs. And—Can you imagine being married for seventy years and then they die?'

'I can't imagine being alive for seventy years,' Harry said. 'What will she do now?'

'Do?'

'Will she go into a home? Aren't her eyes bad?'

'She hates those places.'

Lane laughed. 'I like the sound of this woman.'

Harry took his hand away and the absence felt like a weight. 'God, being old sucks, though, doesn't it?'

'Maybe. But you'd know so much. You'd have seen so much,' Lane said.

'But your body doesn't work. Your ears go, your eyes go, everyone ignores you or tells you what to do. By the time we get that old they'll have legalized euthanasia – there'll be a pill.'

'Except maybe when you are old you will not think the same way,' Marinela said.

'Maybe.'

That night she lay on the sofa in the sleeping bag Harry had pulled from his wardrobe and listened to the unfamiliar sounds of the flat. The hum of the fridge, the traffic outside, the occasional bleep of the pedestrian crossing. She tried not to think about Harry and Lane and thought instead of Bet, lying in the bed she'd shared with Jack, staring at the ceiling, feeling how slowly time moved when you were on your own.

BET

The morning after the funeral, Bet woke with a headache. It felt as though there was a vice fixed around her skull and someone was tightening it and then tightening it again. The gin. She hadn't had a hangover in years, she had forgotten what it felt like. But it was more than the gin and she knew it. Jack in that coffin in the cold chapel. Jack being lowered into the ground. The flat empty and her body hollowed out. She couldn't even get herself out of bed. Just lay there, looking at the ceiling, her mind like a blank wall. Jack had always slept on the right. Bet on the left. She could sleep in the middle now if she wanted, but she'd stayed on her side. She stretched out her arm into the empty space beside her. Cold sheets. He had gone too quickly and she couldn't get any of it straight in her head.

The phone rang on the bedside table a few times but she ignored it, and when the door-knocker went, she ignored that as well. Tommy had a key. If he wanted to fuss, that was his concern.

'Bet?'

Bet sat bolt upright. 'Jack?' she said.

The noise of the letter box pushed open. 'Bet? It is me, Marinela. Are you OK?'

Bet closed her eyes, her shoulders slumped.

'Bet?'

'Go away,' Bet whispered.

'I call someone?'

'No.' Bet turned and lowered her feet to the floor. Jack used to put her slippers by the bed each night so she could slip them straight on – she had no idea where she'd left them, so she walked barefoot to the bedroom door, unhooked her dressing gown and made her slow way along the hallway.

'Bet, I am calling someone.' Marinela's voice sounded high-pitched, worried.

The police. Social services. Tommy. There was no one who could help.

Bet unlocked the door and pulled it towards her.

'Oh Bet, I was worrying.' The girl wore a thick white jumper with a roll neck, skinny black jeans, a coat that didn't look warm enough. She was so young. She could do anything. And there was Bet, in her nightie and dressing gown, her hair all over no doubt, her head pounding.

She ushered Marinela in, followed her to the kitchen.

'Let me get dressed,' she said.

'I will make tea. Toast? Eggs? Have you eaten?'

Bet shook her head.

'It will make you feel better.'

Except even the thought of eating made her feel sick.

She stood at the bathroom sink for a long time, looking at herself in the mirror. Jack is gone, she told the old woman facing her. He's gone, you are on your own, and that's the long and the short of it, there's no use in wallowing around feeling sorry for yourself. You drink that much gin you get a headache. You're married for that long it's not going to be easy when it ends.

She squeezed toothpaste onto Jack's brush and scrubbed at her teeth until they felt clean. Then she splashed cold water onto her face, under her arms. Come on, Bet Chalmers, she told herself. Pull yourself together.

She emerged to the smell of toast and the sound of eggs hissing and spitting in the frying pan. Bet stood at the kitchen doorway and watched Marinela at the stove. She wanted to say something to her – tell her she mattered, that Bet was glad Jack had talked to her in the cafe, that she had made things better somehow – but then the girl turned and smiled, and told Bet to sit down and she would pour tea and the eggs were nearly ready, and Bet just nodded and said nothing.

'The man I told you about came to London,' Marinela said, setting a plate in front of Bet. Two eggs. Toast. More than she could possibly eat.

'He's a lecturer at my old university, I told you that?' Marinela said. 'In Romanian literature. I took one of his classes.'

'He's here?'

Marinela sat down and shook her head. 'He said he'd left his wife, but he hadn't. I told him to go.'

Bet took Marinela's hand and turned it over. 'They say everything that's going to happen to you is written on your palm, don't they?' Her fingers traced the lines across Marinela's skin. 'Life line. Love line. All that.' She paused. 'I mean, it's nonsense, but.'

'The man who gave you the flat,' Marinela started, then faltered. 'The American? I was thinking about him.'

Bet said nothing for a long time, then, 'Kit and I used to write to each other. For a year or so. Sometimes we'd go over the whole thing again and again. Sometimes we'd pretend I hadn't refused to leave – make plans we knew we'd never actually see through.' She smiled. 'I don't suppose it was a good idea, and I stopped it once Tommy was born, but it was nice. A little bit of make-believe.'

'Stefan keeps sending me messages, says he's going to die,' Marinela said. 'Says that he'll jump off something, or hang himself. He won't die, will he?'

Bet sat back in her chair and folded her arms. Kit had never threatened suicide, only talked about his disappointment, his confusion. I thought you loved me, he'd written. I thought you were fed up of Jack, of London, of all that mundanity. He was the kind of man who used words like mundanity. 'I have no idea,' she said. 'But I know it's not your responsibility. I know that. Don't you worry yourself about it. Men can be such drama queens.'

Bet surprised herself with her hunger. She ate both eggs, and three pieces of toast. Maybe she had had no dinner last night, she couldn't remember.

'Bet, I do not want to bother you,' Marinela started, when their plates were empty.

'But.' Bet almost smiled.

'I had to leave,' Marinela said.

Bet blinked. 'Leave where?'

'The flat.'

The flat. She had told Jack about it and what had he said? It didn't matter. None of it mattered. All that weight, and then nothing.

'You don't like it?'

'Tommy came round,' Marinela said, her voice so low Bet could hardly hear it. 'He said I had to go.'

'Did you tell him to mind his own business?'

Marinela looked at the floor. 'He took the keys.'

'Last night?' He must have gone straight from dropping her off. Drunk. Had he been drunk?

Marinela nodded. 'I wanted to tell you it is OK,' she said. 'You were very kind to let me stay. Thank you.'

Tommy. Bet tried to feel angry, but she couldn't find the

energy. If she told him Jack didn't care, he wouldn't believe her, and what did it matter any more?

And then it came to her, the idea so fitting and fully formed it must have already been there, waiting at the back of her mind.

'I will give it to you,' she said.

'Give?'

'Yes, give. I don't need it.' Bet pushed the image of the two women in the lounge of The Willows out of her mind. 'No ties. No conditions. Give.'

Marinela stood up, took Bet's plate and her own to the sink and turned on the tap. Bet waited.

Eventually Marinela turned. 'You cannot do this,' she said. 'It is not right.'

'I've decided.'

'I am not family.'

'I wasn't family to Kit.'

'But I'm not—You don't even know me.'

Bet flinched. 'I know you well enough.'

'They will say I stole it. Tommy won't let you.'

'I'll do it all properly. Find a lawyer. Get everything signed and sorted out.'

Marinela turned back to the sink and Bet listened to the sound of her washing the plates, the water dripping off as she lifted them onto the draining board.

'I don't understand,' Marinela said.

'I want you to have choices.'

'About what?'

'Life. A long time ago I had a choice. It was between one man and another man. They were both good men, but that was my choice: Jack or Kit; Kit or Jack. This gives you as many choices as you want.'

'Things are different now,' Marinela said.

'Different and the same.'

For a while, neither spoke.

'You know I can't, don't you?' Marinela said at last.

'It can be a home, or it can be something you sell. It's up to you. I'll phone a lawyer today. Tommy can't do anything about that. He'll say I'm loopy, but I'm not.'

'Bet.' Marinela walked back to the table and put her hand over Bet's. 'Tommy said you need the money for a care home.'

Bet thought of The Willows again – the heat and the smell, the green carpets and wipe-down chairs. 'I'm not going anywhere,' she said.

'It's too much. Far too much.'

Bet turned her hand over so their palms met. She squeezed and Marinela squeezed back.

'Humour an old woman,' she said. 'Won't you?'

MARINELA

Marinela checked her phone as she left Bet's flat. A text from Harry: *There's a room in my friend's flat going, in Elephant and Castle. Call him.* And then a contact – Freddie M. She went into the little park opposite, sat on one of the cold metal benches and dialled Freddie's number. He sounded distracted, but kind, said he was in for the next hour if she could hurry over.

'I am very near,' she said.

'Great. Flat 7. Buzz on the silver panel thing. What's your name again?'

'Marinela.'

'Marinela. Cool.'

And there she was, walking towards Walworth Road, pulling her coat around her but still shivering. She could not take Bet's flat. She couldn't. Tommy would call the police. There would be all sorts of trouble. Maybe they would send her back to Romania.

She stood waiting for the pedestrian lights, looking at the boarded-up building on the other side of the street. Her stomach felt wrong, as though she had eaten something bad. It must be worth half a million. More than that. She couldn't think about it. She couldn't not think about it. What would she do? Sell it? Live there for ever?

I want you to have choices.

But it wasn't right. Bet was old. Sharp, yes, but old.

She turned down a side street towards a building clad in yellows and oranges, as though it was permanently on fire. Behind it loomed the cranes on the cleared land of Jack and Bet's estate.

'It's not the biggest room in the world, but this is London, right?' Freddie was wearing cycling leggings and a cycling top with some brand she'd never heard of emblazoned across the back. He was tall, skinny, moved his hands in wild circles as he talked. 'There's just me and Suz, and then you if you take it. We like a drink but we're not big party people.' He turned to look at her and she blinked. Smiled.

'Me too.'

They stood in the doorway to a small room. Magnolia walls. Queen-size bed stripped of bedding. A white wardrobe. A narrow beech-laminate desk. A rectangular window that looked onto the building site behind.

'What do you do, Marinela?'

'Photography. I am studying photography.'

Freddie nodded. 'Cool. Lots to take photos of there.' He gestured towards the window. 'Though you've missed the best bit – the whole place coming down.'

Marinela thought of Jack and Bet listening to the roar and groan of the demolition from their dark ground-floor flat.

'Used to be what, a thousand, two thousand flats there,' Freddie said. 'A proper dump though, apparently. Concrete. Thugs. You know. Anyways, I'll show you the rest of it, see what you think.'

She followed him into a narrow lounge with a brown sofa and a couple of bean bags, a TV and a thin-framed bike propped against one wall. Then the kitchen, also narrow, but clean and new-looking. A strangely large bathroom with a bath and shower, a poster from the Tour de France above the toilet.

'I'd offer you a cup of tea, but I've got work,' Freddie said.

'Thank you.'

'I'll have to talk to Suz, but I don't see any problems if you want it. Harry said you need somewhere quickly?' He lifted the end of his sentence into a question.

'It's very nice.'

Freddie pursed his lips. 'Well, stuff goes fast, so let me know, right?'

Marinela nodded. 'I will message you. Today.' She nodded. 'I just need to think for a moment.'

'Sure you do. I've got to shoot, Marinela. Been good to meet you.' He took her hand and shook it, and she let herself be ushered back to the front door.

On the street, she started to walk without thinking, found herself searching for a view onto the building site. Still just flat ground. The start of foundations. Marked squares of poured concrete. Low lines of bricks. Men in work boots and yellow jackets. She wondered what it would be like to be one of them. Did they think about what they were doing, what it would look like in the end, or did they just follow their instructions for that day, and then the next, and then the one after?

She could stay in Islington. Bet could get the keys back from Tommy. They could go and see a solicitor. She could have her own place. A place that no one could tell her to leave. Her parents had bought their flat in the nineties, after Ceaușescu. The same as everybody else. The deals were too good to say no to, her dad had told her. He'd said it hadn't made much difference in truth, just meant he had to fix the boiler when it broke, and pay for the hallway to be redecorated. But now, the prices were rising and it was hard for people her age to find the money to buy. Same as everywhere else. She had already bought plastic trays and tongs for her planned darkroom, looked into shelving units and second-hand enlargers.

Nothing was that easy, she told herself. Nothing. She thought of her grandmother, sitting on the front step of her house, shelling peas. You make your own way in this life, Marinela, she would say. *A fi pe picioare tale.* You need to be on your own feet. That is what matters in life – that when you get to the end you can look at it and say I made this, on my own.

She carried on walking, heading, she realized, for the shopping centre. She went in on the ground floor, past the shoe shop, the computer cafe, the mobile-phone booth. In the cafe she ordered coffee and a cheese sandwich. The place was nearly empty and she chose the same table she had sat at with Jack all those months ago. It would be good, she thought, to have him there again, his calm voice, his light blue eyes, the way his face creased and smoothed as he spoke. What would he say? Whatever you choose, Marinela, it's your choice.

You make your own way, child. Don't be beholden to a soul.

She wanted to say yes. For Bet – for the way her eyes would light up when she told her, for the lightness in her step. For herself – how easy, a flat in London, a patron, a life made simple. She watched people walking past outside the cafe window, dark coats, heads lowered. Stefan would tell her she was a fool to even hesitate. Life is hard, he'd say, don't make it any harder. But she had already decided.

When she had finished her sandwich and drunk to the dregs of her coffee, Marinela took her phone from her pocket, found Freddie's number and wrote: *I would like to have the room, please. Marinela.* Then she went to Harry's number and wrote: *I have taken the flat, thank you. Maybe one or two more nights at yours? Or I can go to a hotel? M.*

She sat and waited.

Cool. Will talk to Suz and call later. F.

Quick work! You're very welcome to stay. Harry x

She would take him for dinner, she thought. Somewhere nice. To say thank you. She would be happy for him and Lane. The money she'd saved for the darkroom would help with the rent. She'd stop working in the club, find another job – a photographer's assistant, or something in a cafe. She was on her own and for some reason the thought lifted her heart.

BET

'If you've come here to gloat, I don't want to hear it.' Bet sat hunched in her armchair, glaring at Tommy.

'She called me – you gave her my number?'

Bet shrugged.

'I've given her the keys so she can get her things.'

'You threw a girl out on the street in the middle of the night.'

Tommy shifted his weight. 'It was evening. And anyway, it's all ended well.'

Bet snorted.

'Have you eaten?' Tommy asked. 'I brought pasties.'

Bet closed her eyes. The girl had been so reasonable. So kind. I appreciate it, Bet, I do, I can't tell you how much, but I cannot take it – I do not want to take it. There was a story about her grandmother, something about standing on her own two feet. She was being foolish and Bet said as much, but the girl's mind was made up, and who was Bet to ask her do anything she didn't want to do?

'I'll get plates,' Tommy said.

Bet had wondered, over the years, what might have happened if Kit had given her the flat when she was still young. Would she have woken up one morning, waited until Jack had gone to work, and Tommy was at school, then packed a bag and left? It wasn't worth thinking about now. None of it was. Tommy could sell the bloody thing and do what he wanted with the money.

He'd brought beef and onion pasties and Bet ate hers quickly, despite herself, feeling the pastry turn her lips slick with butter. When they were done, Tommy cleared his throat.

'We're going out,' he said.

'It's snowing.' The light outside had sharpened and paled, thin flecks of snow lacing the air.

'I've got the car.'

Bet shook her head.

'There's somewhere I want to show you.'

A quick flare of anger. This was it now. He would sell the flat, deposit her in some over-heated, over-crowded home that smelt of feet and bleach and God knows what else.

'I'm fine here,' Bet said.

'I think you might like it.'

'I don't want to.'

'Mum.' Tommy was in front of her now, holding both of her hands in his. 'Please?' There was something in his voice that reminded her of him as a kid, always looking up at her, wanting her attention. Maybe she hadn't given him enough attention.

'It's not far,' Tommy said. 'A nice little drive. Get you out of the flat.'

Which was exactly what he wanted to do.

Bet pulled herself to her feet. What did it matter, really? Jack was gone and he wasn't coming back. Marinela would go before long. It was just her and Tommy and there was nothing to be done about that.

They drove in silence. South, she thought, or maybe east, grey streets turning white with snow as they passed, the air muffled and quiet. Eventually they drew to a stop on a quiet residential road. Trees evenly spaced along the pavement. Cars parked tight to the kerb.

Tommy switched off the engine and sat for a moment.

'So, I've been thinking,' he said at last. 'About what you've been saying, about wanting to stay in the flat, about not wanting to go into a home.'

Bet said nothing, watched a woman in high heels leading a tiny black dog along the opposite side of the street.

'I get it,' Tommy said. 'I do.'

Bet glanced at him. Her eyes felt worse than ever today and it was hard to make out his expression without turning her head to one side.

'I only kept on about it because I thought it was the right thing for you,' Tommy said.

Bet raised her eyebrows.

'But I'm not some monster who's going to lock up his mum, am I?'

Bet tapped her fingers against the dashboard. 'So what, you're moving me to the suburbs?'

'I just want you to keep an open mind. Can you do that?'

Out of nowhere, Bet thought of the wicker chair that used to be by the window in the Islington flat; remembered sitting there one afternoon, completely naked, and Kit walking towards her. Brazen. She could hardly believe it even now, but she could remember standing up and showing him how the wicker had pressed her bare skin into an intricate red and pink pattern. How he had insisted on kissing every last line and corner. Maybe she should have been that way with Jack – should have taken all her clothes off and sat in the living room waiting for him to come in from work.

'Mum?'

'Yes. Yes, I can do that.'

'OK. And look, there's the agent.'

Bet let Tommy open the passenger door and help her out.

'Mr Chalmers? Mrs Chalmers?' A bright-eyed young man in a suit and tie approached. 'Happy New Year to you.'

The man shook Tommy's hand but not Bet's, then turned towards one of the houses.

'Just look,' Tommy whispered as they went inside. 'That's all I'm asking.'

It was a terraced house with a large garden. And in the garden was a granny flat. That's what the agent called it, with a light laugh. She wasn't a granny, Bet felt like telling him. Never would be.

'So you'd come through the main house, of course,' the agent said. 'But then you're all independent out there. Kitchen, bathroom, little sitting room. You're never more than a few metres from an emergency alarm.' He turned to Tommy. 'You can have that alarm go straight to your phone, or there are companies that—'

'Yes.' Tommy took Bet's arm. 'Shall we go and have a look?'

It was small. Clean. Light. Warm. The living room had large windows that gave onto the garden, the lawn mottled with snow, a handful of trees, their branches outlined white.

'There's a library just down the road,' the agent said. 'Shops too – and a hairdresser I think I'm right in saying.'

Jack would have somewhere to walk to in the mornings. Bet flinched as she thought it, putting her hand against the window to steady herself.

'Mum?'

She swallowed. 'I'm fine.' Her voice bright. Her stomach churning. Jack. She wanted to lie down on the floor and cry, kick her feet and flail her arms the way kids did. She wanted him back. She wanted to do it all over again and get it right this time.

'Do you want to spend a bit of time here on your own,

Mum?' Tommy's hand on her arm, his voice kind. His voice like Jack's she thought with a start. 'I can take another look at the house.'

She said nothing, kept her palm on the cold windowpane.

'We'll just be inside. Are you OK to make your own way in?'

'I'm not a cripple,' Bet snapped.

Tommy dropped his arm to his side and turned to the agent. She watched them walk back towards the house, no doubt talking about difficult mothers, ageing mothers, what a bloody problem they were.

There was no furniture, nowhere to sit, and she needed to sit down. Bet lowered herself, as carefully as she could, onto the floor by the window. She might never be able to get up from there, but no matter.

'What do you think, Jack?' She said it out loud, closing her eyes against her own voice in the empty room. 'Has our boy lost his mind?'

Her here. Tommy in there. The two of them almost together. She hated the thought of it, she told herself, and yet she wasn't sure that she did. She'd never got it right with Tommy, from the very beginning. She wasn't the doting mother to match Jack's doting father; could never make the whole thing sit right. And yet maybe this was her chance. Maybe she could make it better, however late.

They didn't speak on the car journey back, but when Tommy pulled up outside Bet's flat, she turned and said:

'I think there's a pack of mince pies left over.'

And Tommy simply nodded, turned off the engine and followed her inside.

'Can we afford it?' Bet asked, when they were settled in the living room.

Tommy took an audible breath. 'With the flat, and my

savings, and your pension. Plus I'll be working another five years at least. We should just about be able to cover things.'

'And you want it?' she said, carefully.

'I think it could work.'

'Me in the garden?' Bet said. 'Like a grumpy old gnome.'

Tommy laughed. A loud, bright laugh.

'I'm serious,' Bet said.

'You don't want to go into a home, I get it,' Tommy said. 'But your eyes are getting worse. This flat isn't suitable. I think this other place is a good solution.'

Bet swallowed. If she left this flat she'd be leaving the last bit of Jack – the smell of him, the memory of him walking from one room to another, brewing tea, falling asleep in front of the television. They would give his clothes and his shoes to a charity shop. He wouldn't be moving with her.

'You don't have to decide now, Mum. Think about it. I just want you to think about it.'

Tommy. She wanted to reach out a hand and touch him, but that wasn't how things were with them.

'I should have been a better mum,' she said.

'Don't.'

'I should have done it all differently.'

'You did just fine.'

'I always felt you wanted something from me and I didn't know what it was or how to give it to you. I didn't even know if I wanted to give it. Jack was always so much better at it than me.'

'Mum, stop.'

Bet lifted her mince pie to her mouth and nibbled the soft pastry edge. 'I'll think about it,' she said. 'I will. I'll think about it.'

MARINELA

She took photos. Hundreds of them. Every angle of the Islington flat. Her stuff in the kitchen cabinets – the same stuff in boxes on the kitchen counter. The bed made – the bed stripped. The bathroom shelf lined with her shampoo and shower gel and make-up – the same shelf empty. She took photos from the street; sneaked into the back garden and took photos from there. Once she had started it was as though she couldn't stop. She had no idea what she would do with them, but she let herself carry on until she was done, until there was nothing else to see.

And then she left. Three cardboard boxes in the back of a taxi and she didn't live there any more.

I'll be down the road from you, she had said to Bet. We'll be neighbours. And Bet had nodded and smiled and looked so disappointed Marinela had wanted to cry.

Her new room was small enough to look almost full once she'd unpacked her boxes. She put the cactus on the window-sill, the glass bowl and the photo of her grandmother on the narrow desk, the red cushion on the bed and the rug over the small patch of visible carpet. Maybe Stefan was right, she thought, stepping back and surveying the space – it helped to have things around the place, it kept your feet on the ground.

Freddie was rarely at home, as far as she could tell. He breezed in and out, Lycra-clad, a courier bag slung across his back. Suz worked at some advertising agency in town – left in a suit each morning and came back late clutching a sandwich or take-away noodles. Marinela had plenty of time on her own and it suited her fine. She took photos in this flat too. Her room mostly. The light changing through the day. The view through the window onto the building site, still no walls or windows to be seen, just foundations and machines. She started taking her camera to the club and photographing the girls in the dressing room. They were wary at first, but then she brought in prints and they passed them around, examining the details of their faces and bodies, grinning and laughing. Our little photographer, they started calling her. We're going to be in the Tate one day. And it was the best work she'd done, she could see that, their faces swimming up from the developer in the university's darkroom. She had decided to leave once she'd got the photos she wanted, but there was no hurry.

She saw Harry a couple of times in the university cafe, passed him in the corridors. Smiled, waved, said a few words, but little else. Each time it made her sad. And so a couple of weeks after she'd moved she sent him a message. *There's a Chinese place on Walworth Road. It's meant to be the best in London. I would like to give you dinner to say thank you for helping me. Not a date, just friends. M x.*

He didn't answer that day and Marinela told herself he wouldn't, tried to stop checking her phone. She woke the next morning to a message sent in the early hours. *That would be nice. Thanks. When? H x.*

That afternoon, Marinela walked over to Bet's flat. She cleaned the kitchen. Hoovered. Made a chicken casserole.

'Sit down, girl, what's got into you today?' Bet said eventually. 'You're like a whirlwind.'

Marinela sat at the kitchen table, her heel tap-tapping against the floor. 'I asked Harry to have dinner.'

Bet raised her eyebrows. Smiled. 'I wondered how long that would take.'

'But he has a girlfriend, Bet. It's just dinner. It's just to say thank you.'

'It's never just dinner.'

'I shouldn't have done it?'

'Not at all. You like him?'

Marinela stood up, took a cloth from the sink and started wiping the surfaces although they were already clean.

'What are you cooking?' Bet asked.

Marinela shook her head. 'A restaurant.'

'Very nice.'

'I thought I might wear your dress.' She glanced at Bet and saw a smile flash across her face.

'Well, you make sure you kiss him, do you hear me?'

'Bet!'

'You only get one shot at things, Marinela. You're young, but that doesn't go on for ever. He's a nice boy.'

'He's got a girlfriend.'

'Well. Nothing's set in stone, is it? People change their minds. Now put that kettle on and make an old woman a cup of tea, won't you? And then sit down with me. Tell me what you've been doing. I'm not going to have you on hand for ever, am I?'

'I'll visit,' Marinela said, sitting back down. 'I will come every week. I have an idea for some photographs.'

Bet held her hand to her face and laughed. 'I am too old.'

Marinela shook her head. 'No, you are beautiful.'

On Monday night, Marinela put Bet's dress on again. The satin clasped her tight around her waist, hips, chest. She drew shimmering green powder over her eyelids and painted her lips a dark, almost plum red.

Harry was waiting for her outside the restaurant, which took up the ground floor of a block of student accommodation. The large, half-frosted windows glowed onto the dark street. Two stone dragons flanked a wide red door studded with brass.

'The best Chinese restaurant in London,' Harry said, 'here in Elephant and Castle. Who would have thought it? It's nice to see you.' He kissed her on one cheek, then the other.

Marinela laughed, and felt herself blush. 'Nice to see you too.'

She followed him into an entrance hall with a semi-circular pond backed by red marble, fake rocks and potted plants. Plastic fountains shaped like lilies threw out water, the sound echoing off the walls. They walked into the bright restaurant, sat by the window and ordered a beer she'd never heard of. Marinela could think of nothing to say. The dress felt too hot, too over-the-top.

'Did I tell you about the meeting?' Harry asked.

Marinela shook her head.

'With some local residents. They're objecting to the developer's plans.' He gestured towards the building site across the road.

'But they are already building.'

'Some of it. But there are other plans, other opportunities to change things. They've promised affordable housing and they're not honouring it – that should be grounds for objection, if nothing else. And the shopping centre, the new college, that's all up for grabs too.'

Marinela watched him as he spoke, his eyes bright, his hands dancing along with his words.

'It is another project?' she asked.

'It's what we should be doing,' he declared. 'Students. Academics. We shouldn't be just sitting in our offices in our universities writing about how terrible everything is. We should be out there, on the ground, doing things.'

Marinela smiled. 'You are a good man.'

Harry blinked. 'Not really.'

'No. You are.'

'I'm just blathering on. I'm sorry. How have you been?'

Marinela shook her head. She could cry, she thought, right there in the restaurant, but if she started she wasn't sure she'd be able to stop.

Harry waited. The beers came in bottles and they poured them, frothing and fizzing into tall glasses.

'Bet wanted to give me the flat,' Marinela said.

'Serious?'

Marinela nodded.

'But?'

'I said no.'

'Wow.'

Marinela took a long drink. 'You think I am stupid?'

'No. Not at all. Well, maybe.' He grinned. 'It's worth, what? Half a million? More?'

'She said she wanted me to have choices.'

'And you said?'

'It didn't feel right. I need to make my own way.'

'Very noble.'

'You do think I am stupid.'

Harry looked at her then, held her gaze so long she felt she'd stopped breathing. 'I actually think you're very wise,' he said eventually. 'I read so many articles about housing and property, and how we're all trained to want to own our own place. Except there are writers who argue it's actually a burden, a trap. Money can be toxic. It's not always what we need even though we're told it is.'

'But a home. We need a home, right?'

'And you've got one, no?'

Marinela thought about the cactus on her bedroom windowsill and nodded.

'So there you are. Homed. Weightless.' Harry raised his glass. 'Let's drink to that.'

The waiter brought their dim sum and they ate in silence, like an old married couple, Marinela thought, as though everything had already been said, as though there was all the time in the world. She finished her beer and took a breath.

'Are you in love with her?' she asked.

Harry looked up. 'What?'

'Lane.'

Harry lifted the last pork bun from the bamboo steamer and lowered it onto his plate.

'I'm sorry.' Marinela blushed. 'It is not my business.'

Outside, a bus wheezed past, its top deck lit a lonely blue. Shadows of passers-by flickered behind the frosted glass. Music played quietly from somewhere – a tinkling piano, violins.

'Do you love him?' he asked after a long pause. 'The Romanian guy.'

Marinela shook her head. 'I did for a long time, but no. Not any more. I told him to go. It's finished.'

Harry sipped his beer. 'Lane and I went on a few dates,' he said. 'She's nice, but I don't think we'll be going on any more.'

Marinela felt her heart hurry against her chest.

'So—' Harry fidgeted with his chopsticks. 'So if you wanted to maybe go out sometime.' He flicked her a glance. 'I mean, I know we're out now, but if you wanted—'

She needed to say something, but she couldn't. All the English words suddenly knotted and tangled inside her mind. She kept thinking about Bet, sitting in the armchair with the TV on, her head drooping to one side, snoring gently. And then her grandmother, too thin, too pale the last time she'd seen her. And then the strip club, the way the lights only lit up their immediate surrounds, leaving patches of darkness in between.

'It doesn't matter,' Harry said. 'Just ignore me.'

A waitress came to take the empty bamboo trays and their stained plates. Harry smiled and thanked her, made some comment about the weather.

'I work in a strip club,' Marinela said, watching Harry's face for a reaction. There, a tension at the edges of his eyes, and again at his mouth.

'Not as a cleaner,' she said, feeling as though she was driving blind, hurtling into the dark. 'Not as a barmaid. I take my clothes off. I don't work in a pub. I lied.'

There, the slightest of blushes.

'I dance on a stage and take my clothes off.' She shrugged. 'I'm going to stop soon, I've decided, but still, this is who I am.'

Harry blinked, drained his beer. Behind the bar, a waiter tipped change into the till – a noisy avalanche of coins.

'Say it then.' She sat back in her chair.

'Say what?'

Marinela couldn't look at him. She stared instead out of the window. Above the frosting she could see a brightly lit crane, and far beyond that the Shard, glittering white, with a red light winking near its summit.

She stood up. 'I go to the bathroom,' she said, and walked quickly along the length of the restaurant, past the bar, out into the chilly foyer with its water fountains and marble.

The toilets were cold too, choked with air freshener, empty. The music was louder there, a melancholy tune – violins soaring and falling, soaring and falling again. She leant both hands against the row of sinks and stared at herself in the mirror. Cropped dark hair. Her eyes big with liner and mascara.

If you wanted to go out sometime. She looked into her own eyes. All she'd needed to say was yes. One word. Nothing more complicated than that.

'I thought you'd done a runner,' Harry said, when she finally sat back down.

Their main course had arrived, and he started to spoon food onto her plate. Now she was looking at him and he wouldn't meet her gaze.

'I didn't run,' she said at last.

He glanced up at her. 'No. You didn't.' A pause, and then he grinned, gestured to Marinela's plate. 'Tuck in. It looks good.'

Marinela lifted a piece of beef with her chopsticks but didn't put it into her mouth. 'Bet said: you make sure you kiss him.'

Harry let out a loud laugh of surprise. 'Well, I agree with Bet,' he said. He shovelled food into his mouth and chewed, looking at Marinela, still smiling. 'Are you OK about the Romanian guy?'

Marinela nodded. 'I should never have let him stay. I blocked his number. He will find someone else. He is the sort of person who will find someone else.'

'OK.'

They ate in silence for a while.

'You don't care that I am a stripper?'

Harry blinked. 'No, I don't.'

They ate until they could not eat any more, until their stomachs were sore with it. No dessert, no, they laughed to the waitress. Just coffee.

And then they were out on the pavement, back in the cold January night, Walworth Road buzzing with traffic. The skeleton of a new building stood across the road to their right, no walls yet, just concrete floors and thick concrete struts reaching top to bottom. Buckets and rolls of cloth bunched up in the corners. The ground around it churned and rough, machines waiting for the next day to start.

'Come.' Harry took her hand and pulled her across the road as the lights changed. They stopped by the wire-mesh fence and looked across the cleared space.

'She's so sad now he's gone,' Marinela said. 'I mean Bet.

Imagine, seventy years with someone and then they're not there any more. I'm not sure she knew how much she loved him until he'd gone. Does that make sense?'

'Course it does. That's what humans do, isn't it? We've got something and we ignore it or take it for granted and then it goes and only then we understand how much we need it.'

'She will be able to sell the flat and be comfortable.' Marinela slotted her fingers through the gaps in the fence, one finger in each space.

'And you will make your own way in the world.' Harry swept an arm in front of him.

'Yes.' Marinela laughed. 'Yes I will.'

Harry arranged his fingers into the spaces next to Marinela's. 'There's a play on next week,' he said. 'At The National. Maybe we could go together?'

'Is it horribly serious?'

Harry smiled. 'Maybe a little.'

She released her fingers and looked at him. His eyes dark; his hair mussed up the way it always was; his shirt – white with tiny blue flowers – open at the neck.

'I would like to come. Thank you. I can be horribly serious.'

Behind her, the foundations for new glass and steel apartment buildings. In front of her, a half-finished block of flats, each of them worth hundreds of thousands, millions of pounds. And here, close enough to touch, close enough to kiss, Harry.

'I look forward to it,' Harry said.

And then she kissed him, or he kissed her; it didn't much matter.

BET

There were still things to do. I's to be dotted and T's to be crossed. Legal things she had no interest in understanding. But it was all in progress. She was leaving Elephant and Castle for a granny flat out towards Bromley. She was leaving Jack, but he would approve, she was sure of it. Her and Tommy, together and apart. And though she hadn't said as much to her son, there were days she found herself almost looking forward to it.

It was late March, three months since Jack had died. A bright, blue-skied morning. Chilly, but with the slightest hint of warmth to come. Bet had started sleeping later than she used to, lying in bed and letting herself drift in and out of consciousness. Then she'd take her time getting ready. A bath some days, if she had the energy to get in and out of the damn thing. A cup of tea and a piece of toast. The radio chattering away on the kitchen windowsill. Her eyesight had got no worse and no better. She managed.

Bet sipped her morning tea and watched a sparrow flutter against the window as though it wanted to get in. Nothing here for you, little bird, she told it. She had started talking to things – the teapot, the curtains, the furniture. There was no one to hear, so what did it matter? And she had the idea that her voice might vanish otherwise – or maybe it was she that would disappear; Tommy or Marinela would knock one afternoon and there would be no one there to answer.

She would go to the shopping centre. The idea slipped into her head and stayed there. She hadn't been for years, and she'd never understood Jack's daily pilgrimage. She remembered when the centre was built. Such a fanfare about it. Kids running up and down the escalators. Light glittering off the floor tiles. The glass roof opened to the sky. She'd been sucked in along with everyone else – American design, the future of shopping. But it had never worked, not like they said it would – the top floor half-empty from day one, and the other shops struggling to stay in business.

She couldn't walk there, so she called a taxi, asked for it to come in an hour, and got herself ready. She put on the grey dress she'd worn for their anniversary party. It felt loose around her stomach. Marinela kept on cooking her Romanian food. Vinegary soups. Fried sausages. Tiny pies filled with cheese. Cherry cake. Bet would try them all, a mouthful, a sliver. You must eat, Marinela said. You must keep strong. And then she laughed and said, you are making me into model granddaughter, and Bet had had to press her fingers against her mouth to stop herself from crying. She'd never been one for weeping, but these last few months the tears would be in her eyes and out onto her cheeks before she could do anything about it.

She drew a dusky pink lipstick over her mouth and dabbed a beige eyeshadow onto her lids. She considered the same low heels she'd worn to the party, but decided on her sensible black flats instead. Old lady shoes, her stockinged feet puffing out of the tops. Her black coat. The turquoise scarf Jack had given her for her birthday. Her stick. She undid each lock and stepped out into the tiled hallway, took a breath. Spring. She could smell it.

It would be a new start, Tommy kept saying. For both of them. On good days she almost agreed with him, but then she'd be hit by worry – what would she do? Would they argue all day? Would he end up hating her? I don't want you to feel trapped, she'd told him last week. He'd leaned forward and kissed her cheek and said, I don't. Do you? And she'd touched her face where his lips had been and said no, no I don't.

In the back of the taxi, Bet took in the familiar streets at the edges of her vision. When they reached the estate she wanted to close her eyes, but made herself keep them open, for Jack's sake. Nothing to see, except those long wooden boards along the length of the street, covered in promises and pictures. The noises had changed too, a few months back. No more groaning, falling walls. No more destruction. They were starting again now. Brick by brick.

The taxi driver got her as close to the centre as he could – the New Kent Road entrance, by the Coronet. She stood on the pavement in front of the theatre's blue sign. She'd gone there with Nell and with Jack, though never together; another version of herself, who she sometimes felt so close to, and other times was sure must have been someone else – that young woman with her smooth skin and flawless stockings and easy smile.

It was slow going. Small step by small step, from the pavement, down the ramp, through the scrappy market stalls, to the ground-floor entrance. It wasn't an easy place to walk slowly – the noise and bustle made her feel rushed and unstable, but she kept herself going. One foot in front of the other – that was how things got done.

And there she was. Inside. The air warmer. The light brighter. She'd shopped here all those years when they were still in Larcom Street, and then on the estate. She knew the place.

As she made her way along the wide corridor she wondered if they missed him – the people who worked here, who would have seen Jack each and every day if they'd been paying attention. She would have liked to ask them, but she didn't trust herself not to cry, and she didn't trust them to say what she wanted to hear.

The Sundial Cafe smelt the same as it always had – fried eggs and chips. She ordered tea, milky with two sugars, toast and jam, and the woman said she'd bring it to her. The tables and chairs had changed, she was sure – more colourful than they'd used to be, laid out differently. Bet chose a table with red seats either side, sat facing the window.

Jack. There were days she woke up and forgot he'd gone. She'd turn to look at him in bed, or lie there waiting for the sound of the toilet flushing, or the kettle boiling, or him humming to himself. And then there were other days she woke with that concrete feeling in her bones and veins, when she'd try to slip back into sleep just so she wouldn't have to acknowledge the truth of it.

The woman brought her tea and toast and Bet picked up a slice and nibbled at its crust. She imagined Jack here, maybe in this seat, looking out of this window, watching all the people – every colour under the sun they were these days – going about their business. He'd had a doughnut, he'd told her, the day he met Marinela. He hadn't thought much of it. American nonsense. She'd said something mean, she couldn't remember what exactly, but she wished now she had just smiled and said she'd never liked them either.

The flat would be sold. The money put in a bank account with Tommy's name on it and she never needed to think about it again. She still wished that Marinela had taken it, but the girl seemed happy enough. In love too, which was nice to see – that glow coming off her, her voice bright with laughter. She'd promised to come and visit every week, and maybe she would, to start with at least.

Bet stretched out her legs under the table and sat back in her chair. She might stay there until lunchtime and then order a bacon sandwich and another cup of tea. If she had a little nap in between no one would mind, no one would even notice. That's what she'd always loved about London – you could do what you liked and most of the time people were too busy, too caught up with their own lives, to pay you much attention. Maybe she would come back tomorrow and do the same thing. Jack would laugh – all those years of coming here on his own and now here she was, an old woman with dodgy eyes, sitting in her husband's favourite cafe drinking sugary tea and eating toast and strawberry jam, letting the world go on around her.

Acknowledgements

The idea for this novel came from a story told over dinner by a family friend. I have changed it, probably beyond recognition, but I am grateful for that initial spark of inspiration.

I am lucky to have a great network of supportive writers and readers in my life. Thank you to those who have read, commented, and cheered from the side lines, especially Emma Claire Sweeney, Paul McVeigh, the Inklings writing group, and my fellow writers at Hawthornden Castle where I worked on an early draft of this novel.

I wrote *Jack & Bet* as part of a Ph.D. in Creative Writing at the Open University, generously funded by the CHASE consortium and even more generously supervised by two brilliant writers: Sally O'Reilly and Derek Neale. Thanks to both of you for your insights and support over the years.

Thank you to my agent, Cathryn Summerhayes, my brilliant editor, Francesca Main, her assistant Gillian Fitzgerald-Kelly, and the whole Picador team.

Thank you to Alexandra Oanca, Clara Casian and Ana Bors for your help with all things Romanian. To Jean Betteridge for advice on housing matters. To Andy Barry and the Elders Company at the Royal Exchange Theatre, Manchester, for teaching me about ageing with energy and joy. To Eva Sajovic and Rebecca Davies for our sustained collaboration making work in Elephant and Castle. You can watch our award winning film, *Unearthing Elephant*, on Vimeo: vimeo.com/222385394.

And finally, thank you to my family, for everything, and especially Matt, for your endless support and encouragement, and Sam, for your joyous distraction from the whole business of writing – I wish you could have met your great grandparents who this book is dedicated to.